THE LAST DANCE IS MINE

Bill Horner

THE LAST DANCE IS MINE

BILL HORNER

Autobiography with resource information by the Multiple Sclerosis Society of Canada

OPTIMUM PUBLISHING INC.
MONTREAL • TORONTO

Published by Optimum Publishing International Inc., Montreal

Legal Deposit
National Library of Canada
4th quarter 1992
Canadian cataloguing in publication data

Horner, Bill
The Last Dance is Mine
ISBN 0-88890-228-X

1. Horner, Bill, 1941- . 2. Multiple Sclerosis--
Patients--Biography. 3. Miners--Ontario--Biography.
I. Title.

RC377.H67 1992 362.1'96834 C92-090161-1

Cover design: Peter Knowles
Cover Photography: Pierre Brunet—Publiphoto

For information address:
Optimum Publishing International Inc.
Box 237, Victoria Station,
Westmount, H3Z 2V5

Printed and bound in Canada on acid free
environmentally friendly paper.

TABLE OF CONTENTS

This book is dedicated to my wife Esther for her undying faith and encouragement

ACKNOWLEDGEMENTS

I would like to thank **Michael Baxendale** and his editorial staff at *Optimum Publishing* for publishing this book and providing insight and advice on the text. He had faith in the project after many others turned it down. The *Canada Council* also recognized the merit in my book and provided tangible support.

Thanks are also due to the *Multiple Sclerosis Society of Canada*, for providing support information included in the appendix. The *Society's* communications director **Deanna Groetzinger** was an early believer in my book and was kind enough to go on the record by writing the foreword. I sincerely appreciate her help.

Dr. George Rice the renowned neurologist of the *MS Research Clinic* at University Hospital, London, Ontario has written an excellent summary of the known medical facts as they relate to the disease. I believe its inclusion in my book will provide valuable insight for those who want to know more about this mysterious illness. I appreciate his important contribution and applaud his dedication to MS research.

Finally, I wish to thank the *Thunder Bay Writer's Guild*, *HAGI Attendant Care Workers,* past and present, **Terry Bellavance** and **Simon Hoag** of the *Ontario March of Dimes*, the *Happy Handicap Club of Thunder Bay*, **Jim Farrell** and **Bill Prendergrast** who taught me the techniques of writing, **Ginger Morey** who helped me to learn to use the word processor and **Monica Fadyshen** for her technical assistance and inspiration.

Bill Horner

FOREWORD

The book you are about to read, is first and foremost a revealing autobiography of inimitable readability. That it provides insight into what it means to have and live with multiple sclerosis is a distinct bonus. *The Last Dance is Mine* is the portrait of one courageous person's battle with a very tough opponent. While at once a very personal and intimate story, in many ways it is also universal. Like author Bill Horner, tens of thousands of Canadians have to learn to deal with the mysterious symptoms of MS that come and go, as they try to keep their job and fulfil their responsibilities as husbands, wives, parents and neighbours.

The actual diagnosis of MS was a shock to Bill and his family. Like so many, he looked for logical reasons why he, a young, robust hard-rock miner, should suddenly have to cope with a potentially disabling disease. But he found no logic, no answers when he asked "why me?"

FOREWORD

Multiple sclerosis is the most common disease of the central nervous system affecting young adults in North America. MS is highly variable in the way it affects people. In Bill Horner's case, he was eventually unable to use his arms and legs. For others, MS is more benign. For years, they may have no outward signs of multiple sclerosis after it has been diagnosed. Approximately, one third of people with MS have the mild or benign form. Another third have a "relapsing-remitting" variety in which there are sporadic attacks followed by periods of complete or almost complete recovery. The remaining third have the chronic progressive form of MS that Bill Horner contracted. MS attacks are followed by incomplete recovery, and a gradual worsening occurs over the course of time.

The Last Dance is Mine is not a story of despair. Through perseverance and plain stubbornness, Bill fought back against the disease and found new love and a new life. It wasn't easy; increasing disability, marital problems and rebellious teenage children broke up his home, and for a time he became very bitter. What brought him through was his honesty, his zest for life and the love of those around him. It is also what makes his book such a compelling narrative.

The *Multiple Sclerosis Society of Canada* is pleased that its chapters in Sudbury and Thunder Bay were there to assist Bill, even in a small way, in coping with multiple sclerosis. The *Society* offers a number of services for people who have multiple sclerosis and for their family members. In a special appendix to this book the publishers have included useful information such as addresses and phone numbers of *MS Society* offices in Canada and the services they offer. Also provided is information on the *Society*, world wide. For those who would like to know more details about MS, Dr George Rice has written a valuable question and answer sequence.

FOREWORD

As this book goes to press there is no cure for multiple sclerosis but there has been an enormous acceleration of research during the last five years. The answer will be found, and in the meantime, the *Multiple Sclerosis Society of Canada* will continue to assist the tens of thousands of Canadians who have multiple sclerosis.

Bill Horner's story, told so eloquently in *The Last Dance is Mine* provides insight into what it means to have multiple sclerosis. The challenges imposed by the disease compelled the author find an inner strength that he did not know he had. This process gave Canada a gifted writer who may otherwise not have developed his craft. While Bill does not wish to be considered an inspiration to others, many will find he fits that description. Not only did Bill learn the skills of an author, but having been denied the use of his hands and fingers, he wrote this book by using a mouth piece on a word processor. His "never give up" attitude has freed him from the darkest moments of a disabling disease and allowed him to find a way to keep dancing.

Deanna Groetzinger,
The Multiple Sclerosis Society of Canada.

PROLOGUE

This is what I remember. Through a thick fog, I saw people in white floating around me, talking. I couldn't move, but they moved about freely. Someone was holding me by the shoulders and shaking me, shouting "Mr. Horner wake up!" I knew I should answer but the pain and the heaviness held me back. I wondered where I was, who all these people were standing over me? My mind was full of questions. I felt a terrible pain in my groin and heard myself scream.

The rest I saw through a tunnel, as if it were happening to someone else. The dim fluorescent light, the faces staring down at me, the buzz of machines, the whiteness.

"You're going to be okay." said a male voice. In my confusion he seemed to be speaking incredibly slowly.

"You pulled out of it remarkably well, considering. We don't think you've done yourself any permanent injury. Of course there is a wait and see period but right now I can say you are a very lucky man."

Quickly, my mental fog dispersed. The realization of what had happened seared into me. Up to then I hadn't fully remembered. Still immediate pain outweighed it. "My groin," I mumbled groggily, "It feels like it's on fire."

"It's the catheter," he said. "We had to irrigate your bladder to make sure all the toxins are flushed from your system. We pumped your stomach, too, so you may have a raw throat for a day or more." The sound of his voice faded in and out.

Gradually, my mind came into focus. "How long have I been here" I had to ask.

"Today is Monday. You were brought in Saturday evening. I'm Dr. Winslow and this is the Memorial Hospital." His reassuring hand touched my shoulder.

"We'll be moving you out of intensive care as soon as there's a bed ready. I'll be in touch." Dr. Winslow hurried on to continue his rounds.

Moments after the doctor left, an orderly appeared. I winced at the stab of pain as he withdrew the catheter from my bladder. As the pain slowly subsided, I had to smile bitterly at the awful mess I'd got myself into.

When I'd first contemplated suicide, it wasn't fear of dying that bothered me so much, it was fear of living. Multiple sclerosis had taken so much from my life, I couldn't see clearly what was left. I worried if I botched the attempt, I would end up seriously disabled. Even now, when I had the doctor's reassurance that no real damage had been done, I still feared living.

While waiting to be wheeled out of intensive care, the constant beep...beep...beep of a heart monitoring machine drew me into an almost hypnotic trance. My thoughts slowly drifted back to when my troubles began.

ONE

The Year was 1963. Joyce and I had been married since October 10, 1959. I was madly in love with her and she with me. We were childhood sweethearts. I had known for years the sparkle of her hazel brown eyes, the sheen of her dark brown hair, her gentle shyness and happiest smile. I also knew the sudden flash of her fiery temper.

Our first son, Allen, inherited his parents bashfulness. The day he arrived in the world on April 11, 1960, I stood over him perplexed at his wrinkled, peach face and bald head. Joyce lay in her hospital bed with Allen cradled proudly in her arms. I was so happy I buried my face in her warm belly and wept.

Gordy arrived a year and a half later. His grin and his large brown eyes could melt the coldest heart. He was born with blocked tear ducts and until an operation corrected the defect six months later, tears streamed steadily down his cheeks. He was our 'Sad-Sack.'

We lived in Creighton Mine, a small mining town ten miles west of Sudbury at the very heart of the world's richest nickel deposits. There was no hint of those underground riches when you entered Creighton. The narrow streets were paved with crushed mine rock that turned to a dingy slop in rainy weather. Grass grew between the wooden planks on the sidewalk. Huge corrugated pipes filled with sand meandered through the middle of town, supported by a wooden trestle that rose above the rooftops. The sounds of mining were always there in the background—like the roar of traffic in the city—the murmur of compressors pumping air down to the miners, the thump, thump, thump of the mill crushers over at Seven Shaft.

Creighton sat at the end of a dead end road. In this town of wooden houses and dusty streets, three mine shafts dominated the view at the north end; shafts Three, Five and Seven to Creightoners. Those weather stained giants were the gateways to the underground world. Over by the water tank, clusters of red and green tarpaper shacks perched on hills of black granite. Across from the Catholic church, rows and rows of pastel-coloured farm houses decayed beneath too many layers of cheap paint. And in most backyards stood the familiar outside toilet.

The house we rented was directly behind Takala's Garage, whose yard was always cluttered with derelict trucks and cars. Our cedar-shingled house was small, old and smelled of dry rot, but to a young married couple just starting out, it was a palace.

One work day morning was much like any other. The alarm clock sounded as the grey light of dawn stained my bedroom window. Joyce stirred only enough to roll over and bury her head deeper into the pillow.

I rose reluctantly, sitting groggily on the edge of the bed rubbing my eyes, drained and tired. It had been another restless night when sleep did not come till the wee hours. A tingling sensation had crept into my lower right leg a few days ago. I could feel it now. There was no pain to speak of but my leg prickled steadily, mildly, as though a swarm of mosquitoes were biting. I hadn't told Joyce, but my leg almost gave out on me during the usual quitting time stampede to the punch-out clock. I had to grab the arm of the man in front of me to keep myself from falling on my face.

I pushed myself off the bed and stood up. I felt nothing at all below the knee. I stamped my foot, trying to shake off the numbness, and Joyce woke up.

"Why all the noise?" she mumbled.

"My damn leg's acting funny. Seems like it's getting worse. Those nerve pills Magruther prescribed don't do a thing except make me tired. Whenever he's stuck for an answer it's either aspirin or nerve pills."

"Why not get a second opinion?" Joyce said. "Take the day off, go down to Lively and see a doctor there. I'll go with you."

"Jesus, Joyce, you know I can't afford to stay home! After an eight month layoff? Our savings are all used up." I had never been one to spend any more time in the Doctor's office than I had to.

"Suit yourself," she said, stifling a yawn, "but what if it's serious? What then? You could end up staying home longer than an extra day. Remember when Grandma Marion had her stroke? That started with a numbness."

"Grandma Marion was in her seventies. Strokes happen to old folks, not to young guys. I'm only twenty-two!"

I fastened my trousers and went outside to the toilet. As I walked gingerly over the gravelled path in my bare feet, my left foot tingled from the sharpness of the stones, but my right foot felt nothing. Maybe, I thought, I should listen to Joyce and stay home. I shrugged off my fears and headed for work.

I worked at the copper refinery—a huge, squat structure situated halfway between Creighton and Sudbury along Highway 17. Copper was the main product but gold, silver and platinum were also separated in the process of copper refining.

The tankhouse was a building longer than a football field, filled with a honeycomb network of rectangular tanks. The tanks were lined with lead because each contained a hot, acid solution used in the process of separating copper from the other metals. Every day a section of these tanks was drained and cleaned to make room for a new batch of copper. Cleaning those tanks was how I earned my living. I was a mudman.

When the acid solution is syphoned off, a foot of heavy sludge, mostly precious metals, remains at the bottom. I would climb into each tank and muck it out. With a rubber squeegee I'd push the blackish grey slop down a drainage hole. The work is dirty, hot and dangerous.

A mudman must balance himself on narrow, six inch boards that separate one tank from another. The job requires the skill and agility of an acrobat On this particular day I was lacking in both requirements.

Even after three years in the tankhouse department, I had not grown accustomed to the acrid smell that pinched my nostrils, nor to the concentrated heat which immediately formed beads of sweat on my forehead and bare arms.

As I headed to my workplace that morning, I passed by the sheetflopper crew already hard at work stripping and straightening copper sheets. They would work furiously on piecework; each strike of the flatbar cracked like a gunshot resounding to the furthest corner of the building. Overhead, huge electric cranes rumbled back and forth plucking dripping sheets of pure copper from the tanks of solution.

My partner Walter stood watching all the hubbub while the crane operators prepared our section for cleaning. He was anxious to get started. He wiped his brow with his brown stained apron. When he saw me he grinned, "Let's go, Horner, we'll muck out the shit, then fuck the dog, huh?" Once we got through our allotted tanks we could shower, then hide out in the basement 'till quitting time.

The numbness persisted in my right leg. I had to be careful climbing into the tanks. I was balanced between two tanks full of hot solution trying to adjust the steam syphon when without warning, my leg just buckled beneath me and I pitched into a tank. I screamed like crazy as the scalding liquid engulfed me. I had enough sense to keep my head above the surface and my eyes tightly shut. I scrabbled at the lead side of the tank thinking of men I knew whose eyesight had been damaged by the acid solution.

Above my own screams I heard Walter yelling, "Help! My partner fell in the tank!" Powerful hands clutched me under the armpits. Walter and the foreman hauled me out of the hot solution. They half carried, half dragged me to the nearest emergency shower. The foreman tore off my rubber boots and stripped me while Walter got the shower turned on. The icy water rained down on all three of us as they held me up. I was trembling uncontrollably. The foreman realized I was close to shock.

"Try to relax," he said calmly. "Let the water wash away the acid and cool down your body. You'll be okay."

The few seconds in that tank had turned my skin a beet-red colour. To the crowd of onlookers, I must have resembled a lobster freshly plucked from boiling water.

The first aid attendant pushed his way through the crowd. "You okay?" he asked.

I shrugged. "I think so."

"Can you walk, or shall I call for a stretcher?"

"I'll walk," I said. I didn't think I was a stretcher case.

The eyes of the workmen followed us as I limped toward the first aid station. The attendant noticed my limp.

"Did you hit your leg when you fell?"

I nodded. It was a lie of course, but as I was ignorant of the company's policies on such matters, I was keeping my mystery affliction to myself until I got some definite answers.

Doctor Magruther didn't offer much satisfaction when I limped into his office on my way home.

"It could be arthritis," he said, after a lengthy examination. "That might be what caused your leg to give out on you. I'll give you a prescription. Come see me again in two weeks."

"You mean I no longer have a nervous condition?" I remarked in a tone laced with sarcasm. His answer was a cold stare over the rim of his bifocals.

During the three weeks I was off work the affliction continued. In fact, as time went on, my leg began acting stranger than ever. I kicked my left ankle so many times with my right heel, I was left with a bloody ankle bone. The longer I stayed home the more I worried about it. I began to wonder if I would ever work again. Sometimes, to ease the boredom, I tried to help Joyce with the housework but my lack of balance was frustrating. One thing about staying home, I saw a lot of my family and, my in-laws.

Gordon, my father-in-law, dropped in daily on friendly fault finding missions directed mostly at me. Gordon had a sombre face with Diefenbaker jowls and a bulbous nose the shape and texture of an overripe pear. Known for his critical eye and taste for drink, he made up for it with his wry sense of humour.

One day he sat at the kitchen table, looking around for something to gripe about.

"You want coffee, Dad?" Joyce offered.

"Yeah, maybe I will," he muttered. Joyce placed a mug in front of him and before she could pour the coffee, Gordon grabbed the mug and rinsed it under the tap.

"Got dust in it," he said, wrinkling his face. Joyce looked at me and I looked back at her.

"The nerve of the old fart," I thought.

After double-checking his coffee for floating objects, he wrapped his lips around the rim of the mug and took a sip. Then he started on me.

"How in hell can you have arthritis? You're too young. Besides, I know arthritis, a lot of it runs in my family and it don't act that way."

"Magruther said it was arthritis," I replied, getting my guard up. "According to you, Doc Magruther is always right. He can do no wrong."

"Well, doctors are human too," he said, "if you were to ask me, I really don't think there is all that much wrong with your leg. If you've got arthritis, I've got St. Vitus Dance."

"I suppose you figure I purposely fell in that tank just so I could stay home from work?"

Gordon shrugged his shoulders, making me angrier. He knew it, too. That did it! I slammed my coffee mug down on the table. My neck and ears reddened.

"And while we're on the subject of blowing shifts," I retorted. Wasn't it just last week that you missed two in a row?"

Now it was old Gord's ears burning red. He was still being raked over the coals at his house for that recent drinking binge. I was almost sorry I brought it up, but he had it coming.

Gordon downed his coffee and got up to leave. I didn't think he'd say any more that day, but it wouldn't be Gordon unless he got the last word. "There's a rip in your screen door," he said, "if you don't get it fixed you'll have a house full of bugs." Gordon really got under my skin. After he left I turned to Joyce.

"Your old man's got his nerve accusing me of dogging it," I said. "He has no idea how it bothers me that I'm not bringing home a paycheque." Joyce knew that, but she also knew her father.

"Don't let him get to you, Bill. Actually, he's as concerned as you are. Dad cares a lot about us and the boys."

"He certainly has a strange way of showing it. All he ever does is stick his nose into our affairs and criticize the way we live. What's it to him if I want to buy a case of beer or treat us to a movie. That's our business, not his. I'm not a kid any more."

"Don't be too hard on them, Bill. They're really good people at heart. It's just taking them a while to adjust to the idea that their little girl is married."

"But Joyce, it's been three years."

"Yes, it's been that long alright. But some parents take longer to adjust than others. After all I am their only daughter."

"Maybe you're right," I said, "They mean well but it's awfully discouraging when they find fault with everything I do. If you ask me I think your old man still holds a grudge against me because you were three months pregnant on your wedding day."

I don't think Gordon ever got over that. Then, when Joyce was pregnant a year after Allen was born he was on me again. "Just because your old man had eleven kids," he reminded me, "don't mean you gotta screw yourself away from the table the way he did."

TWO

After a month of weakness and tingling sensations, the pain in my legs disappeared as suddenly and as mysteriously as it had first appeared. On the way over to see Magruther about returning to work, I tested my leg by walking the few blocks to his office. I had to know it wasn't all in my mind. But my leg proved to be as good as ever. In fact, I was so relieved and elated, I felt like skipping all the way.

Magruther was as baffled as before. "Whatever it was," he said, "has arrested itself. You can go back to work next week, but if you have problems call me."

He adjusted his bifocals and filled out a return to work slip. As he swivelled in his chair to hand it over he said, "I have a strong suspicion that the numbness in your leg is neurological. We won't know for certain till we've eliminated all the other possibilities. In the meantime, let's hope this is the end of it."

Monday morning I was back in the tankhouse—back to my old job as mudman. Only now things were different. There was a gnawing fear in my gut whenever I worked around the tanks, and each day I entered the tankhouse, my fear grew. I knew that for my own sanity I had to get off the mudman job.

I discussed my problem with the union rep.

"You don't have the seniority to bid on another job," he said, "your only alternative is to transfer to the mines."

I wasn't fussy about working in the mines. My father was a miner and had been for twenty-five years. How many times had I heard him talk of the dangers underground, of men being crushed to death by cave-ins or falling five hundred feet down an ore pass. Dad worked on the trams and he'd seen more than one accident. He saw his partner severely injured by a runaway car. Mining required a special breed of man, someone courageous like my dad.

Yet the more I thought about underground, the more I began to like the idea. Being a miner couldn't be any worse than being a mudman. Besides, miners were paid a lot more; and if I transferred to Creighton Mine I could walk to work.

When I approached the personnel man he explained that transfers usually take time.

"The way it works," he said, "is that before another man can be hired for Creighton, we must first consider your transfer. It could happen next week or next year. We don't know."

Summer turned to autumn and my transfer hadn't come through. I was still a mudman and still apprehensive about working around the tanks, but so far my leg was holding up. There had been no recurrence of my mystery illness. And now that I was working steadily, life around the house became more bearable. There was money coming in to catch up on our debts and some left over for Joyce to buy winter boots for the little ones.

Gordon's attitude toward me got better, too. Though he continued to find fault, I knew he was trying to be helpful. Slowly,

I was learning not to be so easily offended. So when he invited me to go deer hunting that fall, I realized he might be finally accepting me as his son-in-law.

We headed out before dawn on a snow rutted road west of Highway 17. At each hill the back of Gordon's pick-up swished side to side in the wet snow, slowing to a crawl. I wondered if Gordon's old '51 *GMC* was going to make it, but I knew enough to keep my doubts to myself.

As Gordon wrestled with the steering wheel, he gave me a few pointers about hunting deer. It was my first time hunting big game so I grabbed onto every word. He told me to watch out for buck fever.

"Buck fever?" I said. "Never heard of it."

"It's when a guy freezes on the trigger," he replied. "I seen it happen to my brother two years ago. He was guarding a runway when a ten-point buck pokes his antlers through a bunch of tag-alders. That's when buck fever hit him. He froze, bug-eyed and speechless, and never fired a shot. Instead, he ejected every shell onto the ground." Gordon's grip whitened on the steering wheel as if he could see it all through the windshield.

"By the time he got his head in gear," he went on, "the deer had bolted over the next ridge. I could a kicked his ass all over them hills, the silly bugger."

It was dark when we parked the truck. Gordon handed me one of his big game rifles—a 303 calibre British Lee-Enfield. He was amused at the nervous way I held the gun. It was a cumbersome relic left over from the second World War.

"Keep the safety on her," he warned, "I don't want my ass shot off with you trailing behind."

"There he goes again, the old fart," I muttered under my breath. Though I'd never hunted deer before, I did know how to handle a rifle. Soon we were tramping through the woods. Blobs of snow dropped from the heavy trees in front of us.

The grey morning mist hung behind the trees and in the folds of the ridges, flattening the rugged country into facades, like row upon row of cardboard scenery.

Gordon placed me on a grassy knoll where I had the best possible view of the ridges that ran on either side of me.

"I'll stand watch over there," he said, pointing his mitt to another hill some two hundred yards away.

"If there's deer around, they'll either pass by me or head in this direction. Don't move and don't smoke."

My eyes followed Gordon's red hunting cap until it bobbed out of site over the next ridge. The excitement grew inside me and I imagined each clump of snow or twig falling from a tree to be a deer about to emerge from the woods.

In all the times I wandered through the woods, I'd never come upon a deer. The only deer I'd seen was the one my father had shot and strung up by the neck in the garage at home. No remnant of the shy, graceful animal remained as it hung with staring eyes and lolling tongue. I wondered if I could ever be responsible for such degradation.

I loaded my gun and the first hour went by. There was no sign of any movement except two squirrels playing in the brown and white snow-laden trees.

The game became dull. I rocked back and forth on my heels and toes to ward off the nagging cold that was slowly creeping through my thin rubber boots.

As the cold crept up my legs and stiffened my fingers I checked my rifle again and felt the trigger to make sure I could pull it should the moment come. Bored, uncomfortable and cold, resentment towards the creature that caused me so much discomfort welled up inside me. It would serve the deer right to be shot.

A twig snapped; there was a crashing through the trees and suddenly, not one, but two deer appeared across the clearing.

My heart was pounding its way out of my chest cavity. I slammed a shell into the chamber and raised my rifle. Both deer were now broadside and only twenty yards from where I stood.

"Hey, you stop!" I yelled.

Immediately, as if trained, both deer froze and remained motionless. I squeezed the trigger and a clump of snow spattered from the branch inches above the head of the lead deer.

At the crack of my rifle, both deer leapt for cover. As they sprinted for safety I followed them along the barrel of my rifle and got off another shot, but I was nowhere near the target. The white flags disappeared into the thicket.

I was still trembling in my boots when Gordon came puffing up the hill. "Why all the shooting? Did you see one?"

I showed him two fingers. "T-two," I stammered.

Gordon's eyes got as big as mine. "Two!" he yelled.

Then he noticed how close the tracks had passed.

"Two fucking deer almost ran you over and you missed?" I knew he was pissed off when he threw his cap on the ground and kicked at it.

"Jesus, Bill, no one on this earth can be that lousy of a shot. Why didn't you clobber them with your rifle butt?"

I stared at my boots and grinned sheepishly. Later, when we were sitting around the fire drinking black tea and eating tough beef sandwiches I told Gordon the whole story—how both deer had stopped when I yelled. He grinned at first, then his loose jowls shook with laughter.

"Well Bill," he said, trying to contain himself, "at least you didn't get buck fever."

THREE

My transfer to Creighton finally came through in the spring of 1964. On Monday morning, May 5, I followed the gravel road that led to Number Five Shaft. A diesel locomotive, hauling fully-laden ore cars, rumbled along at my back, its whistle screeching as it approached the crossing on George Street.

The crisp morning air was exhilarating. Scattered puffs of clouds floated idly on a dawn sky. It promised to be another bright spring day. But the weather didn't matter to me. This was going to be my first day underground. In Creighton Mine almost everybody's father was a miner, and going underground was a part of growing up. Still, I had to admit, that day I was a bit edgy. As I approached the mine, the looming headframe, silhouetted by a rising sun, cast a long dark shadow directly in my path.

I showed my pass to the security man at the gate, and he pointed me toward the personnel office. When the required paperwork was over, I was introduced to the shift foreman. He only grunted and left. And there I stood, wondering what I should do next.

There were dozens of miners milling about; and every one of them stared at me. Few had anything to say, let alone a cheerful remark. I've always been shy and felt terribly self-conscious.

At long last, after most of the men had disappeared, the foreman returned. He was followed by a grey-haired, heavy-set man.

"This is Bulkhead Pete, the nipper boss," he said. "That means he's in charge of supplying timber to the stope crews. You'll be working with him."

Pete had a pudding face and small round eyes that bored their way through thick dark-rimmed glasses. His great pot belly hung over his belt like a pan of over-risen bread dough.

"Remember," warned the foreman. "Stick by his side! We don't want you getting lost down there."

Pete was an even bigger man than my former partner, Walter, but if he was huge, he was also friendly.

"First day, Laddy?" he asked in a kindly Scottish brogue. "Well, don't worry. I get all the greenhorns."

'Greenhorn' didn't sound so bad when he said it.

"Most are a wee bit nervous. But ye'll find it ain't all that bad."

Like a barnyard goose I followed Pete through a set of swinging doors into the collarhouse. The immensity of the room dwarfed us. It was a storehouse for machinery and supplies. At the far end of the building, a row of trucks piled high with timber sat on steel rails.

"That's the loading station," Pete explained. "Everything that goes underground, all the men, all the supplies are loaded onto the cage here." He pointing to a huge rectangular box that dangled on the end of a wire rope. "That's the cage," he said. I was shocked to realize this was our elevator into the deep black below.

"Four thousand!" called a voice on the loudspeaker, and it made me jump.

"That's ours" said Pete.

Before I knew what was happening, I was packed in with forty grubby miners. Stale sweat mixed with the stench of soiled clothes. My chest grew tight, and I felt I couldn't breathe.

"Here we go," someone said.

And "go" we did! The floor fell away, and our crowded cage dropped like a stone. A wind rattled up my pant legs and I could hear the cables squeak and squeal like terrified pigs.

"She needs new brakeshoes," said some wise guy beside me.

We dropped forever. The further we dropped, the quieter it got. The men even stopped shuffling and coughing. Down, down, down.

Finally the cage started to slow. I felt the pressure start to build; in my knees, in my crotch, in my ears. Then it came to a stop. Or rather, it bobbed up and down like a yoyo on the end of a very long string.

"Last stop!" said the cagetender and threw back the door. I caught a whiff of the air, it smelled used.

Straight ahead I could see a big, low-roofed open space with tunnels running through it to the ore body. Every once in a while I could see the light from a miner's helmet in the blackness of one of those tunnels like the wink of a firefly in the night.

Riding the cage had been bad enough but as I stepped onto the level my fears heightened. What if I should stray from the others?

"We'll go to the lunchroom and have some tea," said Pete, "the foreman will give us a list of workplaces to check for supplies."

We followed the other men who walked two abreast down a narrow tunnel. We made a sudden turn and entered a room carved out of rock. It was about fifty feet long. Actually it was just another tunnel but it was whitewashed, and wooden benches lined either side. To me it was close enough to a palace because it was filled with light.

Bulkhead Pete and I sat together on one of the benches. The foreman had told me to stick to his side and I did. While the men around us poured cups of coffee and unwrapped sandwiches, Pete reached into his shirt pocket and pulled a small tin out the size of a hockey puck.

'Copenhagen,' it said on the label. He yanked back his lower lip and shoved a pinch of it into a ready-made pouch, then he passed the can to me.

"Here, Laddy," he said with a wink, "guaranteed to kill the bugs." It smelled wonderful—like sweet licorice flavoured with rum.

"No thanks," I said. I had smoked the odd cigarette but couldn't see the enjoyment of shoving the stuff in your mouth raw.

I looked closely at the rugged characters around me. Because of the heat most of them had stripped to their undershirts and their tree trunk arms and barrel chests only hinted at their strength. These men were as solid as the rock they mined. They seemed cheerful enough, for the granite walls echoed with laughter.

"Hey Pete," one of them hollered across the room, "got yourself another greenhorn, eh?"

"First day," said Pete, adjusting the snuff under his bottom lip.

"Think ya kin make a miner outta him?" the heckler wanted to know.

Pete let go a gob of juice. Most of it splattered between his boots; the rest stained his chin.

"If they made a miner outta you," smiled Pete,"they can make a miner outta anybody!" That brought a chorus of laughter. Pete turned to me.

"I gotta warn ya," he said, "these crazy buggers are forever teasin' and playin' practical jokes, especially on new guys. But they don't mean no harm. Just don't let them get to ya."

Pete gave me a tour of the benches from where we sat. Timber Tom, Jackleg Louie, Boxhole Bill—next to them, Hooknose Mike—I must admit there didn't seem to be more than that to Mike's whole face!

"You'll get to know them all," said Pete, "and you'll find they're a pretty good bunch." He looked them over as if they were all his kids.

"A lot of people look down on a miner like he's some kind of worm," he said in a more serious tone, "what they don't know is there's a closeness among miners you don't see anywhere else. It's dangerous work. That's why we look out for one another."

As we were finishing our break, a young man walked the length of the lunchroom, handing out cigars to each man he passed. He was a good looking chap with wavy black hair, and his face beamed. When he got to me he stopped to introduce himself.

"Name's Joey," he said, "and last night my wife gave me a son... our first!" And he beamed even more. I smiled and thanked him.

"I'm sure glad you're on this level," he said. "Not too many guys my age here. I'm up in 48 stope. We'll talk some more when you'n Pete make the rounds."

Though I knew I'd never smoke it, I tucked away my cigar—the first thing I'd shared with my workmates. Just having it was enough.

Joey was 21 and had just bought a house for his growing family. He had been underground since he was eighteen and by now he was making good money. Enough to raise a family and have a good life so long as he was able to go down the mine each day. Our lives were alike in lots of ways. I thought that he might make a good friend.

Pete and I were the last to leave the lunchroom and as we walked along the main drift, there wasn't a soul in sight. The men had all disappeared into their workplaces like prairie dogs into their dens.

The drift had been illuminated as far as the lunchroom, but now, except for the light on our helmets, we were in total darkness.

The earth here was greyish-black; but now and again specks of ore reflected rainbows in our tiny helmet beams.

I noticed the walls of the drift were more and more wet the further we went. Droplets of water appeared on the roof. Everything glistened. Where minerals leached from the rock above, they formed cone-like stalactites on the ceiling. It reminded me of an eerie cave I'd read about in an adventure novel. At any moment I expected to be attacked by bats.

Then we came to a recess cut in the drift wall. In it was a trap door with a wooden guardrail. It was a manway, Pete explained; a set of ladders which led to the stope. A stope, he told me, was a big room heavily timbered against cave-ins where the main job of blasting and timbering was done.

"I want you to wait here," he said, "while I check to see if this crew needs supplies."

I watched Pete open the trap door and start down the manway. His light quickly dwindled to a faint glow, then to blackness. Suddenly I was very much alone. Everything was so still, so devoid of life. I almost believed I had strayed into prehistoric times, when the ore seams were being laid down. The silence, the stalactites, the glistening roof were beautiful. I was entranced.

Pete's light appeared again. "They'll be needin' timber," he said, puffing heavily, "but first we'll check 48 stope. Then we can do both places." The sweat ran down his face.

"This time you come with me." I followed Pete up the manway for about forty feet then through a trap door which brought us to a large opening cut into the ore body.

The stope reminded me of an underground parking lot. It had wooden pillars a foot thick every eight feet. At the far end was the actual working face, where the uncovered seam of ore gleamed in our lights as we approached.

Two men were bent over their air drills. They looked like machine gunners crouched to repel an attack. The pounding of steel against rock was ear-shattering. We came upon them unnoticed; but when Pete shook his helmet light, the drilling stopped. One of the men was Joey.

"Well, I see Pete's giving you the grand tour," he said with the same natural good humour he'd shown in the lunchroom, "if you're like me, you're probably thinking it's a hell of a way to make a living."

"My first day in this hole, I hated it!" Joey looked around. "Thought about quitting many times. Maybe someday I'll regret that I didn't." He laughed. "But I'm making good money working with Big Red. And I'll be needing it now."

Red was a moose of a man, as big as Pete but not as sloppy. His face was polka-dotted with freckles, and he had rusty hair to match.

"Take the new kid'n show him around," he told Joey. "I want to talk to Pete about what timber I'll be needin'."

"This is called a square-set stope," Joey explained.

"Usually two men work a stope, the leader and a driller. Working on piece work, we get paid a bonus for the ore we produce."

He had a way of explaining the job that didn't make me feel stupid.

"The floor we're on is called the mucking floor. This is where the drilling is done when we blast, the broken ore falls to the mucking floor. From there it is dragged to the chute by giant scrapers," Joey finished.

When we got back to Pete and Red they were both staring seriously at the roof of the stope. Small bits of rock trickled down through the wooden bracing.

"She's groanin' like hell," said Red with a look of concern.

"The supports are taking a lot of weight," Pete agreed.

"We'll put up more bracin'," said Red, "but you boys better nip back and get us a good supply of timber."

I thought I was in good shape until that day. The timber Red and Joey needed was big stuff. Some beams weighed as much as I did. And they had to be carried or dragged through low, narrow drifts with water or slime underfoot. My throat was dry, but the rest of me was soaked.

Pete, though he looked like an oversized dumpling, was incredibly strong. Some timbers that I couldn't even budge, he carried without effort. When he'd see me struggling, he'd pull out his box of snuff, and with a sly grin he'd say, "here, Laddy, just a wee bit, and ye'll be throwin' them timbers around like they were matchsticks." Then he'd chuckle.

My back was aching, but with less than a half-hour to go till lunch, we managed to nip up all the timber Big Red had ordered.

I was never so glad to see lunchtime. I wanted to cry, to lie down, to run away but I didn't have the strength to do anything but eat.

As I slumped down on one of the benches, the conversation floated around me like a stream.

"Drunk on the weekend?" someone asked me.

I smiled a "no" rather than said it.

"Haulin' timber's nothin'," said another, "wait 'till ya get on the drills." The others broke into laughter.

What could I do but grin? I didn't have the strength for anything else.

By the time lunch was over, I felt a little better. As Pete and I got up to leave, I realized that Joey and Big Red weren't there. I glanced down the length of the lunchroom, thinking they'd come in ahead of us. But neither of them were around.

This had just occurred to me when from outside the lunchroom came a faint sound. Instantly the hubbub ceased. I held my breath to listen. It was a kind of moan and footsteps... shuffling steps. Big Red staggered through the doorway. His helmet was missing and blood streaked his face. His arm dangled awkwardly at his side.

The men stood in silent shock. Then Red spoke the word that electrified them all.

"Cave-in!" he managed, "the whole damn place has come down." He grimaced with pain. "I dove down the manway but Jo-Joey..." he struggled to catch his breath, "...is still up there."

The foreman was the first to swing into action.

"Look after him," he shouted to two of the men, "and phone surface! Tell them there's been a cave-in at 48, and there may be a man in there yet. The rest of you, come with me."

We waited in the drift below 48 manway while the foreman went to check conditions above. We waited.

Finally the foreman came back.

"Looks bad," he told us. "From what I could see, the mining floor is completely buried." Someone cursed. "And part of the mucking floor with it," he said, and his eyes turned hard. "I couldn't find Joey. No answer when I called."

I couldn't believe what I was hearing, so I looked from face to face, hoping to find some kind of sign of a terrible, practical joke.

"First thing we'll do is remove some of the debris," said the foreman, bringing me back to reality. "Then we'll try to get onto the mucking floor. We have to hope he made it that far."

"The ground is still not settled in there, and there's more of it could come down," he warned, "For Chrissakes, be careful!"

Despite thick dust, unbearable heat, and cramped conditions, the men worked feverishly. *We* worked feverishly. In this emergency, new guy or not,I was just another miner.

Finally, enough debris was cleared away to make a passage through to the mucking floor. It was a shocking sight. Huge support timbers lay splintered from the massive weight of the cave in.

Slowly the miners moved ahead. Inch by inch they cleared the debris. New timbers were needed to shore up what space was gained, it was up to Pete and me to get them.

We searched the mucking floor thoroughly; but no sign of Joey. He had to be on the floor up above.

"There's blood over here!" Someone cried. Droplets of red oozed from the floor above, through the cracks between the planking.

Slowly, and with painful caution, the men cut the boards away. The veteran miners must have expected the worst, but they didn't show it in the way they worked.

When the last board came free, Joey's crushed body fell from above into waiting arms.

I saw him for the last time then; before he was covered with a blanket and put on a stretcher. It was not Joey, I told myself. A dust as fine as flour filled his mouth and his nostrils. It was hard to believe that we had ever talked, that a few hours before, he had been a proud father. I had to turn away and retch.

The cage was waiting to take us to surface. The body was placed gently on the floor. That morning I had stepped out of the cage as a greenhorn. Now I rode to the surface as part of an honour guard for a miner's last ride.

In what seemed no more than a few minutes, the darkness was broken by a burst of daylight shining through the wire mesh. Suddenly, the air was fresh again.

I waited until the body was removed. Then, not knowing what else to do, I wandered outside. The sun shone warm and bright. I wondered what sun Joey saw, because I didn't like to think of him in the dark. I didn't like to think of him down on forty-eight, on 4000 level—down in the worst darkness of all.

Mining is a dangerous business. Miners and their families have lived with the danger for generations. No matter how 'safe' they say the mine is, the danger is always there. It is part of what makes miners a close bunch. The danger is even an attraction to some. But the death of a friend or loved one down in a mine is not glamorous. In the years that followed there were more deaths, some of the victims were men I had got to know well. Each time it happened I felt a deep hurt but none effected me more than the death of poor Joey.

FOUR

For the longest time after that day I had second thoughts about my new job. Joey's broken body remained in my dreams to haunt me. Eventually, I adjusted to my role as a hardrock miner.

It was hot and dirty down in that stinking blackness but in the sunshine of the surface, things were different. I was satisfied with my life. Joyce seemed to share the feeling. On Saturday nights we went dancing at the Cabrini Hall or gathered with friends at our house to play cards or party. There was singing, guitar playing, more drinking. Our friends would stay till dawn. Joyce and I would make love then sleep till noon. On Sunday afternoons we'd bring the boys along and rejoin our friends at one of their houses for a barbecue and more partying.

Are the sound effects there? The snaffling of beer caps and the strumming of guitars. Can you hear the deep-throated laughter of adults mixed with high pitched squeals of the kids who play tag around the lawn chairs? Can you smell the aroma of highly seasoned char-broiled steaks, and the smoke from the barbecue?

Stop the clock at eight on a warm evening in May—one of those nights when the sounds of dogs and children fill the air and when darkness comes and the sounds falter and die suddenly in the streets. We arrived home from one of those all day barbecues. Joyce tucked the boys into their bunks while I put on the water for coffee.

Soon the boys are quieted down and the house is silent except the gurgling sound of the coffee pot. Joyce joins me at the kitchen table but her face is sombre; a tear appeared in the corner of her eye.

Then she says to me quietly, "Bill, we are going to have another baby. The doctor says I'm due in September."

I was shocked into the wrong response. "Oh, Jesus, no!
What happened to your calendar? You said it was safe."

Suddenly Joyce's control broke altogether and she leant into me, her head against my shoulder.

"Oh Bill, I don't know if I can handle another child. I can barely cope with the two we've got. I never dreamed married life would be like this."

We held each other close. My body surged with love for her. She was trembling, crying. In the breaks between her bouts of sobbing, I was aware of the gurgling coffee pot.

We had not planned the first two children and now Joyce was pregnant again. I could see us once again being tied down by feeding schedules, more diapers. As far as I was concerned, this new life in her womb was an intrusion, an unwanted complication in our lives.

* * *

That summer we bought ourselves a tent trailer to do some camping at Fairbanks Provincial Park. The park was a half hour drive from Creighton and a summer playground for a lot of the miners. Usually, on a Friday evening, Joyce and the boys would be waiting for me at the mine gates with the trailer hooked up and everyone raring to go. The only stop along the way was at the beer store in Lively.

After working underground all week amid the rat-tat-tat of drilling machines I longed to get out into the fresh air among the tall pines.

I well remember the summer weekends we spent there. Afternoons, we'd all head down to the beach to claim a spot among the tangled mass of bodies slowly frizzling in the sun. What a joyful madhouse. When the sun had reddened our bodies and heated the white sand hot enough to scorch the soles of our feet, we'd dash into the cool, spring-fed waters of the lake. The boys had no fear of water. They thrashed around like gaffed lake trout.

After a light supper back at our campsite, we'd bathe in mosquito repellant and gather around the campfire to toast marshmallows and sing campfire songs.

It was such a night, when I first accepted our unborn child not as a complication to our lives, not as an intrusion, but as a natural extension of our family.

One of those firefly nights, after the boys had been bundled up in their sleeping bags Joyce and I went skinny-dipping. The full moon skimming over the lake, seemed to focus all of its shimmering light on Joyce standing knee-deep in the water—the skin stretched drum tight over her tummy. Suddenly, she took my hand and pressed it to her swollen abdomen. "Feel it?" she said.

My hand moved steadily upward. "There are more attractive areas," I asserted.

"Not there, here," she laughed and brought my hand against the throb of life within her. The baby took up the cue and thumped the wall of Joyce's belly.

"I hope it's a girl," I said, patting her belly. I then carried Joyce to our blanket on the ground and made love to her while the fireflies winked in the hush of the night.

Teresa Ann Horner was born on September 15, 1964. The contractions began the night before. Joyce was calm and full of courage as I rushed her to the hospital. She laboured for sixteen long hours, finally giving birth at noon the following day.

It was a gift well worth waiting for. When I held my daughter in my arms afterwards, she was as fragile as porcelain. When she looked up at me and smiled with bright, sparkling eyes, I felt a sense of wonder.

We kissed, Joyce and I, very gently, and we wept together in our joy. We were both twenty-three years old, and life seemed marvellously good to us.

* * *

By 1967, I had been a miner for three years, and was 'hardrock' a miner as any of them. There were easier ways to make a living but considering my limited education, few that paid as well. I tolerated the damp, the dark, the sweat, the wrestling of huge equipment and machines not just for money alone. It meant independence and the satisfaction of being my own boss.

In my short time underground I'd learned a little about most aspects of mining. I preferred driftman's work. Driftmen work as a two-man team, blasting tunnels through the rock, developing ore for the other miners to produce. Driftmen have eyes only for the unconquered ground ahead of them. They are probably at greatest risk, working at a task that takes great nerve. In the hierarchy of the underground they are the kings.

My future as a miner brightened when I was accepted as a member of the Ontario Mine Rescue Team. Rescue Team members are trained for disaster work. If a mine disaster occurs, a team must be available, trained and equipped to effect rescues in contaminated air.

The rescue team became my goal the first time I saw them in action. Members of the Creighton team had come to use a mined out portion of our level to practice their rescue drills. They were dressed in black coveralls and white helmets. Except for their eyes, their faces were hidden behind facepieces. Attached to those facepieces were corrugated hoses which lead to oxygen cylinders strapped to their back.

I was highly impressed as they filed smartly past, and I continued to stare wide-eyed long after they had faded into the darkness like aliens from another planet. These men were the front line soldiers against mine disasters. That day my mind was made up. I was going to be one of them.

On a bright spring morning in April, I arrived at the rescue station in the little town of Frood Mine to begin my training. To qualify, a new member had to be between 22 and 44 and in good health, both mentally and physically. He had to be courageous,capable of performing long and arduous labour and familiar with underground conditions.

The rescue station was a two-story building perched on a rise overlooking the red brick headframes of Frood and Stobie mines. Scarring the barren landscape behind them was the Frood open pit, an enormous cavity, two miles wide and a quarter mile deep.

From where I stood, the clanging of cage bells could be heard resounding through the crisp morning air. Close by, a return air raise shaft spouted gusts of used air, its grey-white mist streaking the pale blue sky.

In the rescue station I took a seat in the classroom along with a dozen or more other recruits. They were all from other mines in the area. A quick glance around the room told me that most were as jittery and nervous as I was.

Our instructor, Harry Moorehouse, made the introductions all around. Harry was an average size guy, heavily tanned with a little pointed moustache. A ghost of a smile creased his kindly face, as he got down to business. "Glad to have you chaps aboard," he said, "this course was designed to teach you the basics of rescue and recovery work following a mine fire. I will be assessing you to see what kind of stuff you chaps are made of. But before we get into it, I'll warn you now that it'll be a rough go for the next five days."

His sharp-eyed glance flicked from face to face. I could have sworn it hesitated for a moment on mine. "Some of you might wish you'd stayed home—but those of you who can keep your balls up and see it through will be real rescue men."

The first two days of our basic training were spent in the classroom learning about poisonous gases, classification of fire extinguishers and testing and wearing oxygen breathing apparatus. Harry had us marching around out of doors five men linked together with standard four foot linklines. He stressed the importance of working as one unit, "the idea of the linkline is to keep you chaps together when travelling in strange territory or in atmosphere where visibility is limited."

On the third day we headed down into the depths of Frood Mine to put into practice what we had learned on surface.

Our field training was conducted on one of the upper levels mined out years ago. Now it was only visited by fireguards passing through on routine inspections. The level was old and smelled even older.

Dank stagnant air filled my nostrils as we followed behind Harry who guided us to the refuge station. On the way we passed by a side drift where rusted hulks of worn-out ore cars sat in the dingy gloom. A heavy wooden door infected with dry rot creaked noisily on rusted hinges. We brushed away a bit of the dust on the benches and sat awaiting further instructions.

"Today we're going to find out what it's like to fight an underground fire," Harry said, pacing among us. "Somewhere on this level I've piled some wood and tarpaper which makes one helluva fire. When I return it'll be up to you chaps to find it and put it out."

"This exercise should be a piece of cake," he continued, "but there are hazards. Do not remove your facepiece under any circumstances. Breathing that smoke for even a few seconds could mean your life. Are there any questions?"

We were silent, looking for answers in each other's faces, wondering what we had got ourselves into. As Harry was leaving the station he turned and looked directly at me. "Horner," he said, "you are the captain of the first team. Pick four other men and have them ready to go when I get back."

I was stunned. I had made myself as inconspicuous as I could, knowing Harry would eventually get around to appointing captains. Now, what I feared most had happened. Why he chose me I'll never know. I certainly didn't consider myself a leader!

I was still trying my damnedest to remember all the proper procedures a team captain must follow when Harry returned.

"O.K. Horner," he commanded, "get your team under oxygen and let's see some action."

Weighed down with fire extinguishers and other equipment, my team advanced into the level. A maze of drifts criss-crossed in front of us, but we found the right one. Billows of black smoke engulfed us. Our light beams were useless. I knew then what it felt like to be blind.

Completely adrift and leading four others, I stumbled into a drainage ditch that ran along one wall and heard the splash and curse of those behind me. I had just got us out of the ditch when I ploughed into an ore car almost knocking myself out. Suddenly I had a powerful urge to rip off my facepiece, but I didn't. I knew better.

Fearfully, I moved ahead bouncing off the walls as I went. Though we were all together in this mess, I felt lost and lonely.

My confidence waned. I felt like the blind leading the blind as we probed vainly onward step by step. We were moving so slowly I worried that we might run out of oxygen before we even got near the fire.

Then I remembered a simple manoeuvre Harry had taught us when travelling in heavy smoke—staying on the rails. I cursed myself for not thinking of it sooner. By sliding one foot along one of the steel rails, I managed to keep myself and the team in the centre of the drift until we stumbled upon the fire and put it out.

To my heartfelt relief, the smoke cleared and I could see again. Moments later, Harry arrived on the scene. "Jolly good show, chaps!" he said. "Bit of a shaker, wasn't it? But you've pulled it off and none of you are the worse for it."

Harry's statement wasn't exactly correct. When the air was tested and pronounced safe enough to allow us to remove our facepieces, one of the men had puked in his. The sight nauseated the rest of us. Harry's words must have been firmly implanted in this man's mind. Had he removed his facepiece rather than be sick in it, it would have meant certain death.

The next three days were spent underground marching for hours in and out of endless drifts. We crawled, squirmed and wriggled up and down manways. We learned to read maps. We practised the proper techniques for constructing barricades, improvising from materials at hand.

Through sheer determination and grit most of us endured this rigorous training schedule. By the end of it, only three of the original group had quit. Two more were considered: "Unsatisfactory rescue material." I came close to that fate myself.

Nevertheless I squeezed by. I beamed with pride as Harry presented me with a certificate from the Ontario Department of Mines stating I was a qualified member of the Ontario Mine Rescue Team.

FIVE

Nineteen sixty-seven was Canada's Centennial year. We celebrated by moving into a company house on Edward Street at the north end of town. It was a two bedroom frame house, painted canary yellow with chocolate brown trim. A green picket fence enclosed the grassy lawn, a definite improvement over the plot of clay and crushed mine rock we had at the other place.

The rent was a lot cheaper too—$19.00 a month. We were used to paying $45.00. Although it wasn't a newer or bigger house, we were thrilled to have it. What really excited Joyce and me was the three piece bathroom, complete with inside toilet. Joyce delighted in being able to bathe in privacy, no longer having to suffer the inconvenience and uneasiness of bathing in the kitchen in a galvanized tub. Yes siree, we were certainly moving up in the world.

But it was not all celebration that year. Not long after we settled into our new residence my mother developed cancer. A malignant tumour was discovered in her lower abdomen. The tumour was removed but the cancer had spread. "Nothing more can be done," her doctor informed us. It was only a matter of months.

I was stunned. Over many years she'd complained about pain. She'd told us many times; for our own reasons, none of us really believed her. I guess we didn't want to, especially my father, who was to keep a constant vigil at her bedside for five months.

When I think of it now, I remember that her belly always protruded; long after Janice, the last baby, was born. Often, I heard her retching her guts out in the bathroom. The cancer was probably growing in her then—growing gradually as a ship on the horizon grows taller only after you have forgotten about it for awhile. I was devastated. Other people got cancer, not my mother.

Each time I visited her in the hospital I could see how she was wasting away. She became so gaunt that her wedding ring slipped off her finger and was lost. Her lips were parched and cracking. She continually ran her tongue over them. She became dehydrated, unable to draw any liquid from the straw I held for her. When she screamed in pain, I wanted to run from the room and just keep on running till there was no more screaming.

In unguarded moments, deep bitterness welled up inside me. A mother who had denied herself for her eleven children was now losing everything—her clothes, her shoes, her tongue and skin, her mind.

The first boyhood memory I have of my mother is watching her come rushing in from the cold, from hanging out the clothes or bringing in an armload of firewood. She stood with her back to the old 'Findlay' wood stove to warm herself. Then, when she thought no one was looking, she'd hike up the back of her dress and rub her cold tingling legs.

My mother was a gentle women with hazel-brown eyes and dark brown hair. She rarely hurried, her regular gait was sort of a shuffle. She walked as she did everything else...languidly.

She was hooked on cigarettes. Most days, she smoked fifty, rolling her own from a tin of *Sweet Caporals*. The cigarettes were as thin as knitting needles to economize. Sometimes they got lost between her nicotine-stained fingers.

Because of her shyness, she was as careful with her affection as she was rolling her smokes. Her heart was large enough to accommodate loads of love for all her children. She could never really show it with a hug or a kiss. When I think back on those days, I think of how much I longed for a tender embrace or a peck on the cheek.

Now as I stared at her shrivelled body lying in a coma, her breath coming in laboured gasps, I found it hard to believe that I, her son, so healthy and strong, could do nothing to save her.

Strangely, I cannot remember the exact hour of her death, but I do remember that it was in the wee hours of the morning of September 5th. All through the night close relatives gathered in the hospital lounge because we knew she was very low and sinking.

Uncle Maurice and Aunt Terry were there. Beside me sat Uncle Joe, smelling as though he had braced himself up with booze. My sister Sue paced the corridor, crying, silently soaking her immaculate handkerchief.

Grandma Marion, partially paralysed by a recent stroke, had us all kneel to say the rosary. During the chanting of Hail Marys, her shoulders shook and a high screech escaped her murmuring lips. That was enough for my brother Bob, he got up from his knees and fled for the elevator. I followed. We both needed some air.

I coaxed him to the cab of my pick-up where I had a bottle of brandy stashed. He hadn't wanted to break down in my presence but he was so overcome by grief that he couldn't keep it in any longer. A low moaning sound filled the truck. I didn't know what to do except pass him the bottle.

After a long pull on the bottle we both felt better.

"Dammit, Bill," he managed, "why her? She is only forty-nine years old..." He buried his head in his hands and cried some more.

I had never seen my big brother cry before, and though I felt uneasy, I envied him. I loved Mom dearly, yet I could not shed one tear for her.

The funeral mass was held on a sunny day in September—a day that belonged half to summer and half to autumn. More than two hundred people came to Pope Pius X Church for the funeral.

My five brothers and I were pall bearers. Bob and I were in front, next were Len and Ken, then Bryan and Danny. Mom had carried each one of us; today, we carried her. We laid her gently at the foot of the altar amidst baskets and baskets of gladioli and pink and white carnations.

As I turned to go back down the aisle, I caught a glimpse of my father sitting in the front pew with Grandma Marion. He seemed smaller and older, his face dulled with pain. He was fifty-seven. He and Mom had been married for over thirty years. It was hard to imagine him without her by his side.

Father Delaney stood at the pulpit and read Mom's eulogy with a voice so soft and sincere that each word he spoke brought me closer and closer to tears. Still I didn't cry.

But later that night, when Joyce and the kids were asleep, I pulled the pillow over my eyes and mouth and there in the darkness I finally began to weep. I wept in rage at this cancer that had ended her life so soon and so painfully. I wept in sadness for the words we had exchanged and for those I had left unspoken even at the end: "I love you, Mom."

SIX

In the long evenings of summer Joyce and I would take the kids down to Vermilion River to fish for pike and catfish. The river was four miles behind Creighton over a gravelly road so bumpy and full of potholes that it was dangerous to drive more than twenty miles an hour. But we always enjoyed the ride.

We picked wild blueberries that grew at the side of the road to eat later with milk and sugar. When it was too hot to fish, we went to nearby Meatbird Lake to barbecue supper and refresh ourselves with a cool evening swim. We were a tight knit family and life was good.

My son Allen turned eight that spring. Quiet and reserved, he loved to tinker with electronic gadgets. Gordy was seven, adventurous and outgoing, a big hockey fan. He idolized Bobby Orr. They were good boys with very different personalities. I was certainly proud of them.

Teresa was four, a delightful child right from birth. As my children grew from childhood to adulthood, I tried not to favour one more than the other—to love each of them equally, but Teresa was such a good baby, I have to admit she was the apple of my eye.

It was at this time that we made another addition to the family. Sheba, a black Labrador was given to me by a friend bent on finding her a good home. A pure-breed from champion stock, she was a family pet as well as a hunting dog. So gentle, she could hold a raw egg uncracked in teeth that could snap a broomstick. She loved to play with the children, to run on a beach and plunge headlong into the water after a stick or ball, but Sheba was at her proudest when retrieving ducks.

She would huddle quietly at my side in a duck blind and together we'd scan the skies, waiting for the ducks to come streaking into my decoys or to fly within shooting range. There was hardly a fowl that Sheba failed to retrieve. We travelled miles of wooded trail together. A man could ask for no better companion.

On July 10, 1969 contract negotiations between the company and the union broke down and we were out on strike. Picketers with placards manned the mine gates. Helicopters buzzed food and supplies to supervisors locked inside, and food vouchers were distributed to union workers. These were the definite signs of a long strike.

We were given a food voucher for thirty two dollars a week. It wasn't much but somehow we managed. We ate a lot of potatoes, drank tea and Kool-aid. Beer and steaks became a luxury. Smoking was too, but each week we treated ourselves to a tin of tobacco which had to do us till the next voucher.

As the strike dragged on the town grew quiet. The men on the picket lines idled away the hours pitching horseshoes or playing poker for matchsticks without enthusiasm. Everyone moved slowly. They ambled up to the post office, shuffled in and out of the three stores in town, taking their time about everything.

For the striking miners, free time each day was twenty-four hours long. There was no hurry, for there was nowhere to go, nothing to buy, and no money to buy it with. An atmosphere of gloom settled over Creighton, with very little optimism for the future.

Somehow that summer seemed hotter than most. Rain was scarce. The heat seemed to bake into the streets. A tanker truck sprayed a molasses coloured oil on them each week to stifle the grey, choking dust. Blueberries wilted and died on the vine before ripening. Meatbird Lake turned murky green from the throngs of bathers who sought relief from the scorching heat.

My dad saw the strike as an opportunity for a vacation. He owned a little cottage about sixty miles east of Creighton on Lake Washagami and that's where he was headed. On his way he stopped by our house and invited us to join him. "Lots of room there to park a tent trailer," he said.

I had been there once before, back in '62. Dad had asked me to haul in a truckload of camping stuff for them and for the nine kids staying with them that summer.I had driven there at night, after working the day shift. I didn't recall much about Washagami except that it was deep in the bush and isolated.

Considering the heat, Dad's offer couldn't have come at a better time. The following day we were on our way. The children were excited, looking forward to the long ride in the great blue wagon. I was annoyed when their crayons melted and made a drippy mess on the back seat of my new station wagon.

Joyce was the last one in, and when she slid into the front seat next to me I had to admit she looked pretty damn good for a mother of three. She had on a pair of tight shorts that showed her pretty legs and a skimpy blue halter top that accented her trim figure. She caught my stare and said jokingly. "I know what you're thinking, Mr. Horney, but you just keep your thoughts to yourself and your eyes on the road."

My reply to that was a joking leer and a sly grin.

I turned north off Highway 17, for the next twenty miles following a tattered ribbon of bush road that wound over steep hills and over corduroy logs that bridged swamps. I could have cried out loud each time my new wagon crunched into a pothole.

The drive seemed endless. When we were deep into the interior, a news flash interrupted the music, announcing American astronauts have landed on the moon.

The sudden elation I felt for Neil Armstrong and his courageous crew gave me goose bumps—but at the same time I wondered if it was as much of a journey for them to reach the moon as it was for us to reach Washagami.

By late afternoon we finally arrived at the lake. Dad waved from his cottage landing as we drove up. When I stepped from the car, I was immediately struck by the absolute quiet and remoteness of Washagami. It was as though we had stumbled onto a lost world.

In front of Dad's cottage the pristine water rippled onto a sandy beach. I walked with him along the water's edge.

"Washagami," he said, "is an Indian word meaning clear water." Beneath the surface I could count every pebble on the lake's gravelly bottom.

Looking around me, I could understand why Dad always talked up Washagami and why he and Mom had planned to make this their home someday. It was utterly beautiful—a rugged beauty that captured our heart.

Where did the day go? Here we had lost all sense of time. The wind was dying down and the sun had fallen behind the tops of the pine trees. Joyce and I worked quickly to set up housekeeping inside the tent trailer. There were sleeping bags to unroll, pots and pans and kids' pyjamas to unpack, food to stow, the gas lantern and stove to set up.

By the time darkness fell, we had managed to store away the last of the articles in the tent trailer. As the big yellow moon skipped moonbeams across the black water, we settled in for the night and for the summer.

At Washagami, life stood still. We ate when we were hungry, stretched out in the grey-white sand to soak in the sun, and splashed and played in the lake when the sun grew too hot. In the evenings we fished for walleye off Bald Island or searched for raspberries in clumps of bramble bushes along the roadside.

Out on the water, the sun sparkled and the air was clear and warm. The thrust of Dad's outboard motor ruffled the hair of Allen and Gordy looking over the windshield. A down of spray covered their faces. I noticed how Joyce's eyebrows swirled in interesting little clumps as she smiled into the wind.

It was also a time to get to know my father. He was more or less a stranger to me. To earn extra income for a house full of kids, he moonlighted as a backyard mechanic, repairing neighbourhood cars. Mom had commented one time that when he wasn't underground, he was under somebody's hood. His schedule was so heavy he had little time to spend with us kids.

After Mom's death he was depressed for the longest time. He never spoke to any of us about his grief. It was his alone. He and Mom were very close. As far back as I can recall, every Saturday night they used to sit at the kitchen table sharing a bottle of Hudson Bay rum and playing crib till the early hours of morning. This was the Saturday night ritual, it was always just the two of them.

Evening in Dad's cottage was a time of warmth and togetherness. Sometimes other family members joined us at Washagami. When the mosquitoes chased us inside at twilight we'd all gather round the long wooden table for a game of hearts.

I still laugh out loud when I remember how my brother Ken, who was always a bit jumpy, would fling his cards in the air at any sudden noise. Or remembering Bob going down to the lake in the black of night to fetch water for tea and coming back sopping wet with lily pads hanging from his shirt collar.

When we tired of cards we were entertained by Dad's master storytelling. When Dad told his stories, he laughed, his eyes watering in merriment. Often his tale focused on a family member, who would redden while the rest of us held our bellies in laughter. Sadly, summer was coming to an end, and the beginning of the school year was just around the corner. Before we headed back to civilization, Joyce and I talked about the possibility of buying some lake front property when the strike was over.

Dad took us on a tour of the lake to show us what was available. There wasn't all that much to choose from. The first parcel of land we explored sat dangerously high above the water surrounded by great patches of rock. There was another spot Dad suggested we should look at. It was a mile up the lake from Dad's cottage, sheltered in a bay between two jutting points of rock. The land sat only a few feet above water level with a gentle slope to the water's edge. Huge red pine studded the shoreline.

"It's lovely," Joyce cried the minute she saw it. It was the right place.

As Dad cut the motor and coasted to shore, six loons fishing among the water lilies flew out of the bay, uttering their strange plaintive cry. It was mutual, without a word spoken between us, Joyce and I knew this was the place where we would build our cottage.

SEVEN

The multicoloured lights of the Christmas tree brightened the living room. Joyce had holly over the pictures and a big spray of mistletoe was hung over the doorway. The supper table was decorated with our best china on a paper cloth of jolly Santa Clauses. The whole room glowed and the smell of delicious roast turkey filled the house.

"My, how dashing you look," Joyce had told me earlier when I stepped from our bedroom dressed in a white shirt and black suit, with a narrow wine-coloured tie. I like getting compliments from my wife, but she was the one who deserved them. She fairly sparkled in her dress of red fluff and sequins.

Joyce had just finished the last of the meal preparations. I helped her set out the wine, put the pickles and cranberry sauce in their serving dishes, and brought in a basket of bread rolls fresh from the oven. A call of "wash for supper" brought the three children scurrying from the bedroom. They had been there most of the day playing Snakes n' Ladders and building with their Lego sets.

Across from me sat Gordon, working on his fifth drink. His suit coat hung from the back of his chair and his tie was askew. Whenever he had a few, Gordon's his hair fell over his forehead like corn silk. In a slurred tongue, and true to form, he proceeded to tell everyone how much he loved them—even me. Each time he got that way, Laurette, my mother-in-law, glared at him. "Gordon," she barked, startling everyone at the table, especially Gordon, "You have had enough!"

Not a Christmas has gone by that Joyce and I haven't had her parents over for supper. And it always ended like that. It really didn't bother Joyce and me to see them bicker this way. In fact, we had grown accustomed to their antics over the years. Even the kids were amused to see little 'Nanny' yelling at big 'Papa.'

It would have been impossible for anyone to put a damper on our spirits that year. The strike had ended in October, and that meant we could go ahead with the dream we both held in our hearts—to build our cottage on Lake Washagami.

How wonderful it is to realize a dream when you are still young. At first, our dream seemed more like a wild fancy. We had no money for such a wonderful luxury. Through the credit union I managed to borrow three hundred and seventy dollars to purchase the property and another four hundred for surveying costs.

This Christmas, our family gift to each other was the cottage.

Of course, we still needed building materials. The government criteria for purchasing crown land was that a building of at least 280 square feet must be erected within a two year period or the land reverted back to them.

That spring we had great plans. It always came back to the same thing; how could we afford building materials? Then around the end of April, I heard about a four-room house about to be put to the bulldozer.

In Creighton, it was standard company procedure to demolish any of their houses they felt would cost too much to repair. Sometimes though, a house scheduled for demolition would be given away to the person willing to accept the responsibility for tearing it down and clearing away the debris afterwards.

I was flushed with excitement the day I came home and told Joyce the house was ours. It was just a tarpaper shack—but it meant free lumber.

"Isn't that a lot of work?" she said, wrinkling her brow.

"It certainly is," I agreed, "but I've got two weeks vacation coming. I can do it then. Besides, it's the only way I can see us getting lumber. You do want a cottage, don't you?"

"Do I," her eyes brightened, "I've never wanted anything so much."

For two whole weeks I worked from dawn till dusk with hammer and crowbar. Gradually the house surrendered to me, board by board and nail by rusty nail. When I had torn down enough lumber to fill the back of my old pick-up, I'd haul it home, then go back for another load, and then another. Finally, I had one complete house stacked in my back yard.

Next, I rented a five-ton truck from Takela's garage and hauled the lumber to Dad's place at Washagami. Every weekend that summer Joyce and I spent working on our cottage.

After we squared and levelled the bearing timber, the walls went up quickly. The old lumber was solid but rough and difficult to use. We put the studding on the sides, spliced planks for joists, ripped up two-by-sixes when two-by-fours were essential. By the time I finished the roof, Joyce had nearly sheathed two walls.

On that particular weekend there was hardly a whisper of air. The sun scorched our backs. Alone, just the two of us, we shed our clothes and raced into the water to cool off. Afterward we sprawled out on the rain-washed rocks and ate our lunch of cheese sandwiches and drank cold beer from the cooler.

All the time I worked on the cottage, Joyce was by my side. She handed up the boards I nailed into the rafters. She peeled the pine logs we used to tie in the walls. Her help heartened me, for the situation called for all the strength we both possessed. I admired the way she helped me saw and hammer hour after hour and the effortless and graceful way she packed lumber from the pile and shouldered roofing paper up the ladder.

Our dream was taking shape and it was wonderful to watch. Near the end of the summer, we had the main camp standing. We started on the porch, using peeled spruce and cedar posts. Allen and Gordy nailed down the plywood flooring. The frame went up in a day, the roof the following night. We all worked together. A warm sense of family unity flowed steadily among us.

The weekend when the porch screens were installed Joyce and I stood back and surveyed the summer's work with the glorious feeling that comes with achievement.

"Looks like we got ourselves one beautiful place," she said as we threw our arms around one another.

We celebrated that memorable day by opening a bottle of red Chianti and christened the cottage 'Horner's Hideaway.'

* * *

Around 8 o'clock in the morning of August 20th I was back home in Creighton when the sound of rolling thunder woke me from a deep sleep. The large poplar tree outside my bedroom window bent harshly from the fury of the wind, the yellow leaves of late summer whipping away. Lightening flashed and a clap of thunder knocked out the power. All three children scurried into bed with Joyce and me. The house was dark and quiet.

We peered out the bedroom window to watch the storm. The full turbulence seemed to be moving swiftly some distance away. The rain struck in a torrential fury. Almost instantly rivulets of water rushed down the driveway.

"Wow Dad," Gordy cried, "we got our own river!" As the children watched in awe, we huddled a little closer.

The storm raced through the country attacking the night with sporadic cracks of blue light and thunder with such violence it seemed the whole world would come crashing down.

The sound died away. As quickly as it came, the storm moved on. Sunlight slashed through the clouds and a rainbow of colours shimmered on the puddles.

I lit up a cigarette and turned on my portable radio to catch the 9 o'clock news. The words I heard made me leap from my bed.

"A freak hurricane has struck the town of Lively," the announcer said, "latest reports indicate at least one dead, two seriously injured." My family lived in Lively.

"I have to get down there right away," I told Joyce, yanking a sweater over my head, "I have to be sure the folks are okay."

As I approached Lively from the hill by the water tank, I could see where the hurricane had cut a quarter mile swath through the forest, smashing trees, leaving behind a tangle of gnarled and twisted roots. A rug of brown, shaggy moss made the ground look like old animal hides. Across the highway, the sudden savage wind had bowled over cars, toppled chimneys, and lifted houses off their foundations. Half the town lay devastated.

Many people were out in the street, quite a few still in pyjamas. They talked in small groups or wandered up and down the cluttered street, checking the wreckage, stunned and confused.

I moved quickly, my heart racing. When I turned the corner on Sixth Avenue, I was relieved to see Dad's house still standing. The front window panes were gone and a patchwork of shingles had been blown off the roof. Other than that, the house seemed to be okay.

Grandma Marion was shuffling to and fro on the front sidewalk, clutching her rosary. She burst into tears when she saw me. "Oh dear," she cried, "It was dreadful! We could have all been killed...I was in bed when it happened... Oh dear." She cried some more. I held her a moment until she stopped crying.

"Thank God Danny and Janice are alright," Grandma said, dabbing at her tears with a white hanky she kept in her dress sleeve, "they're inside cleaning up the broken glass."

All my worry was gone now that I knew my brother and sister were alright. As I looked around me, I realized just how lucky they were. Dad's garage had been flattened and his tools swept away. The neighbour's house, directly behind his on Birch Street, was now missing the second story. A spanking new pre-fab, next door to the Quinn's was gone altogether—the remnants of it scattered across the golf course. Dad was underground for the dayshift. I could only imagine the look on his face when he came home and saw all this mess.

The miners didn't go underground that afternoon. Instead we were sent to Lively to repair the damaged rooftops temporarily in case more rain came. We had to work quickly, nailing down plastic sheeting before darkness fell.

It was the kind of work I found extremely tiring on my legs—climbing up wooden ladders with heavy rolls of plastic. By the end of the shift my right foot was dragging and there was a slight tingling sensation in my hands and legs. I ignored the feeling. It had been a long, stressful day. All I needed was a good night's rest.

EIGHT

Thanksgiving weekend was celebrated amidst a blaze of colours at Washagami. Joyce and I were observing our eleventh wedding anniversary with some time alone at the cottage. The children were staying with Nanny and Poppa.

On our way I stopped at the *Canadian Tire* store and bought Joyce a light gauge shotgun. Over the summer months we had watched partridge strut around our half-acre like chickens in a barnyard. This weekend we planned to shoot a few for supper. I had my own recipe for northern fried partridge served on a bed of wild rice that was pretty damned good.

The morning was clear and bright. Our hunting jackets matched the glorious red hills. Around us the world was richly coloured; the dark greens of balsam and spruce contrasted with the extravagance of poplar and white birch.

We stopped in a poplar grove. The ground was covered by a leafy green plant with red berries. I told Joyce we should stop and listen. I knew that if partridge were around they could be heard clucking through the woods. It was almost impossible to see them, so heavy was the foliage.

"If we're quiet, they'll start to move again," I said, "our noise will make them stay still, frozen in one spot."

We listened to the hum of the forest. I nudged Joyce, and pointed my finger. Looking where I pointed, she caught sight of the wary staring eye of a partridge, its brown body camouflaged by the surroundings.

"Go ahead," I whispered, "no, pull the hammer back first. Hold the gun tight, like I showed you."

She fired. She missed.

The whir of wings beat the air as I fired at the slowly rising bird. Feathers sprayed out from its white-etched tail and the bird dropped some thirty feet away.

"The next one is yours," I told Joyce trying not to smile.

"I know," Joyce answered, "I'll remember what to do.
Wasn't that bird kind to wait."

"Just dumb," I said, "they're tame before they're shot at."

It was around noon before Joyce got her turn. Now we each had one. I managed another before we headed back. Not bad for a morning's hunt and more than enough for a great meal.

The day had grown warm and humid as the sun sparkled through a canopy of leaves over our heads. I suddenly felt exhausted. My right foot dropped whenever I went to lift it over a log or a clump of grass, causing me to stumble.

"Are you feeling all right?" Joyce said, glancing round in time to see me catch my balance. "You sure are walking funny."

I had to pause a moment to rest. "I don't know what it is," I admitted, "I was okay a moment ago, but now I feel bushed and my leg tingles." I leaned my gun against a tree and rubbed at my leg.

What in the hell was going on? I cursed inwardly. My leg was acting the same way it did the time of the hurricane. I recalled too, that ever since then I hadn't been sleeping all that well either.

Besides the insomnia, other peculiar things were happening that had me baffled. I almost panicked one morning the week before when, as I tried to get out of bed, I opened my eyes to a twisting ceiling and a whirling room. I attributed that incident to a few drinks I had the night before. Then there was the persistent cramps in both my legs. But a lot of miners have that. We blame it on the heavy rubber boots we have to wear.

Back at the cottage I plunked down into my favourite arm chair by the wood stove and rested while Joyce made us lunch. For the rest of that day I kept the weight off my leg as much as I could.

The next morning, although the numbness persisted, I felt great. Maybe a good rest was all I needed to feel like my old self again. I began the day full of vim and vigour. Then the strangest thing happened.

I was boarding up the windows as a precaution against the onslaught of winter. When I went to drive in the nails, my aim was nowhere near the nailhead. I swung my hammer again and again. For every blow that hit the target, three missed. I had lost my eye-hand coordination. Joyce laughed when she saw my futile attack at the elusive nail. "Trade your hammer for a shovel," she kidded.

I answered her with a grin, but I was beginning to realize this was nothing to grin about. This was serious.

Besides the lack of coordination, I felt a prickly sensation from my wrists through to my finger tips, as if they'd gone to sleep. I was more baffled than ever and now I was getting scared out of my wits.

For the rest of the weekend, Joyce and I teamed together to complete the work that had to be done—at least I could hold the boards while she drove home the nails.

Perhaps I was being more stubborn than wise when I returned to work the following day. I had to fight off an overpowering feeling of lethargy as I forced myself up from the bed. The strength had returned to my leg but the pins and needles sensation had spread from my hand down the entire right side of my body.

I swallowed hard to clear my ears as the cage swayed down the shaft. The rocks blurred by. An occasional rush of water from the ceiling was the only indication that our destination was more than a mile underground.

Mike Cranston and I fixed the lights on our helmets in anticipation. When the cage came to a stop, we entered the dimly lit station on 5200 Level, a warm and humid part of the mine. Without a word we strode into one of the black tunnels. Our nostrils had long ago become accustomed to the smell of the dank, damp earth and to the burnt powder fumes hanging in the air.

We were the only men working on the level. Except for the sound of our footsteps sloshing through water and the reverberation through the rock of a far away drill, it was a world of silence. Any sound was a violation.

Mike and I had been drift partners for more than two years. We had learned to respect each other's privacy, moods and weaknesses. He was powerfully built, about my age and a native of Manitoulin Island. His easy-going, laid-back manner was typical of his fellow Islanders. This morning, Mike seemed to sense my brooding mood. His good natured banter broke the silence between us: "Your ol' lady not good to you this weekend, eh Boy?"

I smiled weakly. He knew he should say no more. We walked for another twenty minutes down the haulage drift, finally reaching the crosscut where we were working, driving a drift through to a large ore-body.

While Mike scaled the newly broken ground from our previous blast, I oiled and set up the eighty pound stoppers. Stoppers are drilling machines used to fasten a wire mesh to the ceiling with rock bolts, forming a continuous canopy overhead. Mike and I knew our routines. Not a word needed to be spoken.

Soon the low-pitched scream of compressed air filled the narrow opening and echoed over and over down the hall. We did not notice the noise, nor did it bother us.

For lunch Mike and I remained in the drift. Too much time would be lost hiking back to the lunchroom.

My mood was getting me down so I decided to share my problem with Mike, whose big grubby hands were wrapped around a roast beef sandwich.

"I've been thinking of getting out of drift work," I said.

"What the hell you talking about?" he said between bites, his eyes widening in surprise. "Me an' you been drift partners for a coupl'a years an' makin' goddamn good money too. You gonna give it all up?" Then in a softer tone he added, "What's botherin' you, Boy?"

"That's just it, Mike," I replied, "I don't know what's bothering me. All I know is I just don't have the strength to continue this kind of bull work. I was thinking to transfer into mechanical... It's a lot easier."

In a lowered voice I told Mike about the odd sensations I'd been experiencing these past few weeks.

"Keep your mouth shut about this, o.k., Mike? I don't want anyone to know, at least until I get some answers."

Traditionally, miners are very concerned about keeping fit enough to stay on the job and bring home a good cheque. It takes a healthy body to do the tasks required down in a mine. Without our health we come to think of ourselves as less than whole men, not properly able to provide. I didn't want anyone casting doubt on my physical abilities.

We managed to make our blast at the end of the shift. By then the work and the heat had me exhausted. When we walked the long drift back to the station, I was no match for Mike's stride. My right leg dragged and sometimes I'd stagger with a stiffening gait.

The next day I didn't show up for work. Instead I went to Lively to get a second opinion from a doctor down there.

When I tried to explain my weird symptoms, they sounded so bizarre that he became surly and short-tempered. He actually refused to believe anything was wrong with me. Before even attempting to make a diagnosis, he began to criticise me. "You moose hunters are all alike," he said sharply. "As soon as the season rolls around, you make up these phoney illnesses expecting me to write out a doctor's slip." His accusing eye bored right through me, leaving me stunned and speechless.

"I'll let it go this time," he continued, "but don't make a habit of it. I'll see you in two weeks."

Often, when I think back to that day in his office, I can only attribute his rude manner to the fact that I had presented him with questions he could not answer. I suppose many doctors think of themselves as infallible healers. In this particular doctor's case, I can see now that he must have felt angry and frustrated when the healer's role was denied to him.

NINE

Everybody knew something was going to happen, the way you feel a storm in the air long before it hits. I first heard it from Mrs. Moore, the lady who ran the post office. "Most of the houses in Creighton are coming down," she said.

"Something to do with improper sewage is what I gather..."

Shock and anger were all over the faces of the miners when rumours of it reached underground. It was the main topic of the lunchroom

"A crock of shit," Tiny Connors said. "Creighton is the richest nickel mine in Canada, maybe the world, yet this bullshit company expects us to believe they can't afford proper sewage treatment for our homes. They'll tear 'em down instead. Don't give one God damn about us. Just goes to prove we're just another badge number to them guys."

After my time off, I felt strong enough to return to work. However, I did not go back as a miner. I began my new job as a second class garage mechanic over in Three Shaft. I still had to go underground but toting a tool box was much easier than wrestling an eighty pound jackleg drill.

By this time most of the strength had returned to my leg even though the tingling sensation remained. In the back of my mind I had the strangest feeling that whatever I had was here to stay—bubbling away like an evil brew—working against the strength in my body.

As soon as the snow melted, the company bulldozer began bashing down the first houses, leaving emptiness in its place. One by one, they all followed. The buried house sites were marked by stumps of blackened timbers and low depressions of tumbled-in cellars.

One day I arrived home from work to find Joyce sitting at the kitchen table clutching a sheet of official-looking paper. Her eyes were red-rimmed, her face ashen grey. "What is it, Joyce? What's the matter?"

I snatched the letter from her grip. Every word made me sick. Even though we had watched the houses around us being torn down, we hoped somehow ours would be spared. It was in better shape than most. But now, the notice to move out had arrived.

"I don't understand why they would do this to us," Joyce cried. She looked me straight in the eye, as if I concealed the answer. Her hands trembled, she bit her bottom lip.

"We worked so damn hard to fix this place the way we wanted it; now they're going to tear it down on top of us. Why in God's name can't they leave things the way they are?"

Almost a year had gone by since we moved up on 'Snob Hill.' This part of Creighton was considered the newer section of town even though the houses were built just after World War II. It was nicknamed Snob Hill, because at one time this was the prestigious part of town. The new fashionable homes had been set aside for company bigwigs—supervisors, engineers, mine captains.

The row of identical, two-story houses had long since lost their newness, and with the newness went some of the prestige. Common folk had invaded the hill. Now the houses we proudly occupied would be torn down.

Joyce and I talked long into the night. We were disappointed to lose the house, but we knew we could make it okay somewhere else.

* * *

It was a bitterly cold night in January and not a soul stirred beyond the frosted window pane. It was a night to stay indoors and watch television, which was exactly what the kids were doing. Joyce was curled up in her swivel rocker crocheting a yellow and blue afghan she planned to use as a covering for the sofa. I was doing what I usually did after supper, rest. I had disappeared upstairs to lay down for a while. It seemed lately that the simple exertion of eating a meal left me utterly exhausted.

As the cold moonbeams fell through my window, partially lighting up our bedroom, the Disney theme song 'When You Wish Upon A Star' drifted up from the television downstairs. The soft sounds of the melody blended with the quiet and moonlight. The serenity of the moment lulled my thoughts back to last night.

Usually, Joyce and I looked with anticipation to our bouts of lovemaking. Last night everything was wonderful—at least it began that way. I kissed her tenderly. She returned my kisses. We embraced and teased and cajoled, brimming with desire.

I was breathing hard as Joyce arched her back to guide me into her warmth. Before I could bring our love act to a climax, the ecstasy faded. I was unable to maintain an erection.

I rolled over on my back and stared into darkness. This sort of thing had never happened before. Why did it happen now?

Joyce put her head on my chest and clung to me. "Don't worry," she said, "these things happen. Everything will be alright."

"I am sorry," I said, "it's not your fault. I just can't understand..."

Joyce soothed me and talked to me and told me I could be a little tired. "Go to sleep," she said, "you'll wake up in the night as good as ever and we'll start again. Go to sleep. Just relax..."

The jangling phone on the night table scattered my thoughts. It seemed louder than usual. I felt an immediate sense of alarm. My intuition was right; the voice on the other end said that smoke was rising from Number Nine shaft. A rescue team was needed immediately.

I arrived as the rescue truck was being unloaded at the substation. I joined in to help the other team members. Not one of us had ever experienced a real mine fire, but we'd been through enough drills to know what we had to do.

On a long wooden table we inspected each piece of equipment to be taken with us. A safety lamp to determine oxygen deficiency, link lines, hand whistles, a CO Tester to indicate the amounts of carbon monoxide, and above all our oxygen breathing apparatus. There could be no mistake in a mine fire.

The briefing officer entered to give final instructions. When the door swung open the clamouring of the sound of the cage bells sharpened my anticipation. Only a matter of minutes separated us from experiencing a real mine fire.

"All I can tell you at this time," the officer said, "is that smoke is rising in the shaft from as far down as 5200 Level. This has been confirmed by the cagetender. We know the fire has to be in this area. Your instructions are to pinpoint the source and report back to surface."

During the briefing I took a quick survey of the men around me. A naked light bulb swaying over the table threw Al Simpson's face into solemn relief. He looked what he was, a bull of a man with a bull's strength. He could hustle up a stope ladder with a jackleg drill strung over each shoulder. Next to him sat his younger brother Royce, known for his darting brown eyes and his lightning reflexes. Royce had a feline air of independence yet was unfailingly gentle in his manner.

If I felt a need for reassurance, I had only to look at two stocky round-faced boys who sat together at the end of the table. Carson and Leo were prime examples of the stuff of which mine rescue was made. These two sat in companionable silence with such calmness it appeared as if nothing in the world could unhinge them. I felt a wave of respect and affection for these men.

The briefing officer appointed me as team captain. He concluded that since I was more familiar with the area, I should lead the way. This was the moment to call on my five years of mine rescue training. It was my moment. I seized it with apprehension; my bowels constricted a little more.

We shuffled into the cage. Wisps of smoke rising at our feet. Donning their facepieces, the men became faceless and indistinct, like figures in some sombre dream. There was no sound except for the slither of the cage gliding over the shaft guides and the heavy hiss of breathing through the oxygen apparatus.

As the cage dropped deeper into the shaft, I hoped my leg would hold out. The echoing of the cage bells snapped my mind back to the present as the cage bobbed to a stop and the heavy steel door creaked open at 5200 Level.

Smoke greeted us at the station. It was like a steaming fog, which our light beams could penetrate.

Before advancing further, I inspected the gauge of each team member's oxygen apparatus. Then, I snapped an indicator tube into the CO Tester to determine the amount of carbon monoxide in the air. It read 3000 parts per million, enough to render a man unconscious within seconds. My hands were slimed with sweat as I gave my team the order to advance into the murky gloom. A thorough inspection of the level revealed nothing. There was smoke but no fire. A tour of 5000 Level proved to be the same as 5200 except that we ran into much heavier smoke.

By this time we had been under oxygen for more than two hours. A quick check of our pressure gauges told me that we had enough oxygen in our tanks to investigate one more level.

On 4800 Level the smoke billowed thicker and heavier the further we went. The apprehension knifing at my guts vanished in the excitement of the pursuit. About a mile in from the station we heard the distinct sound of fire snapping and crackling in a heavily timbered section of the mine. There was another sound too—the crashing noise of ground caving in where fire had weakened the support timbers.

We could not advance any further. We had only to report to surface to report our findings. Our mission was over.

On the way back, my apprehension returned. My leg started to act up. There was dragging, and a stiffening gait which caused me to stagger. I stumbled on as best I could but there was no way I could keep up.

Panic engulfed me. I knew that our oxygen supply was dangerously low and at this rate the whole team was in jeopardy.

I signalled the team to a halt so that I could talk to Al, the vice-captain. "You're in charge," I yelled, motioning to my leg. "I injured it back there. You and the other men will have to carry me."

Though my voice was barely audible through the facepiece, Al nodded. He got the message.

With one man on either side of me I was carried back to the station where the cage was waiting. Only minutes passed before the warning bell sounded on one team member's oxygen bottle.

We were all relieved to breathe the fresh, cold air on surface. No one was more relieved than I. My rescuers showed deep concern as they fussed over my leg. I couldn't help but feel a little foolish and embarrassed. I had come to fight a mine fire and ended up being a burden to four other men.

* * *

This time, when I entered his office, my doctor wasn't as callous. He was more understanding, more attentive when I explained what happened underground.

For the longest time he sat thinking, drumming his desk with his fingers. I was half expecting to be sent home with another batch of nerve pills. He spoke at last.

"There is a new doctor in town. His name is Rastogi. He is reputed to be an excellent neurologist. I'll make an appointment for you."

The seriousness of his tone made my heart flutter. I had a strange feeling he suspected something serious.

TEN

My appointment with Dr. Rastogi in March resulted in a month of tests and then more tests. In the meantime, after a few weeks rest, my leg had regained most of its strength, my vision had long since cleared, but numbness persisted in my fingertips.

An answer to my mystery illness wasn't long in coming. The final test was a spinal tap. When the results returned from Toronto, Rastogi called me in his office. "Bad news, Mr. Horner," he said without wasting any time. The spinal tap had confirmed his diagnosis: Multiple Sclerosis.

I was stunned. The doctor was still talking. "When you complained about the numbness in you hand and the leg weakness, well, I suspected."

When I regained my composure, my mind filled with questions. "What causes it?" I asked.

He only shook his head.

"Treatment?" I asked, "a cure?"

"Not yet," he said. He sounded ashamed.

"Will it get worse?" I asked, not really believing that it would.

"It is usually progressive," he said, "I'd be lying if I said it won't get worse. But we know one thing. It is neurological. Stress or overexertion may trigger an attack at any time. We can't predict when the attacks might occur or what parts of the body will be affected. We can't even tell how bad you'll be once you've had them."

This was an awfully difficult sentence to live under. What is stress after all? And how much is too much?

* * *

Three months had passed since the day when I was told I had multiple sclerosis and life had gone on as if nothing had changed. So what was wrong with a little hike in the woods?

Allen sat stretching on the edge of his bed. Through half-opened eyes, he peered at the bedroom window.

"Dad," he said, "are we going fishing in the dark?"

I had to laugh at the expression on his face.

"No son," I said, "but we are fishing for bass. Bass bite best early in the morning, and it's a long way to the lake. You boys hurry and get dressed, while I start breakfast."

We planned to fish in Northwest Lake that day. It was in the same area in which Gordon had introduced me to deer hunting. A twenty-five mile drive would take us to the very end of the road. From there we would walk, following a well-trodden path for two miles. For another two miles, we would have to trek up and down over very rough terrain through unmarked bush—a long way for two young boys.

You can figure a mile in the Northern Ontario wilderness is like ten miles along a cleared bush road. No one should even think about trying it unless they are in good shape. Once I took a buddy from the mine in there with the promise of great small mouth fishing. After eventually making it back to the road he leaned against the truck and panted: "Horner, I don't give a damn how many fish we caught in your bloody lake today. You'll never catch me putting a foot into that bush again as long as I live".

But the boys and I were going. I knew the lake was loaded with fish, and I had promised the boys I'd take them there when school was out for the summer.

"Eat all your breakfast," I told them, dishing out the eggs. "I don't want you getting hungry on the way. Besides we have to get to the lake in time to give the fish their breakfast, right?" I gave them a wink, and the grins they gave back I can see even now, they are filed away in my memory forever, as if I had taken a photograph.

After a forty minute drive, the road came to an abrupt end. A rundown farm with a ramshackle house sitting on a little knoll guarding the roadway. The lone occupant was working in her miniature garden. She watched as we approached, then waved when she recognized me. I returned the wave and said, "Hello missus. How are you this morning?"

"Veddy goot, veddy goot" she answered pleasantly. Her garments were those of an old country farm woman—a printed calico dress, a tattered black knitted sweater, and an old kerchief that framed her faded white hair. Heavy brown stockings covered her short stumpy legs. Her feet were planted in black rubber boots that came almost to her knees.

She noticed the fishing rod in my hand. "And where today?" she asked.

"I'm taking my boys to Northwest for some bass."

"Such small boys to take so far in the bush," she said with concern, "maybe their legs will not stand up to such a journey. Blue Lake is not even half that far."

"Don't worry missus," I answered. "Judging by the way these guys tear around the yard, I don't think a hike in the bush will be too hard on them. Besides, a lot of people fish Blue Lake. These days a person's lucky to catch even small ones there."

"Well for sure they will be tired coming back," she said, grinning at the boys. "It is hard to carry all the fish a boy might catch."

We said goodbye and headed for the trail.

The first part of the trail ran parallel to a cedar swamp. The woods beside the trail were almost impenetrable. Here and there a shaft of sunlight sliced through the trees. Now and again a startled rabbit scurried away through thick undergrowth. The forest had all our attention, and nobody wanted to be the first to break that silence. I could feel the excitement surging through Allen and Gordy as they walked ahead of me.

Over the next hill, the trail wound down to a small brook. The old bridge over the brook was rotting. I guided the boys as we picked our way across, careful to watch for logs that would not support our weight. Through the trees we could catch the sparkle of Blue Lake, the old lady's favourite.

"Hold on guys," I said reaching for the compass. "Starting now, I'll lead, and I want you to stay close. There is no path, and it's not hard to get lost. Even I have done it."

It had been seven or eight years since I had been in this neck of the woods. Everything was as I remembered it. On the right was the beaver dam. On the other side was a large pine tree. I was beginning to wonder if we were lost, but the sight of that stately pine told me that we were headed in the right direction. We were approaching the grassy hills overlooking Northwest.

I paused a moment to savour the breathtaking beauty; soft rolling hills, dotted here and there with clumps of jackpine and spruce, dark shades of green contrasting with groves of white birch. Best of all—shimmering below us, flat as a mirror—was the lake reflecting its perfect shoreline in the mid-morning sun.

"Gee!" exclaimed Allen, "is that it?"

"It sure is," I said, every bit as excited as he was. I have seen many lakes in the area that were once as clean and pure as the one below us. Progress and pollution ruined most of them. Northwest had been spared because it was far enough away from progress. The lake is too small to land a plane, and few fishermen are willing to trek so far. It was one of tens of thousands of pretty little pot hole lakes that abound in Northern Ontario fed with pure spring water.

"I got one!" screamed Gordy. Moments later Allen echoed the same cry. My boys had done a bit of fishing in the past but it was nothing like the action they were getting now. They giggled with glee every time their rods bent. Their faces exploded in surprise when a bass burst out of the water and tried to spit the hook. Their arms had to strain to bring in the two and three pound fish.

We fished from the big rocks at the edge of the lake. The water was clear and deep and icily cold. We had lures and worms and we would spin cast them out twenty five or thirty feet, let them sink a few feet and while we were slowly reeling in, bang, the bass would hit. If it was a lure they would come right out of the water, dance on their tail, mad as hell that we had fooled them, sometimes spitting it out. When that happened, the tension on the line, suddenly released, would make the lure spring back to clatter against the rocks at our feet. There is nothing like bass for fishing action.

By mid-afternoon we were all hungry so I cooked up some of our catch. I prepared a small fire close to the water's edge. As the flames licked gently at the bottom of the fry pan, I carved up the fillets. While the butter sizzled, I rolled up the fish in flour and placed the pieces side by side in the pan. The aroma promised a good meal. Allen said it all. "Boy," he exclaimed between bites, "this is better than *McDonald's*!"

When the shadows of the day grew long enough, we packed our gear and got ready to head for home. The boys were naturally reluctant. But we had caught our limit and still had all we could eat. I lured them home with the promise of coming again.

On the way back, I kept an eye on the compass while my sons, the excited fishermen, chatted noisily. The thrill was still fresh in their minds. They were happy, and I was too.

We had just crossed the old bridge, less than a mile left to go, when it happened.

At first I only felt a little tired. I told the boys we should stop to rest. But, excited as they were, they couldn't understand. So I let them go on ahead and said I'd follow shortly.

I didn't rest long. When I began walking again, I felt even worse. Suddenly the familiar weakness spread down my right leg. My whole right side became numb.

I wasn't walking any longer; I was dragging my leg with every step. Then I could go no further.

Everything the doctor had told came back in a rush. "Stress or over-exertion may trigger an attack," he had told me.

Was I having an attack? I didn't know and I was frightened. I admonished myself over and over. Why hadn't I listened to him? Why had I endangered myself and the boys?

"So far for such small boys," the old woman had said, but she was worried about the wrong ones. The boys, I thought, they would be waiting at the car, wondering where their slow-poke dad was.

When I tried to walk again, my stiffened leg turned my gait to a lurch and I stumbled along. Still, I had to keep going. Inching along, the time passed so slowly. I was sure it had been hours since the boys went on ahead. When I thought I could go no further, I saw the roof of the farmhouse. The boys were just heading back to find me.

"What happened, Dad?" they wanted to know, "What's wrong with your leg?"

"Okay," was all I could manage. "I'll be okay. I just twisted it, that's all." I could tell them the whole story later, when I had the strength. With their help I hobbled to the car. I got there exhausted, but relieved. After a short rest, I was feeling strong enough to drive. The boys were soon fast asleep in the back seat. The day had been a long hard one for them, too. Silence surrounded me as I drove. I didn't want to think. Still my mind ran over the events of the day; the adventure of the hike, the thrills the boys had known, the closeness we shared.

Driving was automatic. Now on my way home, I felt safe, although the fear of numbness haunted me. I knew my life was changed for good. With the realization of my situation came a sadness. It was a sadness for the loss of Northwest Lake and days like this. I knew I would adapt to that loss with time, but at that moment nothing could soften the pain I felt or dry the tears that came to my eyes.

I never did get to say a proper good-bye to Northwest Lake.

ELEVEN

By the time I went to see my doctor the following week, the strength had returned to my leg and the stiffened gait had disappeared. "It wasn't necessarily an attack." the doctor said. "It was probably an accentuation of the disease already there."

He explained further, "what you experienced in 1963 and again in 1970 was what we call an exacerbation or an attack. Once a person has an attack, he is usually left with a small area of abnormal nerve fibres and there is some difficulty transmitting messages to that area. In your case, Mr Horner, the nerve loss has focused around your leg muscles and has weakened them considerably. I suggest you refrain from walking any great distances."

After the Northwest experience, I learned there were definite limitations to what I could and could not do. I found out that a quarter mile walk caused my foot to drag. If I attempted to go further, my legs stiffened, causing me to stumble or fall.

Then there was the fatigue that drains in a way no person without the disease can understand. The fatigue would come on suddenly, but fortunately as little as twenty minutes of relaxation would restore me. I could understand now why I felt so exhausted after eating a large meal.

A pins-and-needles sensation in my finger tips created a bit of difficulty when it came to buttoning buttons, tying shoelaces or threading a hook onto a fishing line.

I must admit I was somewhat relieved to know that it was multiple sclerosis—something that other people have too. Until then I had never heard of it, at least I could not remember that I had. But hearing I had a known disease made me feel better. Now there was an answer to the strange things that had been happening to me. A man has to know he is not losing his mind when he reaches his hand into his pocket for some change and can't hold on to the change to pull it out again. He needs to know the reason he suddenly sees two, three balls on the table when he's playing table tennis with his brother. Now, no matter how bizarre the symptoms, at least I knew I wasn't going crazy. I had multiple sclerosis.

* * *

In the fall of 1977 the transfer came through. I became a second-class mechanic in the garage located down at 2300 level at number three shaft. The work was a little bit easier for me to cope with and I could ride not walk to my place of work.

The method of transportation to and from work was by bus down a two and a half mile sloping ramp. It took twenty five minutes to ride to work. The slope was so steep that on the way down we all leaned at a thirty degree angle in one direction. On the way back thirty degrees in the other. The garage had seven bays cut into the solid rock. We repaired all manner of vehicles and all the moving machinery. This included scoop trams, jumbo drills, jeeps and buses. In fact we were a fully equipped garage half a mile under the ground.

I had been working there for just four days when I had a bizarre underground adventure, one I would gladly have forgone. It was the end of the Saturday shift, the last one until Monday. I was looking forward to a day off. As the shift ended I was working in the furthest bay from the lunch room where the bus picked up the men and took us on our listing ride up to the surface.

I guess I had my head in the engine of a scoop tram, changing it's oil when I became aware of complete silence around me. Walking out of the bay I looked around. There was no one to be seen. In fact, the foreman's office was locked up and the lights were out. The bus had left without its newest recruit.

There are many emotions that come to mind when one finds himself abandoned two and a half miles under the earth, on a weekend. First, anger:

" Where in hell are they". I said out loud. " How could they miss me?"

Then, anxiety: " How can I last for 48 hours down here?"

Finally, frustration: There was no way, with my MS condition that I could walk out, and the phone, my only link to the surface, was locked in the foreman's office. It was a scary feeling.

As I wandered from bay to bay wondering what was to become of me, I noticed a jeep that was in for repair. Closer inspection revealed the key—in the ignition. Keeping my fingers crossed, I turned the key. What luck! It started right away. I threw my lunch pail in the back and backed her out of the bay.

I wasn't out of the woods yet. It was pitch black down there and this jeep had no headlights. That's why it had been in the garage.

By the light of my helmet lamp I gingerly headed the jeep for the ramp. I was going home.

About halfway up, the tunnel divided. One way led home, the other, who knows? I chose the right fork which turned out to be the wrong fork. After maybe a mile, the road levelled then became bumpy and strewn with rocks. I knew then I was on the wrong track. By the light of my headlamp I could see a vast open space ahead. For all I knew I was about to drive off the edge of the earth into a bottomless pit. By now I was well and truly in the bowls of the mine probably in an abandoned stope with only the light of a helmet lamp to light the way to the surface. My hands shook and my palms were wet. "How the hell am I going to get out of this?" I muttered.

Somehow, I got the jeep turned around and headed back to the fork in the road. This time, I turned left and about twenty endless minutes later I emerged from the shaft at the pit's head. I stopped the jeep, drew a deep breath and looked around. It was dark and deserted. Everyone had gone home. They hadn't even missed me.

From that time on my foreman always treated me well. It would have been worth his job if I had reported the incident. But he was a pretty good guy and it never crossed my mind to go public with my adventure. I think he was grateful but you wouldn't know it. When I told him about it he just shrugged. Miners are not the most expressive of people.

TWELVE

For the next three years the disease remained stable and life went on as if nothing had really changed. Along with my acceptance came a period of practical adjustments. Eventually I had to leave my job in the mechanical department. Not that the work was too strenuous, but I no longer had the fine finger dexterity necessary to make engine repairs.

I transferred back to mining as a scoop operator. A scoop tram is a load, haul and dump machine similar to a payloader. It was introduced underground as a trackless conveyance to haul muck to the ore passes. A lot of the older miners refused to be scoop operators because of the boredom and backaches that came with it. In this sunless world, these huge machines rumbled back and forth all day long from the box holes to the ore pass while the operator rode on the side of it, being continually bucked and jolted over the uneven ground.

I didn't mind the job. I enjoyed the throb of the powerful diesel motor beneath me as I guided the thirty foot dragon through drifts just wide enough to accommodate it. Of course I disliked the ear-shattering noise and the clouds of dust it created. I overcame that part of it by wearing earplugs and a dust mask. The important thing to me was I didn't have to walk. That was the main reason I was satisfied with my job.

Now, more than ever, I longed for the peace and solitude of the cabin at Washagami. I felt so relaxed there. If stress was a major factor in triggering an attack there was certainly little fear of it at Washagami.

Here again I realized I couldn't be the workaholic I used to be, though there were a hundred and one things I wanted to get done around the cabin. "You remind me of a young bull in rutting season," Dad commented one time, when he saw me rooting out an old stump obstructing the roadway. I no longer had the strength it took to do that kind of bull work.

Luckily, Alan and Gordy were getting old enough to share more of the workload. They were both strapping young teenagers with a strength that surprised me. Oh, to be that young again. We worked as a team to carve a road through the bush, build a steambath, and haul in truckloads of fill for landscaping. The boys didn't mind shovelling so long as they could take turns driving the pick-up truck.

My brother Bryan and his wife Joy, spent many a weekend with us. The cottage was small, but somehow we always managed to find room. We had two bedrooms, each only seven feet high. The doors were heavy cloths hanging from the crossbars. Each room had two or three beds, and there was a divan in the living room area that folded out to double size. The main area was the living room, a combination kitchen-dining-cardplaying room. It had a large table, a water pump on the counter, a big black Findlay stove, and not much else.

In the evenings, I'd put on a fire in the wood stove for making toast. We'd gather beneath the warm glow of kerosene lamps and play cards or just sit around and tell funny stories. Bryan was a storyteller like Dad. He could make those cabin walls rock with laughter.

Sometimes at night we'd huddle around a blazing fire by the water's edge and sing-along accompanied by my old Gibson guitar. The sounds of our music reverberated far across the lake and echoed in the distant hills. We had toasted weiners and marshmallows, had hot steam baths and cold beer, and for those who dared, skinny dipping in the moonlight.

It was a beautiful and vibrant world where my family, friends and I shared a full measure of natural beauty, companionship and a true sense of freedom.

THIRTEEN

Winter comes early in the north country and on a cold November night, I lay awake in the grey-dawn light studying the intricate patterns the frost had etched onto the window panes. The house was silent except for the warm air blowing through the heat registers and the soft breathing of Joyce sleeping beside me.

I envied her peaceful repose. I hadn't slept all night. Instead I spent the long hours staring into darkness, trying to be quiet so I wouldn't disturb her.

The previous evening, Bryan and Joy had been over to play a few hands of euchre, which we sometimes did on Sunday night. At first I felt a little tired. At least, that's what I thought. As the evening wore on, I became more and more tired. Weird sensations wreaked havoc with my body. I fumbled with my cards. They constantly slipped from my grasp. My eyes wouldn't focus properly. I could not distinguish hearts from diamonds or spades from clubs.

If it had lasted only a moment, it might have been tolerable, but it didn't. Jolts of electricity, like charged pins and needles were shooting through my body. My breathing became rapid and I began to perspire.

"I can't explain what is going on," I said to no one in particular, "but I feel so terribly strange. I'm sorry, I can't continue to play."

I felt like a real drag when I threw in my hand, but there was nothing else I could do. I could not control what was happening.

"Can we help?" Joy said, her face a mask of concern. "Just tell us what to do, should we call a doctor?"

"No, no" I said, waving off that idea. "Maybe all I need is a good night's rest."

I didn't mean they should leave right away, but Bryan insisted they hadn't intended to stay long anyway. "I gotta work the early dayshift," he said.

"Give me a ring tomorrow," Joy said to Joyce as Bryan helped her on with her coat. "to let us know how Bill is feeling."

After Bryan and Joy left I hobbled as far as the staircase, but from there I had to rely on Joyce's strength to get me the rest of the way. With one of my arms slung over her shoulder supporting most of my weight, we managed to get me safely upstairs and into bed.

"I don't know if we should bother Rastogi tonight," Joyce said. "But if you don't feel better in the morning, I'll call first thing."

The clock on the night table said 8 a.m. Any other Monday morning I would have been underground by now, fuelling up my scooptram for the day's run. But today attempting to get out of bed was utterly impossible. My body was as limp as clothes on a line waving in the air. If this was another attack, it was more severe than anything I'd ever experienced in the past.

I tried to tell myself that it would all go away—it was a flu, it was nothing serious—I could take it. I told myself to relax. Still the fever and weakness grew in intensity. I was filled with a sense of urgency.

Joyce stirred at last. She sat up in bed rubbing her eyes drowsily. "How are you feeling?" she asked,"is it getting any better?"

I shook my head. "I can't move my hands or my feet," I replied, trying to appear calm and brave. "I don't think wc should waste any more time."

Joyce called Rastogi. "Get him to the Sudbury General right away" he said, "I'll meet you there." The ambulance arrived within minutes.

When I was strapped to the stretcher, I could no longer hold in the terror. Joyce could see it.

"It's going to be okay," she said with a reassuring smile. She took my hand in hers. "You are strong, Bill, and I'll be at your side."

Tears spilled from my eyes. I swallowed hard to make them stop. I couldn't break down now, in front of my children. They were confused and frightened after being wakened by all the commotion. "Is Dad going to die?" Teresa asked with a troubled frown.

"Daddy is going to be alright." Joyce reassured her, but as she said it her voice quavered and she had to bite her bottom lip.

It wasn't too long before that I had talked to my kids about multiple sclerosis. I explained to them in a language they could understand that multiple sclerosis is a disease that affects the central nervous system.

"The nervous system," I said, running my finger down the length of Teresa's spine, "is like an electrical cord with all kinds of smaller wires wrapped in an insulation. Somehow this protective insulation is being destroyed. When this happens, the messages travelling through these wires from the brain to the muscles become scrambled, which in turn causes the muscles to weaken."

How much more can you tell a child about a disease as mystifying as multiple sclerosis? After all, the medical profession couldn't tell me much more than that.

As I was wheeled into the ambulance, I managed a weak grin for my three children who stood watching from the porch landing. I was moved by their troubled faces. I could only imagine the fear and anxiety they must be feeling.

While I rode in the ambulance, Joyce followed behind in the station wagon. She was at the hospital to answer questions and to fill out the necessary forms. She was by my bedside when Dr. Rastogi entered the room.

He started right away with a few simple tests, not saying much as he worked. He checked my reflexes with a little rubber hammer, and looked deep into my eyes with a penlight. He told me to squeeze his two fingers as hard as I could, a feat which I found virtually impossible. I had lost the use of both hands.

He spoke at last. "I highly suspect, Mr, Horner, that you are having an exacerbation," he said in a matter-of-fact tone.

"I am going to prescribe injections of ACTH. It is a cortisone drug which should decrease some of the inflammation and stimulate the adrenalin. This drug is definitely not a cure for MS, but in most cases, Mr. Horner, it has helped to minimize the severity of the attack."

From the neck down I was paralysed. I was completely at the mercy of the nurses who had to feed me, bathe me, and shove a bedpan beneath me. To be that helpless after being so independent agitated and frustrated me. I had never imagined the day would come when someone else would be wiping my ass.

For the longest time I did nothing but stare at the yellow-white ceiling. Terrifying questions ran through my head: Would I ever be well again? When would I go home? Back to work? How will I live?

Although I was flat on my back at that moment, I could still think clearly. I had a good life—except for these damn attacks. If there was a way out of this mess, I was going to find it. I had a wife and three wonderful children. I was the bread winner. Who would take care of my family if I couldn't? My duty to them and to myself was to get back to normal as quickly as possible.

After a week of daily injections of ACTH, my body began to respond. I woke up one morning to discover movement returning in my finger tips. If I tried hard enough, I could wiggle my big toe. By day's end I was able to gradually lift my arms off the bed and over my head. What a relief to be able to scratch my nose! The greatest sigh of relief came the following day when I was able to sit up. Whether it was the drug or just the disease itself going into remission no one really knew, but I was on the road to recovery.

I started exercising on my own in bed: leg raises, push-ups, leg and arm extensions, sit-ups. Though the numbness persisted, I had full range of motion in my arms and legs. Apart from the weakness and prickly sensations, it appeared that no other real damage had been done. I didn't know whether or not I could still walk.

Starting physiotherapy was going to be a real challenge. One morning after breakfast, I was transferred from my bed to a wheelchair and portered down to physiotherapy to continue my rehabilitation under supervision.

The therapy department was filled with light and surprisingly, an atmosphere of quiet elegance. The air was cool and fresh, not the foul sick hospital smell. Many patients were in the room. A old man with thinning white hair caught my eye as he hobbled past me. He fixed his sunken eyes straight ahead and moved on. His gnarled hands clutched a walker that thumped heavily on the hardwood floor as he inched forward on his artificial leg. At the far end of the room a group of stroke patients were spread out on a large floor mat engaged in a simple exercise routine. A therapist walked among them offering instruction and encouragement.

I turned my attention to a determined young man on an exercise bike. I was completely unaware that another chair had wheeled up alongside me, when a soft female voice said "Hello."

I turned to see a pretty woman with short, red hair sitting next to me. "My name is Laurie, Laurie Ditor. We've never met, but I know your name. It's Bill Horner, isn't it?" I nodded, somewhat perplexed.

"Don't look so surprised," she said, "I asked one of the nurses who you were when they brought you onto the floor. I'm in room 211, right next to yours. They told me you had multiple sclerosis. Well, congratulations!" She gestured with wide open arms. Her voice was sardonic. "So do I!"

I liked Laurie right away. We didn't get to talk long before she was wheeled away to a row of padded benches to begin her morning exercises. As one therapist took her away, another approached me. She looked to be in her middle forties and her greyish-brown hair held a tight curl.

"You must be Mr. Horner," she said, smiling down at me. "I am Mrs. Quinn, head of physiotherapy.

"You can forget the mister," I said jokingly, "just call me Bill."

"Bill it is," she said, "what we want to do this morning, Bill, is get you standing and perhaps walking a few steps. Do you think you are up to it?"

"Looking forward to it," I said eagerly. I had to know if I could walk again. I didn't want to believe I would stay in this wheelchair.

Mrs. Quinn gently patted my shoulder. "You wait right here, Bill. I'll need some assistance."

She disappeared momentarily, and when she returned a young woman dressed in a white, knitted sweater was by her side. She extended a well manicured hand. "I'm Stephanie Woods," she said cheerily, "Mrs. Quinn's assistant."

I managed a limp handshake, while I feasted my eyes on her. She should have been a model or movie star, not a therapist. Her shoulder length hair was honey blond and her sea-blue eyes stared at me from a doll's face. She was beautiful.

Looking at Stephanie made me suddenly conscious of my appearance, my unruly hair, my attire—the hospital's blue striped one-size-fits-all pyjamas that would have hung loose on a Sumo wrestler. I should have attempted a shave at least, but I didn't think I was going to meet a beauty queen!

"First, we'll get you standing." said Mrs. Quinn, taking me gently by the arm. "Then Stephanie and I will help you walk."

I managed to stand on wobbly legs with one lady on either side to steady me. A sudden wave of dizziness came over me but it quickly passed. "Very good, Bill," Stephanie praised, and her blue eyes sparkled, "Now see if you can walk a few steps."

On legs as shaky as a newborn calf and with about the same amount of coordination, I inched gingerly forward. Each step was more like an exaggerated shuffle. Still each one was a triumph. I was walking, and that was all that mattered.

With Stephanie and Mrs. Quinn cradling my arms I managed a few more steps. Then I experienced a most unusual sensation in my lower extremities. It felt as if something soft had brushed down my legs, followed by a draft of cold air—like being naked with the windows open. "How do you feel?" asked Mrs. Quinn when I stopped momentarily.

"A bit strange," I blurted, my face reddening. "I think I just lost my pyjamas bottoms."

All eyes dropped to the floor where my pyjamas lay in a rumpled heap around my hairy ankles. I was flushed with embarrassment and I wished I could have vanished into the floorboards.

The ladies didn't make a big deal out of it. As casually as you please Stephanie hoisted my pyjamas to their proper place and tied them snugly. "They won't fall down any more," she said, smiling warmly and making me feel a whole lot better.

I wasn't the only one who suffered an embarrassment that morning. After completing my jaunt as a slow motion streaker, I was resting in my chair, waiting to be wheeled upstairs. I looked over at Laurie wondering how she was making out with her exercises. Her face turned red when our eyes met. She looked the other way.

For a moment I didn't grasp why she was acting so strangely, but it suddenly became very clear. She had wet herself and it was trickling off the vinyl covered bench, forming a puddle on the floor.

I looked the other way, realizing how ill at ease she must feel. I fully understood Laurie's predicament. She suffered one of the symptoms of multiple sclerosis I dreaded most, incontinence— the loss of all bladder and bowel control.

Poor Laurie. In our conversations I found out that she was thirty years old, separated with two children, aged six and seven. Multiple sclerosis struck her after giving birth to the youngest. Soon after she was diagnosed, her husband left her for another woman. This bothered me deeply. It was not the first time I had heard of couples splitting up because one of them had contracted MS.

I couldn't help feeling sympathy for my new friend although I knew she wanted none of it. Here she was, confined to a wheelchair in the prime of life with two small children to look after, abandoned by her husband. In the bible it says that we are God's children. When I look at all the suffering and sadness placed upon a person such as Laurie, I can't help but wonder where is his justice? Just how big a sin did Laurie commit that she should be so severely punished?

Looking at Laurie and her situation made me think seriously about my own marriage. I couldn't imagine Joyce ever leaving me because I had multiple sclerosis. Just thinking about it made me shudder. After all, we had shared sixteen wonderful years. It wasn't all marital bliss, but being together that many years had to mean we were doing something right. It seemed only natural that we would always be in love. She was the axis of my world—together we would get me through whatever the hell was going on within my body.

FOURTEEN

"Only twelve more days till Christmas," a voice on the hospital lounge radio reminded me. The normally bleak fluorescent hallways were decorated with holiday cheer. The light fixtures were done up with shiny coloured bulbs that spun and twinkled, and red mesh stockings appeared on the doors, crammed with sticky looking candies and plastic toys. The sound of the radio squeaking out Christmas carols made me anxious to get home to my family.

Dr. Rastogi finally gave me my walking papers. There is nothing more we can do to help your recovery, Mr. Horner. The rest is up to you. Keep up the exercise routine physio gave you and report to my office in a month or so."

Considering it was possible that I might have remained bedridden, I figured I had weathered this attack quite well. I had a slight limp but I could walk short distances without using a cane.

Rastogi said that my blurred vision might clear up, although the tingling sensation in my hands and feet seemed likely to remain.

I left the hospital with a positive attitude and a suitcase full of determination. I had come to grips with living my life with multiple sclerosis. I didn't have the alternative of a cure—at least not yet. I planned to enjoy as much of life as I could. Who knew? This might be the last attack I'd ever have.

I lovc Christmas. That year I appreciated the season even more. I was so pleased to sleep in my own bed again, to gather Joyce in my arms and hold her close, to sit and play with the children and their new toys.

There weren't many presents under the tree that year. If the children were disappointed they never showed it. They understood that my hospital interlude had seriously depleted our finances.

In April, my doctor handed me a return to work slip, which specified light duty work on surface. My days as a hard-rock miner were over. Not that I regretted it. On the contrary, with my strength and coordination deteriorating, it was far too dangerous. In the past few years my fear had grown each day I stepped on the cage. Before now, I had thought seriously about getting out of the mines altogether. Who would have dreamed that the dark uncertainty of multiple sclerosis would be my escape to the sunshine of the surface?

I was transferred to janitorial services at the Copper Cliff smelter, home of the 1250 foot 'Superstack', reputed to be the tallest chimney in the world. "Superprick' is what one politician called it, while campaigning against acid rain.

There were about sixty men in my department. Like me, they all suffered from some form of disability, mostly heart and back problems. They were transferred here from other areas of the company complex. We were nicknamed the "crip clean-up brigade." To give our position a touch of class, we jokingly called ourselves janitorial engineers.

I was assigned to the fitter's shop. My duties included cleaning the lunchroom, polish the foreman's desk, sweeping and mopping the floors, and cleaning toilets. The hourly rate for janitorial engineering was six dollars-an-hour, a lot less than I had brought home as a miner. But it was a job. In fact, with gimpy leg and overall condition, I wondered how long I could hang on to it.

Thinking that far into the future didn't help me to keep up a positive attitude. I had always looked forward—trying to project what I would be doing in a year or five years. Now, I had to change—to learn to see one day at a time. If I can make it through today, then today is complete. Tomorrow I'll start a new day.

Joyce landed a part-time job as a clerk at Fievoli's IGA in Creighton which brought home another sixty dollars a week. With our combined effort, we were getting by.

* * *

I declared multiple sclerosis my worst enemy. Rather than submit to it, I rose each day prepared to do battle. I hunted for cures. Of course I didn't have the money to search the world for it, but I wanted to try. I heard about a clinic in Florida which boasted dramatic results using snake venom. I thought seriously about going but realized I simply couldn't afford it.

Then one day I heard of a Korean doctor, newly arrived in Sudbury, who was rumoured to cure serious illnesses with a treatment called acupuncture. I decided to seek his help.

Doctor Kim ran his clinic from his apartment on Lasalle Boulevard. When I entered the building it surprised me to see the number of people lined up in the corridor and even more crowded into a tiny, improvised waiting room. The pretty receptionist said: "We don't make appointments. Its first come first served." I gave her my name and ten dollars and got to the end of a long line. I did some quick calculating; at ten bucks a head, this guy was bound for unimaginable riches.

When I finally got to see Doctor Kim, I asked him point-blank if his acupuncture cured multiple sclerosis. He hesitated a moment. His eyes studied mine. Then he flashed a pearly grin and his eyes brightened as if my question suddenly registered in his mind.

"Of course," he said, nodding his head vigorously. "Acupuncture cures everything."

He motioned me to the bed behind some plastic curtains and told me to strip down to my shorts. While I fumbled with the fasteners on my clothes he produced a vial full of needles, each about three inches in length and about the thickness of a fine sewing needle. There must have been a hundred needles. I was no longer sure I was ready to be introduced to the ancient art of acupuncture.

I laid nervously on my stomach, as he inserted the needles with a slight twisting motion about a half inch below the skin. I counted at least forty pin pricks as he worked his way along my neck and down my back; a few more in my arms and legs. I watched with a queasy stomach as one the size of a darning needle was inserted deep into the fleshy part of my palm. Ouch!

"Needles need time to stimulate nerves," Kim said, "I come back in twenty minutes." He bowed graciously and vanished behind the curtains.

As I laid there like a pin cushion, I recalled reading somewhere that MS is not a common disease in the Orient. In fact, the disease rarely strikes people of Asian or African heritage—but rather mostly people of Northern European origin. The article said that multiple sclerosis is "the white man's burden," Why this is so remains a mystery.

At first, the needles seemed to help. When putting on my shirt, it was much easier to grasp the buttons. For a while my vision improved slightly and I thought I had better coordination in my arms and legs. I continued the treatments for another month, but when the sessions failed to offer any more noticeable relief, I became disillusioned and discontinued the treatment.

My quest for a cure didn't end there. I decided to give faith healing a try. I saw an advertisement in the *Sudbury Star*:

REVEREND SAM HARRIS OF THE SOUTHERN EVANGELICAL CHURCH CAN HEAL YOU!!!

There will be a Laying On of Hands
Tuesday, December 15, at 8 PM
Sudbury High School Auditorium.
Everyone welcome!

Joyce drove me there, through a veil of thickly falling snow. The city crews had already put up the Christmas decorations, strings of coloured lights hung in garlands from the street lamps, rosy Santa Clauses saluted the wintry silence. How time flies! It was almost a year to the day since my homecoming from the hospital.

It had taken a lot of coaxing to get Joyce to take me to the church that night. When I suggested having this minister lay his hands on me, she winced and stared at me curiously.

"Don't waste your time," she said, "you know that stuff only works if you believe it will. Wasn't it you who told me that your beliefs went out with Santa Claus and the Tooth Fairy?"

She was right. Somewhere along the line I had lost the ability to believe in the Almighty. I wanted desperately to believe that someone up there cares, that someone watches and listens, that I am special and worth healing. I burn with envy of people like Grandma Marion who hold their rosaries and believe in the mercy of God.

Joyce parked as close to the school entrance as she could. With a firm grip on my cane and the other hand entwined around her arm, I picked my way gingerly across the icy parking lot.

Inside, a noisy crowd had gathered. As we found a seat at the back of the hall, the hubbub ceased. A hush came over the crowd as the Reverend D. Harris stepped up to the pulpit.

He had a somewhat harried and shabby look. His wrinkled black suit was taut across his belly; strands of long, grey hair spiked out from his bald pate. In a loud Southern drawl that reached to the furthest corner of the hall, he lashed out a sermon filled with fire and brimstone. His narrow dark eyes stabbed the audience. I'm sure he meant to strike the fear of the Lord into this gathering, but he was boring me. I was about to give up the idea as another lost cause when suddenly the preacher began to talk about faith and healing. My ears perked up.

"When I speak of healing," he said, "I speak from the conviction that healing does not happen unless we have tapped the spiritual part of ourselves—unless we are spiritually whole." His piercing eyes flitted along the rows then came to rest on mine.

"All of you will get sick and die someday," he cautioned, "but for now, some of you will experience a healing tonight. It will happen through the touch of my hand and through your faith in the Lord Jesus Christ."

As he ended his sermon, the sounds of organ music burst forth from a scratchy phonograph record hidden behind the pulpit. As if by cue, a parade of diseased and disabled formed a line up in the centre aisle.

The parade lurched forward on canes or a friendly arm. White-haired old ladies shuffled into line bundled in old sweaters and shapeless coats. A victim of kidney disease was propelled along in a wheelchair, his exposed leg supported on a sheepskin, swollen and purple. I could see determination, hope and faith plainly written on their faces. Joyce jammed an elbow into my ribs. "This is it," she reminded me, "go get your healing."

I heard the sarcasm in her voice. We both knew I lacked the main ingredient—faith!

I got up and edged my way into line. I'd show her. Wouldn't she be surprised if this magic healed me after all. Boy, if I could have bought some faith I'd have gone for the jumbo size.

The line inched forward. I leaned heavily on my cane—thankful that I had brought it along. Since my last attack I found it difficult to stand in one spot for any length of time. At last I was getting close enough to the action. What I witnessed made my palms sweat and my feet grow cold in my fleece-lined boots.

The minister pressed the palm of his hand on the forehead of a white-haired old lady, raising his eyes heavenward and mumbled what seemed to me like gibberish. Suddenly the old lady's eyeballs rolled back in their sockets and her feet went out from under her. It happened so fast I was awestruck. I looked around to see if others had seen it. This guy may not look like much but he had the power alright!

As the old lady lay spread-eagle on the floor, clutching her purse, Reverend Harris focused his attention on his next patient.

I have to admit I came unprepared for the reaction this well meaning fellow achieved—crying, shrieking, fainting! One man threw his crutches on the floor and did a bit of a two-step after he was touched by Reverend Harris. He strutted back to his seat shouting praises to the Lord. It was unbelievable!

I was next. Before he laid a hand on me, he leaned over and whispered in my ear. "What is your problem, son?"

"Multiple sclerosis," I whispered.

The Reverend then turned to the audience and boomed over their heads, "I want to call your attention to this poor unfortunate soul standing here beside me. He uses a cane because he suffers from a terrible affliction." He oozed out the words, "Mult-ee-ple sclero-sis."

The audience reacted with "oohs" and "aahs."

The Reverend bowed his head in prayer,"may the Lord have mercy."

Now that the whole world was aware of my misfortune, the miracle-maker got down to serious healing. He jammed a fist into the small of my back and pressed the other hand heavily on my forehead. His fierce eyes pierced deep into mine. Our noses were inches apart. The pain from his fist was intense. A tingling sensation ran down the length of my spine from the base of my skull to the tip of my tailbone. It was a weird sort of feeling. Is this how it feels when one is being healed? I didn't know.

His spittle splashed in my face. His tongue flickered out words that were beyond me. Just when I thought I would be sick from the smell of his breath, he released his hold.

"I encourage you son," he said, "to give praise to the Lord. When you awake in the morning you will be healed."

I thanked him and headed back to my seat, glad that the ordeal was over. Instead of using my cane as I had on my way up, I tucked it under my arm and marched down the aisle like an army officer. For the life of me, I don't know how or why I did it. I'm not one to go around attracting attention to myself. I just got caught up in all that healing stuff.

"It's a miracle!" someone hollered. "Hallelujah!" cried another. There were words of congratulations and handshakes. I was overwhelmed. Judging by the commotion, I was definitely the hit of the evening.

Joyce wasn't impressed. I caught her look of disdain as I wove my way through a row of chairs. I managed a sheepish grin and plunked down in my chair, relieved to get off my feet.

"Sometimes I wish I didn't know you," she whispered loud enough to be heard across the room. "If I had known you were going to be the court jester I would have stayed home. Why do you do this to me? Why did you pretend to be healed when you're not?"

I shrugged my shoulders. The only reply I could give on such short notice was that I thought it might be good for the Reverend's business.

When I awoke the next morning, I had forgotten about the good Reverend, but as I dressed for work I noticed a big difference in my agility. And I had more energy. There was a definite bounce in my step as I tapped my feet down the stairs. By the time I got to work, a wonderful sense of wellbeing had come over me. An inner feeling of wanting to burst reverberated through me. I felt like a flower exploding into bloom.

I got my chance at the New Year's dance at the Cabrini Hall. Joyce and I rock n' rolled the night away. We brought in the New Year waltzing to Englebert Humperdinck's *The Last Waltz With You*. Dancing with Joyce, I felt so contented. It was going to be a terrific year.

FIFTEEN

For the next several weeks I firmly believed I had won the battle against multiple sclerosis. I didn't know exactly how but I had been healed and I was very grateful.

As the short days of January skipped into February and March, I firmly rejected any doubts about the healing. I flaunted my resurrection like a banner. What better way to do that than to go back into the winter wild ice-fishing with my brother.

Bob and I used to do a lot of fishing and hunting before my troubles began. Many times we packed a lunch of thick bologna sandwiches and a blackened tea pail and took off into the woods in search of game or a quiet, empty lake. In the last couple of years I had to give it up. I no longer had the strength to tramp through the bush or to reel in a fish. It just wasn't as much fun.

As Bob put it, I had become a "box stove collie"; staying inside, warm and dry. He teased me quite often. Having grown up together in a family where showing affection was a sign of weakness, I understood his teasing. He didn't know how else to talk about MS. Even though Bob and I never talked about it, I knew my having multiple sclerosis bothered him deeply.

We could hardly have done better with the weather. It was an astonishingly sunny morning. Ice crystals sparkled like diamonds on the frozen snow and the air was so cold and fresh, it practically brushed your teeth for you.

"We'll head in behind Seagull Island," Bob yelled over the drone of the snowmobile motor as we sped across the lake. "I have a secret hole over there that will guarantee us a couple of trout."

I grinned at him good-naturedly as I clung firmly to his waist. Bob always knew where the fish were holed up. It reminded me of another of the sayings he liked to repeat, "silence is golden." Only a chosen few were ever shown his fishing haunts. Those who were had to swear to God and spit to Death not to tell a mortal soul about it.

The cold air stabbed me with each breath. Tears spilled from my eyes. I didn't mind one bit. I was invigorated by the fresh air, the speed of the machine beneath me, and most of all, the feeling of being back to normal.

It was a wonderful day. Sitting around the ice hole, I was happy to watch my line dance on the end of a willow branch and suddenly curve into the hole. I yanked the line and set the hook. I could feel the fish thrashing on the end of a sixty foot line. It did not stop fighting until I wrested it from the hole and laid it flopping and exhausted on the frozen snow.

By four o'clock we had caught six dandy lake trout, the smallest around three pounds, the biggest, seven.

Winter days in the north are short even in the month of March. Dusk was coming down, ridges of wilderness blocked out the setting sun. With the daylight fading, we packed our gear and headed for home.

The eight mile trail we had followed up the lake was hard-packed and easy going for the high powered snowmobile. On a whim Bob veered off the main trail to find a short cut behind Pine Island. Once we were off the trail, we ran directly into slushy ice.

The machine went willingly for awhile until the ice bogged it down. It sputtered, refusing to budge another inch. A snowmobile is ideally suited for hard-packed conditions but completely useless in soft snow or slush. The kind of slop we were slogging in was the worst kind. It packs tight around the wheels, jams up the rubber belt, and then freezes solid.

It took us more than two hours to push and pull the unwieldy machine onto a firm surface. Pain was stabbing at my legs, back, and all through my body. By the end, I was leaning on the machine more than I was pushing. I was exhausted.

The moon was already peeking through the treetops by the time we arrived at the car. When I climbed off the machine I was stumbling and staggering and ready to drop.

The next morning I woke up stiff and sore. I sat on the edge of the bed and massaged my legs to relieve the stiffness. When I stood up, they wobbled slightly. I wasn't sure if the weakness and stiffness in my legs was from yesterday's ordeal or if it was the disease flaring up again.

It wasn't long before I found out. When I got out of my car at work I barely made it to the security shack before both legs gave out on me. "Are you okay, Mac?" the guard asked, "you been drinking?"

I shook my head. "I don't feel so good. Can I use your phone?" I called my foreman to tell him I couldn't make it into work; then I lurched my way back to my car. I was able to drive after a short rest. Little did I realize as I drove out of the company parking lot that morning, I would never again return. At the age of thirty-six, my working days were over.

* * *

Admitted once more to the hospital, I was highly disillusioned with miracles. Whatever it was Reverend Harris had laid on me, it was not eternal. I felt like such a fool to believe that faith healing had cured me.

At first I couldn't figure out why I had been so strong for the past three months. As I learned more about the unpredictably of multiple sclerosis, I discovered that there were going to be good and bad periods. Other MS victims told me they had had the same experience. It wasn't the miracle of faith-healing that brought me back to normal, but the temporary reprieve of remission.

Multiple sclerosis acts that way. Sometimes it comes on so strong that the individual has to be rushed to the hospital. Other times it insinuates itself into a person's life so slyly that the first time or two it is no more than a puzzling discomfort. After a week or month, it may disappear to return a year or five years later or never again. Sometimes it comes and never leaves, progressing slowly or swiftly to a wheelchair or a life in bed.

This is why no two people with multiple sclerosis look the same or experience the same symptoms. As yet, no one can predict the course of its rollercoaster patterns of exacerbations and remissions.

This stint in the hospital wasn't as bad as the last. The attack wasn't as severe, and I was more familiar with the routine. I took ACTH, the drug which helped me before and worked hard in physiotherapy to regain as much strength as I possibly could. But I hated being in there.

Anyone who has ever flirted with the idea that a few weeks stay in the hospital might not be so bad—the place to recharge one's tired body—had better reconsider. It is not at all like they show on television. They can't show the smell of shit and urine mixed with disinfectant and the terror of the night noises made by the dying.

The hospital routine is set in stone. Up at seven-thirty, breakfast over by eight-thirty, washed and shaved by nine-thirty, down to physio for ten, and back up in time for a tasteless lunch served at noon sharp, hungry or not. After lunch, occupational therapy at two, dinner at five, snacks at seven and lights out by eleven. They hold the keys. They determine when you eat, when you sleep, when you exercise, when and if you leave the hospital. It's an unpleasant and humiliating environment, but the truth is most patients are too sick to care.

The rigidly scheduled days went by formlessly. There seemed to be more seconds per minute, more minutes per hour, more hours per day than anywhere else in the world. Time doesn't move in the hospital, it hangs there with you.

In addition to physio in the mornings, I filled in the long hours with occupational therapy in the afternoons. In a long airy building, patients of all ages were deeply involved with their projects—modelling clay, weaving cloth, making pot holders, doing needlepoint.

With the help of an instructor, I was introduced to the craft of leather-working. I sat down at a long wooden table. I had only to look at the people either side of me to feel hopelessly inept. The exacerbation had increased the weakness and numbness in my hands. The lack of coordination caused me to strike my fingers more than once with the wooden mallet I was aiming at a leather punch.

I had no real desire to learn any kind of handicraft, but I had to do something to stave off the depression and despair that welled inside me. Dr. Rastogi suggested I join the local chapter of the Multiple Sclerosis Society as a place to turn for more information. "You will meet a lot of people in a similar situation," he said. "I think it is highly important, Mr. Horner, that you see how others are dealing with this turning point in their lives."

* * *

My deteriorating health was only one reason for my depression. The other was Joyce. She rarely came to see me. She always had an excuse why she couldn't make it during visiting hours. The few times she did make an appearance, she was tense and fidgeting. She was smoking a lot more than usual, too. Whenever she did that, I knew she was awfully nervous about something. Whatever it was, she wasn't telling me and I couldn't figure it out.

She certainly was not the same Joyce who was so concerned and attentive the last time I was hospitalized. Whatever would I have done without her then? She came to visit every day—twice a day sometimes—sitting quietly, waiting and watching when I was at low ebb, wheeling me around the corridors when I felt up to it.

Sometimes, on a weekend, we'd treat ourselves to a meal down in the cafeteria. We called it 'eating out', out of my room, that is.

Joyce had kept me strong, encouraging me to keep fighting. She reached down over the cliff's edge to rescue me. I don't think I could have bounced back as well as I did without her unflagging support.

On one of her rare visits I noticed how tired and worn she looked. "Is something the matter?" I asked.

She didn't answer right away. She was evading my stare, looking at her hands and turning them over, then back again slowly.

"I worry about you," she said finally, shifting her gaze to the window. "What will we do if you don't get better? I'm scared of what tomorrow will bring."

I reached out and took her in my arms. "Don't be afraid, Joyce. We'll work things out somehow. We always have."

I could understand her fears and uncertainty about the future—our future. What I couldn't understand at that moment was the way she stiffened when I tried to comfort her. And why did she turn away when I tried to steal a kiss?

SIXTEEN

It took four long weeks to get out of the hospital. By that time Easter had passed and the gusty breath of spring was in the air. When I walked out of the hospital I was terribly weak, lurching on unsteady legs. But I was out. I was free.

Joyce was there to pick me up. Her mood remained unchanged. She was quiet, unsmiling. I settled myself into the passenger's seat for the ten mile ride.

I was thrilled to be out of the hospital. As we pulled away from the loading ramp into the crawl of traffic, I had an almost uncontrollable urge to roll down my window and shout to the other drivers, "I'm out and I'm never going back."

All of Joyce's attention was focused on handling the station wagon through rush hour traffic. Finally, on the outskirts of town, near the Copper Cliff bypass, she cast a sidelong glance at me and said "I had Sheba put to sleep yesterday. The poor animal was in constant pain. She couldn't stand any more without toppling over."

The news of Sheba's death saddened me although it came as no great surprise. I knew she had hip-dysplasia. A tear for her formed in the corner of my eye. I was sad for my dog. It was hard to believe that such a beautiful and affectionate creature had to put to death. I was also sad to find so many changes in my life. I'd been in the hospital, but my family had gone on without me.

Rather than go directly home, we drove over to my brother's place. While I was in the hospital, Bryan and Joy had bought a house over on Snider Street near the Catholic church. Bryan could hardly wait to show it off to me. I promised him that as soon as I got out I'd be over to see it. I was glad they were staying in Creighton. We're family, but more than that, we are good friends.

Their small red brick-sided house looked like the kind of house a child would draw—a perfect matchbox square with white trimmed windows all around.

While Joy and Joyce put the coffee on, Bryan showed me around, beaming with pride as he took me from room to room. The house was more than a half century old, but it was their first. There was a good-sized living room and a large kitchen with a small dining area off it. At the back was the master bedroom and a smaller bedroom for their nine year old daughter, Colleen.

Bryan coaxed me to the basement. "You gotta see my workbench and where I'm gonna set up the ping-pong table." I hesitated at the landing before descending. This was my first try at stairs since my attack. Easing my way down cautiously, I realized just how formidable stairs had become. I clung firmly to the handrail while I negotiated each step.

After some cheerful conversation and coffee, Joyce and I got up to leave. Bryan's tour had left me exhausted and anxious to get home.

We went to bed early that night, Joyce and I lying in our spoon position—her back cradled against my chest, my hand cupping her breast. She seemed content to just lie there in my arms and go to sleep, but I had looked forward to more. Many nights I laid in that hospital bed, fantasizing about having sex with my wife in one of our bouts of wild, swirling passion!

I thought after our time apart she would feel the same desire for me as I felt for her. I wanted her to want me, to melt in my arms and make love and blot out my fear and loneliness.

That was not how it turned out. Joyce responded to my advances after a bit of cajoling but I sensed that she was doing it more out of obligation than desire. Still, I figured I had enough desire for both of us.

My stomach muscles and my legs were too weak to straddle her so I coaxed her on top. I was brimming with lust, but as so frequently in the past, I couldn't maintain an erection. Joyce rolled off me in frustration and went to sleep on her side of the bed. I stared into darkness for the longest time, feeling depressed, anxious and scared.

It was a bright sunny morning. The house was filled with the tantalizing aroma of bacon frying and fresh coffee. I ate my breakfast while watching a flock of starlings alight from a distant grove of birch trees and land in our little garden plot right below the kitchen window. I thought maybe I'd go out there later and turn over a bit of soil. I wasn't sure I could do it, but I'd give it a try. The kids were in school and Joyce had to be at work for noon. Pottering around in the garden would be a good way to occupy myself. Taking another sip of coffee, I thought to myself how wonderful it was to be home.

Yet I worried for Joyce who sat at the other end of the arborite table, her breakfast untouched, her face sullen. She smoked one cigarette after another, constantly flicking her ashes on the rim of the ashtray.

"Do you want to talk about it?" I said, pushing my empty plate aside. The suddenness of my voice snapped her thoughts back to the present.

"A-about what?" she stammered.

"About whatever it is that's bothering you. If it's last night, well, I apologize for that. I realize now that I need more time to rebuild my stamina. It will get better. You wait and see."

Joyce crushed out her cigarette and began clearing the table—scraping the leftovers into the garbage container below the sink, putting the milk and catsup back in the fridge, wiping away the toast crumbs. She didn't say a word.

I helped myself to more coffee. When I sat back down again, I was surprised to see long bars of dark clouds appearing over the horizon.

"You've been acting real strange lately." I prodded. "Ever since my last hospital episode I've noticed how you've been so distant. This is not the Joyce I'm used to."

She leaned her hand on the kitchen sink and stared out the small window that separated the red cedar cupboards. The heaviness of her silence was like the presence of a stranger.

When she spoke at last, her words struck me harder than any attack from multiple sclerosis could have.

"I have a boyfriend," she blurted, "I was seeing this guy when you were in the hospital. I think I love him."

I was stunned. I shook my head before any words would come. Was this some kind of terrible joke? Then I heard myself saying: "No, Joyce. You can't do that to me, not now. Please say you're kidding."

"It's true, Bill, every last word of it is true." She seemed relieved to have finally got it all out in the open. "I couldn't break it to you when you were so sick, and I can't keep it bottled inside me any longer. I'm leaving, Bill. After work I'll come back and pack my things."

My throat filled so that I couldn't speak, then I buried my head in my hands and cried as I had never cried before. One person can only take so much pain. A physical beating would have hurt less.

I held my hands over my mouth to try and stifle the sobs. "What about us?" I managed, "don't eighteen years of marriage mean anything to you?"

Joyce turned to face me squarely. She was near tears. "I just don't love you any more," she said, "I'm not sure that I ever did. I'm learning now what real love is."

I wasn't crying any more. I hung my head and stared glumly at the floor.

A clap of thunder startled her. Joyce was dreadfully frightened of storms. At any other time a thunder clap would have thrown her into the shelter of my arms, to cling to me until the storm quieted. A crash of lightning lit the room with a yellow light illuminating her face like a mask of terror, but she remained frozen to the spot.

"It's the disease, isn't it?" I muttered, searching her face for answers.

She nodded, "I suppose you could say the disease was the breaking point. But it's more than that. It's the kids, it's our lovemaking, it's everything. It isn't what I need. It isn't what I want. I can't take any more."

Her hand collapsed to her sides in resignation, tears streamed down her cheeks.She slumped into a chair, wiping her tears.

"You know, Bill, whether you believe this or not, I have really tried hard with this marriage. I have given almost eighteen years to you and the kids. It's time I made myself happy. I don't know why it has to be this way, but just look around you and see how things are falling apart. Our kids are so damn lazy. They won't lift a finger to help me. The boys' bedroom is a goddamn pig pen, and it's a bloody battle to get them to clean it."

Joyce raised herself from the chair and got her blue wind-breaker from the closet. She continued:

"When I came home from work last week, it sounded like there was a party going on in the garage. I opened the door to see and walked into a cloud of marijuana smoke. Gordy and his gang of friends were in there smoking up. I'll lose my sanity if I stay here any longer." She grabbed the car keys hanging by the door. "I have to go to work."

I stared at the closed door, dumbfounded, my mind reeling. In the silence, I became conscious of the rain—single, heavy drops that sounded like pebbles on the roof. The wind was clutching the birch trees. Lightning, close overhead, broke a passage across the sky.

In that moment of despair, I thought about life in a way I had never thought about it before. Never had I felt so deeply hurt and alone. The mystery is why I didn't end it all right then and there. I buried my face in my arms and howled, my shirt sleeves warm and damp.

SEVENTEEN

In the dim quiet of the kitchen I watched the rain transform my garden plot into a soggy mass of chocolate coloured mud. A crash of thunder, a whip of lightning opened up the whole black sky. It was turning into a real shitty day—worse than I ever could have imagined. A damp chill shook me.

It was a hard choice to make, the choice to push myself through this. The harsh reality of living a life without Joyce frightened me. I wanted to die. I didn't want to live alone. Somehow I would make myself carry on—even if it had to be without her.

There was no way my mind could cope with this sudden turn in my life. Just trying to think of everything at once left me drained. I went upstairs to my room and fell into an exhausted sleep.

I was sound asleep when I felt a hand nudge my shoulder. "Wake up Bill," the voice said softly, "it's me, Joyce. I want to talk."

I sat up in bed groggily shaking out the cobwebs, waking up my mind.

"I've thought the whole thing over," she said, "I've decided not to leave. I realized how selfish and unfair I was being to you and the kids. I also talked it over with Mom, and she says you don't kick a man when he's down. If you still want me I'll stay."

I stared wide-eyed, unbelieving. She was actually saying she and I could still have something together. Thoughts flitted through my mind. Why the sudden change of heart? Did she mean it? Maybe I wouldn't be alone after all.

"Try to understand, Bill, it happened at a time when I was needy—you were so sick and I needed someone to comfort me. But I was wrong. Will you ever forgive me?"

Joyce and I had shared a meaningful life together. I honestly don't know how I would have managed had she abandoned me. All I saw in my future was a world of emptiness and loneliness. I took her in my arms and whispered fiercely, "I love you so much."

We both needed time to recover. I tried to get everything back to normal even though deep inside I knew our relationship could never be the way it once was. How could it be? The thought that Joyce had slept with another man sent me into deep bouts of depression.

Not working added to my misery. I knew I couldn't hack it. I was a hazard to myself and to the company. I couldn't even walk around the house without stumbling over my own feet. I didn't want to surrender to the disease, but at the same time I found it almost impossible to adjust to the pins-and-needles assault on my body, the blurred vision, and the overwhelming fatigue.

My doctor broke the news to me when I went for my check-up. "I think it best that you make plans to retire," he said, "you have a year of sickness insurance coming to you. Perhaps by then you'll have some more options. You never know."

He caught me off guard when he asked how things were going at home. At first I was going to tell him about Joyce's affair, but I changed my mind. I was too ashamed to tell anyone that my wife had been unfaithful. Before I could come up with an answer the phone rang, and I heard him say that he would be at the hospital later on that afternoon. While he was on the phone, I gathered up the courage to ask him about my impotence. Although I could feel my face reddening in embarrassment, I had to talk to someone before it drove me out of my mind. And maybe, just maybe, he had a magic remedy tucked away in his little black bag.

He said the reason for my impotence was probably due to the disease but that was not always the case for MS victims. "Sometimes it's purely psychological," he said, "when all a man's energies are directed to worrying about himself, he has precious little energy left to devote to lovemaking. Any emotional state—depression, anxiety—requires so much energy that little is left for anything else."

I listened intently.

"In your next attempt at lovemaking, Bill, try to forget all negative thoughts and concentrate only on pleasurable fantasies. That might help offset your concern about not performing. I also suggest you and Joyce read *The Joy of Sex*. This book comes highly recommended by sex therapists. You both might benefit from it."

Before I left his office he gave me a prescription for anti-depressant pills. "Take them only when you feel you cannot overcome your depression" he said.

Life around our house went on as if nothing had ever happened—at least that's the view we tried to give to the family and to our friends. Joyce continued to work at the *IGA*. I stayed home and did what chores I could; washing, vacuuming, cooking.

I enjoyed cooking most of all. However, with my lack of

coordination, I had to be extra careful around stoves, especially when I removed hot dishes from the oven.

I made sure the kids pulled a bit more of their weight around the house. Their laziness was partly my fault. I should have kept closer contact with them instead of focusing all my attention on my own condition.

I also touched on a few subjects with Gordy while driving him to a hockey game. He was respected for his puck sense in front of the opponent's net, but he lacked good sense when it came to school work. His marks had dropped from honour grades to below average. I suspected marijuana smoking had a lot to do with it even though he swore a joint never touched his lips.

I knew my kids were not the angels they would like me to believe. Joyce had no reason to make up the story about Gordy's smoking up in the garage. On the other hand, I never actually caught him doing it, so I gave him the benefit of the doubt. But I warned him.

"If I ever find out you've been lying to me Gord , it will be the end of your hockey career."

I hoped with all my might that before I was officially put on pension I would get well enough to return to work. As the days grew into weeks and then to months, I realized going back to work was only wishful thinking. A short walk to the end of the driveway left me exhausted and caused my legs to stiffen. I dreaded climbing the stairs, to get to the bedroom or bathroom. Once I lost my footing at the top landing and was headed for a serious fall had it not been for Allen, who was on his way up at the time. His strong arm reached out and stopped me from pitching headlong down the stairs.

Even if I couldn't return to work, I worked at building myself a fortress of resolve. I worked on my home, I worked at being a better husband. I also worked at making people believe that I was coping, even though I felt the whole world was tumbling down on top of me. Behind my apparent tranquillity, I hid my feelings of bitterness, depression, and self-pity. I kept it all bottled inside me until I was alone at night when I would cry into my pillow.

Fear and uncertainty steered me to the *MS Society*. I wanted to meet other people in similar situations to see how they were coping. I needed to know I wasn't alone in my struggle, to gain some perspective. I tried to convince Joyce to come with me but she wanted no part in it.

"Seeing other people with the disease will only upset me more," she said.

EIGHTEEN

The Sudbury Chapter of the *MS Society* held meetings once a month. When I first entered, I was overcome with apprehension. I wasn't uncomfortable around severely handicapped people, I was used to that from my hospital stays. But I had always been self-conscious in the presence of strangers, which in itself is a handicap.

I was greeted warmly at the door by the chairman, Fred Nichols, who introduced me to a dozen or more individuals in the room. As I looked around me I didn't notice anyone that was severely incapacitated by the disease. Two men were in wheelchairs. One woman, tall and slim, stood as stiff as a toy soldier. With some difficulty, she managed to cross the room to the coffee urn and pour herself a cup of coffee. Another lady, across the table from me, sat with her chin resting on her chest because her neck muscles were too weak to support the weight of her head. She seemed to handle it well. Whenever a friend would tilt her head back to assist her breathing, she offered a pleasant smile.

They were a friendly bunch. Soon I relaxed and no longer felt nervous. I talked comfortably about my own situation. I listened while others confided their own experiences.

Paul Marcotte, a balding man with a gimpy leg pulled up a chair alongside me and asked how long I had been living with the disease. "At least seven years," I told him.

"More than twenty for me," he said almost proudly. "When they told me I had multiple sclerosis," he went on, "I was actually relieved. I could never get the damn house cold enough. My wife would be wearing heavy sweaters and I'd be perspiring. Once I knew it was MS, at least I knew what was wrong with me."

One woman told me her reactions when she was diagnosed. "I went through all the stages," she said, "first it was withdrawal, trying to escape from everything around me. Then when the full impact hit home, I asked the question over and over, why me. Then I searched around for every possible treatment. Yes sir, I went through them all. Then one day I thought, oh the hell with it. Avoiding thinking about the disease was worse than facing up to it. Now I've settled into it as I do my rocking chair. I learned to live with it and not make such a big deal out of it."

The *MS Society* was helpful in other ways besides offering comfort and understanding. They organized fund-raising drives to buy wheelchairs and other aids, provided counselling and literature, and raised money for research.

From that very first meeting I became active in our local chapter. I realized how important the society was, especially to newly diagnosed people. I wanted to help pass on the word to others with MS that they were not alone, as I once felt. There were a lot of us out there learning to cope.

Eventually the Sudbury Chapter of the *MS Society* became a family affair when three of my sisters volunteered their time. Carol was the secretary, Joan the membership director, and Marie headed the newsletter committee. My cousin Greg Marion took on the position as chairman. They all committed their time and effort as a way of telling me not to give up hope; that they were behind me in my battle.

At the same time, my marriage was slipping by notches. I constantly nagged Joyce about her past involvement with the other man. I barraged her with questions whenever she dressed to go out for the evening—where are you going? Who are you going with? What time will you be home? She retaliated with sarcasm and coldness. We were quickly getting to the point where it was impossible to forgive any more. I interpreted everything she said as betrayal.

In January 1978, I turned thirty-seven years old. Bob and his wife Gail stopped by to wish me a happy birthday. We celebrated the occasion over a few drinks, and it wasn't long before Bob and I were reminiscing about old hunting and fishing expeditions. We relived them for the benefit of our wives who, to be honest, didn't appear all that interested. Eventually Gail got us on the subject of astrology. She professed that the heavenly bodies had a powerful influence over human affairs. According to her analysis, it was the year of Aquarius. As my birthday is on the twenty-fourth of January, I was headed for all that Aquarian good fortune. It was a wonderful birthday, but Gail's predictions were way off.

The next week life around our house got a lot worse. One night, I had a supper of chipped beef and noodles warming on the stove for Joyce and me. The kids had eaten earlier, except for Gordie, who was going directly from school to the hockey arena to warm up for the big game later on that night. His team was playing the Levack Huskys, their rivals for first place in their division. It was a game I really wanted to see.

Joyce usually served the meal. I didn't trust my balance well enough to attempt filling our plates and dishing them out. When she served only one plate I was puzzled.

"You're not eating?" I asked.

"I'm not hungry," she said, rubbing her tummy. "My stomach is upset. I think I'll lie down for awhile."

"What about the game?" I said, a little disappointed. We always made it a point to cheer on Gordie and his team when they played at the Walden Arena.

"You go ahead," she said, "I'm really not up to it."

The team was warming up on the ice when I got there. I didn't see Gordie out there with the others. I expected he was still in the dressing room. I had just settled down to watch the game when the coach came over.

"Where's Gordie?" he asked.

"He's here, isn't he?" The coach shrugged his shoulders. "He didn't dress with the other guys. I thought he came with you. His playing hasn't been so shit-hot lately but we could use him tonight. We're short on players."

"I'm positive he said he was coming straight here from school," I said. "Maybe I misunderstood. Give me ten minutes to drive back home and see if he's there."

I sped back to Creighton thinking how stupid of me not to check his room first before leaving the house. Sometimes he likes to have a nap before a game.

I went as quickly as I could into the house and downstairs to his room. He was there alright. His black wavy hair protruding from under the blankets.

"Jesus, Gord, you're supposed to be at the arena. What are you doing in bed?"

Getting no response, I shook him firmly, "Gord, wake up!"

He turned over slowly. "I got the flu, Dad," he mumbled. His bleary eyes were glassy and bloodshot.

I leaned over and felt his forehead to see if he had a fever. I thought I smelled alcohol on his breath. "You were drinking."

"No, Dad, I wasn't."

"How come I smell booze?"

"Well...Just one drink, that's all. I thought a sip of your whisky would make me feel better."

I stared down at him for the longest time not knowing whether I should take his word or not.

"Okay, stay in bed and rest," I said finally. "You're not feverish, but you better take it easy. I'll call your coach."

First Joyce and now Gordie. It seemed my whole family was coming down with something.

I had plans of going back to watch the game. On my way out, I looked in on Joyce to see if she was feeling any better. When I peeked in around the doorway, I was surprised to find an unruffled bed and no one in the room.

"Where is your mother?" I asked Teresa who was seated cross-legged in front of the TV, biting into an apple.

"Gone to Aunt Joy's," she said, not once taking her eye off the set. "She said she would be home around nine."

"Joy's house be damned," I muttered under my breath. I was willing to bet she wasn't there at all and that she didn't have a bellyache either.

It was after eight when I pulled into Bryan's driveway. Joyce had to show up there before nine to cover her tracks. I would be there waiting.

Bryan was surprised to see me. We seldom visited on week nights with him working steady day shift. I had a strange feeling Joy knew why I was there, but if she did know something, she was keeping it to herself. She put the coffee pot on and went to bathe Colleen and put her to bed.

The conversation between Bryan and me hovered around his 1970 Ford wagon which was always in constant need of repair. I usually enjoyed teasing him about his repair-daily car. Tonight I was low key and serious. The idle chatter drifted through my mind. Underneath I thought about my dear wife and what she was up to at this very moment. The visions of it tore me up inside.

Shortly before nine, Joyce entered through the back door just off the kitchen where we sat around the table having coffee. Her eyes opened wide in surprise when she saw me. "Where were you?" I asked.

She caught my glare and quickly her eyes dropped to the floor. Her face flushed a rosy red, partly from the bitterly cold night but mostly from the embarrassing situation she suddenly found herself in. "Just walking," she stammered.

"Lying bitch," I cursed under my breath. One thing Joyce bragged about and I had always believed in was her honesty. The blood boiling inside me made my neck and ears redden. I fought to retain my composure. "I think we'd better go home now," I said, "we have things to talk over."

I said goodnight and hobbled behind Joyce to the car.

"So you've been cheating on me all along," I said, "and I trusted you." I called her names I only partially meant, striking her with my tongue. Overcome by bitterness and indignation, I lashed out and smacked her across the face.

The suddenness of my fury surprised me. I had never struck a woman before, and I certainly didn't feel good about it. But neither could I accept all the fault. Joyce bowed her head and remained silent the rest of the way home.

I was upset, but it wasn't a total surprise. Even though she had promised unwavering loyalty, I had suspected all along that she was still involved with someone else.

I guessed that Joyce and her lover had met during her lunch breaks at the Creighton Restaurant, directly across from the *IGA*. I imagined the two of them together in the high padded booths. I had often felt tempted to walk in on them to confirm my suspicions. I couldn't, the restaurant stairs had no handrails. No matter how much I might like to, it was not possible for me to go there.

Later in our bedroom, out of earshot of the children, I told her exactly how things were going to be from now on. Knowledge of her first affair had almost devastated me. Now I only felt anger and contempt.

"You've got till tomorrow to get out of this house."

"This is my home, too. Suppose I decide to stay?"

"There are ways to make you want to leave," I warned. "Besides, you were the one so anxious to trot out of here the time I came home from the hospital. Now I'm making it easy for you. There's the door," I motioned.

"I need time to think things over," she said. "Will you let me have the car keys?"

"You want to discuss it with 'him', is that it Joyce? Well, you do that." I threw the keys at her feet. "Tell him you are his woman now and see if he'll buy the cow rather than get the milk for free."

Moments after she left I yelled downstairs for one of my kids to bring me up some beer. I needed something to stop the tremors that shook my entire body.

"You an' Mom planning a bedroom party?" Teresa asked, carrying a six-pack of *Molson Lite*.

"Yeah, something like that," I answered, relieving her of her burden. She gave me a mischievous grin and headed back downstairs.

The party was over for Joyce and me. As I watched Teresa walk away, I thought about the emotional impact our separation was bound to have on her and the boys. They would survive somehow, just as I would have to.

I was opening my third beer when I heard our car pull into the driveway, her footsteps ascending the stairs. "Well, what did you and your lover decide?" I said when she entered the room, "you don't look too happy."

"I want to make a deal with you, Bill. One that could benefit us both. Will you hear me out?"

"I'm listening."

"First of all you must understand that I need and crave strong, physical love. And even you have to admit..."

"I can understand that there is a lot more to a marriage than just sex," I interrupted.

"Here is the deal I want you to consider," she said. "I'll continue living here and take care of your every day needs. You know yourself you can't make it on your own if this disease gets any worse. In return I want your okay to continue seeing my friend."

"Let me see if I fully understand what I just heard," I said. "You want us to go on living together as man and wife but whenever you feel like it, you'll get your servicing from him. Is that what you're proposing, Joyce?"

She nodded. "That's a crass way of putting it, but yes. It'll be like an open marriage. Both of us can be free to come and go as we please."

"Here is my answer," I said, and almost automatically the bottle of beer flew from my grasp and shattered a ceramic pitcher and washbowl set she kept on the dresser top. "You have until morning." I hissed. "Get your ass out of my room."

"Imagine her nerve!" I muttered, clenching and unclenching my fists. "She must take me for a complete fool to think I would consider such a proposal".

It surprised me even more that I was actually running the idea through my mind. The uncertainty of the disease had heightened my fear of being abandoned. But I would never be that desperate. I couldn't make that compromise. Somehow I would find the courage and whatever else it took to go it alone.

The beer I had drunk the night before sure did a job on me because when I woke the next morning, I was lying fully dressed on top of the bed covers. My head throbbed with a dull ache. I splashed cold water in my face at the bathroom sink then eased my way down the stairs. Seeing the rumpled blankets on the couch reminded me that the night before was the first time in our marriage that Joyce and I ever slept apart by choice.

Her beige overcoat and knee-high boots were still in the closet so she must be planning to return later for the rest of her stuff. Well, good riddance, I thought. I wanted to stick to my decision even though I wasn't sure how the kids and I would manage without her. I wasn't about to bend to her wishes like a whipped puppy. After all, a man's got to have some pride.

I was a real blunderhead as I stumbled around the kitchen trying to make myself a pot of coffee. Opening the coffee canister I spilled most of it on the white counter top. I went to the fridge and stood with the door open for the longest time wondering why I had opened it in the first place. My mind was a complete muddle.

Finally I managed to get the coffee brewing. I was about to pour a mug of it when Joyce burst through the door, tears washing the mascara down her cheeks.

"Oh Bill," she cried, rushing into my arms and clinging to me. "Please let me stay. I've been such a fool to jeopardize all the wonderful years we've had together."

She practically melted in my arms. I can't remember ever being held that way by her.

"I love you," she whispered through her tears, "can we start over?"

This sudden turn of events caught me by surprise. I didn't know what to say or how to react. Her damage to me had been devastating. I wanted to hate her. Yet deep down, I still felt the flicker of love.

So we decided to try again—harder this time. She had made a choice between him and me and I had won. That morning Joyce and I uncorked a bottle of sparkling wine. We toasted our new beginnings with champagne glasses full of pink bubbly and our eyes brimming with joyous tears. Looking at me lovingly, Joyce played her guitar and sang *And Today I Started Loving You Again.*

NINETEEN

For the next few weeks, our misty promises and murky devotions seemed to hold possibilities. Not that I thought everything was going to be marital bliss. I was no longer so naive as to believe patchwork was as strong as our original relationship. I didn't trust Joyce's professed love for me even though she seemed to say it with all sincerity.

On a blustery Saturday night in March, my sister Carol, and her boyfriend Ron invited Joyce and me to attend a dance at the Cabrini Hall. Actually I wasn't enthusiastic about going anywhere. A sudden storm earlier in the day had dumped a foot of snow. A driving wind was swirling and packing it into drifts. I was content to sit in my easy chair and watch the *Leafs* tackle the *Bruins* on *Hockey Night In Canada*. But Carol wouldn't let me off the hook. "It's a surprise anniversary party for Aunt Terry and Uncle

Maurice," she said, "if you're not there they'll be awfully disappointed." Carol knew how close I was to my aunt and uncle, and right away she had me feeling guilty as hell.

"Okay, okay, I'll go" I said, "but let's get there early so we can reserve a table near the washroom." I insisted on it because, with my staggering gait, I would feel terribly self-conscious lurching across a dance floor with everyone staring at me.

I was surprised to see the parking lot jammed with cars by the time we got there. How lucky for Maurice and Terry to be so well loved. So many cars on such a stormy night, that meant a lot of people. Boy, were they in for a surprise!

My first concern was getting from the car to the hall without falling flat on my face. The snow was higher than my overshoes and much higher than I could ever lift my feet. I was pondering my situation when Ron stepped around to my side of the car.

"Here," he said, stooping and presenting his backside. "Hop on. We'll get you in there one way or another. This is one party you're not going to miss."

I got on Ron's back and with my arms and legs draped around his lanky frame, and piggyback style he carried me into the hall.

While waiting for the girls to check their coats I stole a quick glance around the dimly lit hall.

"Look at all those people," I commented "I knew we should have got here earlier. We'll be darn lucky to get a seat, let alone one that's near the washroom."

With one arm wrapped firmly around Joyce's arm and using my cane to steady myself, we filed through the hall-way to the edge of the dance floor, scanning the dim room for a place to sit. All of a sudden the hall lit up in a blaze of light and immediately the circle of people rose from their chairs and began singing, *For He's A Jolly Good Fellow.* I wasn't sure at first but it seemed everyone was looking straight at me!

"What the hell," I said to no one in particular. I looked at Joyce for an answer. She shrugged, she appeared as stunned as I was.

I looked over at Carol who was grinning from ear to ear. "The party's not for Maurice and Terry," she said, hardly able to contain her giggles. "It's a retirement party for you. You and Joyce are the guests of honour tonight. Were you surprised?"

Surprised wasn't the word. I was dumbfounded. I had never been the centre of so much attention and I didn't know how to react to it. My face grew hot with embarrassment and my legs wobbled. Ron noticed that the commotion was more that I might be able to take standing so he took it upon himself to usher us to our table which, by the way, was the one nearest to the men's washroom.

It was a night I will always cherish in my memory. Most of my family was there—brothers, sisters, aunts, uncles and in-laws. Some of the guys I used to work with showed up; many of whom as dear to me as my own family.

Before the evening drew to a close, Joyce and I were presented with a cheque for eleven hundred dollars and a guest book signed by everyone there. No words can fully describe how touched I was by their warm display of kindness, and very few words would come when I was urged up on stage by them yelling, "speech! speech!" My voice trembled and my eyes grew moist. Though I did manage to say thank you, I couldn't utter another sound without breaking down completely.

On April Fool's Day 1978, I received my first pension cheque; two hundred and twenty dollars. I also had a cash settlement of five thousand dollars that came due from a sickness insurance benefit. I needed new transportation. After nine years of Washagami torture trails, the old blue wagon was no longer dependable, so I used the insurance money to buy a new *GMC* van.

Around that same time, Joyce spent a week's vacation with Carol and Ron in Nashville, Tennessee. I could have gone too, but as my condition was more susceptible in hot and humid conditions, I decided against it. I had learned through a few scary experiences that concentrated heat and humidity weakened me drastically.

The worst was in the sauna at the cottage. Perhaps I made it too hot, or I stayed in too long, but my reaction had changed. When I crawled off the wooden bench and tried to stand, my legs folded under me. I sagged to the floor like a limp washrag. Luckily, Joyce was in the change room at the time and managed to get me out. She doused me with cold water and after a twenty minute rest, I was okay again. "No more hot saunas for you," she said.

There was no reason for Joyce to miss out on the trip. The mention of Ron's offer brought a sparkle to her eyes—something I hadn't seen for a long time. Both of us were fond of country music. Joyce bubbled with excitement at the idea of seeing her country idols live, on stage, at the Grand Ol' Opry.

I wanted her to go. I could feel the love and devotion she had promised, evaporating. As she pulled farther away I felt cheated, miserable, and more lonely than ever before. Perhaps a holiday away from me and the children might make her want to come back.

Instead, she got a taste of life without me. The night Joyce arrived home, I anticipated a hug and a kiss and something like, "It's so good to be home." But to my dismay, she just went on and on about how wonderful it was in Nashville.

"I would like to live there," she said, bragging it up like it was some kind of utopia. I felt deflated. What about her own home? What about me and the kids? Weren't we worth a bit of her attention?

Day by day we moved further apart—trying to stay out of each other's way. She no longer wanted to be married to me, to bear the responsibility of my sexual and emotional needs. As my illusions of saving our marriage gradually evaporated, I became even more miserable. It was hard for Joyce too. We'd put so much energy and trust into these second and third tries at our relationship. Our discontent weighed so heavily on our fragile marriage that it was likely to collapse and splinter.

This didn't mean I wanted a divorce. I still loved Joyce and I feared the emptiness I would have to face, if we were to separate. I set out to make substitutions, to repress my feelings, and to keep going even if I was "white knuckling" it. I filled the vacuum of my life as best I could. I began lifting weights again in the basement hoping to regain some of my strength. I kept my limits in mind, so as not to exert myself to the point of exhaustion. The penalty could be another exacerbation. To fill in more my idle hours, I got out my hammer and saw. First, I built a pine hutch to give to Carol for her birthday. I used to enjoy pottering around with wood. My feelings of ineptness made it hard to return to a hobby that requires a strong hand, but I badly needed new accomplishments.

I had good friends, my growing children, the cottage I loved so much. As long as I had these things to fill my life, I felt I would be alright.

Then I became involved with another woman.

I was plucking out a song on my guitar at a party at Bryan's when this dark-haired women sidled up to me. She was impressed at the way I stumbled through *The Wildwood Flower.*

"Could you teach me to play that thing?" she asked, parting her full lips into a sweet smile.

"I suppose I could," I said, never once thinking she had anything more in mind than guitar lessons.

Each Wednesday morning at ten we met in my kitchen where I began teaching her the fundamentals of guitar playing—how to strum and where to place her fingers between the frets to sound the major chords.

I tutored her for three straight weeks. It was all the time I needed to conclude that she lacked any musical talent whatsoever. A sensitive ear was not one of her attributes. One morning she called to say her husband needed the car that day.

"Would you mind coming over here to give me my lesson?" she asked. The way she sang the words, how could I refuse?

I wondered why she didn't walk to my place. I only lived a couple of streets over from her. I figured she had her reasons. Before I hung up I asked if she would mind bringing my guitar in from the van when I got there. I couldn't walk with a cane and carry a guitar, too.

When I drove up she was waiting in the driveway dressed in blue jeans and a white T-shirt. Her shiny black hair brushed her shoulders. As she approached, I could easily see she wasn't wearing a bra. From then on, I found it extremely difficult to look anywhere else.

"You go on in," she said breezily, "I'll bring the guitar."

I lurched my way inside reaching out for a wall or a stick of furniture to steady myself. I aimed toward the living room sofa. No sooner had I sat down than she plunked herself next to me. She yanked off her T-shirt, baring her large breasts.

"I want you to make love to me," she whispered huskily in my ear as she pressed her body firmly against me.

I felt a wave of panic. I had not planned on this.

What if her husband should barge in? How could I explain to him that I came here quite innocently, intent only on giving guitar lessons. I had no idea...

She sensed my concern. "Don't worry," she reassured me. "My dear husband is deep in the mines right now working his ass off. He won't be home till supper time. Relax."

"Are you sure you want to do this?" I said, as she fumbled at my belt buckle. I wasn't at all sure that I did. But then I realized that of course I wanted to. It wasn't so much the sex part I was interested in—even though it had been months since Joyce and I had had sex. What I desperately wanted was caressing, touching, the feel of a sensuous female in my arms. Whether or not I had the ability to do more than that I wasn't sure. And I told her so.

I explained to my guitar student, now apparently my one-women fan club, how the disease had affected my sexual performance—that even at the best of times my erections were fleeting—if I did manage to attain one at all. But she wasn't concerned and her breath came faster as she cupped my hands to her breasts. She had both of us naked now.

"There are other ways to make love," she crooned softly, spreading her lily-white body on the sofa and pulling me down on top of her. The feel of her naked body beneath me gave me immense pleasure and I was content to just snuggle into the nest of her arms. But she had other ideas.

"I need you," she said, her words running together,"we're going to make love."

Then we made love, or rather I made love to her while she lay on her back uttering soft guttural sounds. She was using me to gratify her sexual desires but I never once thought that I was taken advantage of. She wanted me. She needed me. She was treating me like a man and I responded to her wishes like a man should.

It was as simple as that. If my wife would not recognize my needs, why shouldn't I seek attention elsewhere? Anyway what did it matter? Looking down a dark and depressing road, it didn't seem as if there was anything left to lose.

TWENTY

Days went by, different only in the smallest ways——like freight cars at a country crossing, both the beginning of the train and the end too far away to see. Spring was in full bloom, a time of year when I usually felt so vibrant, so alive. This year I couldn't shake my misery, no matter how hard I tried. I still worked out with my weights and tooled wood and made supper when Joyce went to work. I tried to be satisfied with the way my life was going. But I felt so wasted, so isolated. The distance between Joyce and me was becoming vast, the loneliness devastating. I believe this relentless stress played a major role in bringing on another exacerbation.

Like the others that came before, it began gradually, creeping upon me ever so slowly. This time I knew it was coming. I had been through enough of them by now to recognize the signs. First, the fatigue forced me to spend a lot of time sleeping and be barely able to get up in the morning. I was so exhausted I couldn't unbutton one shirt button without resting a moment or two. I could barely walk any longer without dragging my right foot numbly behind me. And, as with the previous attacks, I was terrified.

It was the uncertainty that scared me more than anything—the fear of not knowing how badly off I'd be afterwards. I couldn't cope with the idea of my condition deteriorating even more, and I didn't want to go back to the hospital. Why couldn't I just stay as I was? I would be satisfied with that. I couldn't bear to think about life in a wheelchair—helpless.

I had met many people through the *MS Society* that could bear it; and I took my hat off to them. But I was willing to bet there were others who complained loudly that life had cheated them, as they sat alone by their radios in perpetual rage, finally dying of neglect, loneliness, or by their own hand.

I decided if I couldn't be well I didn't want to live. It had come to that. I could not settle for semi-functioning as a cripple dependent upon strangers. The painful truth was that I could not depend upon Joyce, nor would I demand her help.

There was nothing more to be said. It was my life and I would do with it as I chose. But I would have to act quickly before I became too weak to do the job.

At first I thought about getting behind the wheel of our van and driving it headlong into the open pit over at Three Shaft. It seemed simple enough, and the 600 foot drop would guarantee instant results. But the more I thought about it the more squeamish I became. It was a bit too violent for my liking. Then another idea flashed through my mind after watching a television documentary about teenagers and suicide. It dramatized the suicide of a young couple who gulped the carbon monoxide of their car in a sealed garage curled into each other's arms. I had to squash that idea, too. I didn't have the strength to shut the garage door behind me and I certainly wasn't about to ask a neighbour or passerby to do me the favour.

I finally decided that the easiest and the least painful way out of this world was to overdose on pills. I thought of the anti-depressant pills I had saved from my last visit with the doctor and some valium pills from the time before. There were pills for everything—for depression, for sleep, for death. Why wasn't there a pill to give me back my health? I still remembered what health had been like, although the memory was getting foggy.

I settled on Friday night as the best time to carry out my plan. Joyce worked all the next day, leaving me alone to sleep late. If everything went the way I figured it should, no one would discover my body until Saturday evening. By then it would be all over— at least, it had better be. I didn't even want to imagine the consequences should I fail in my attempt.

It so happened the whole house was mine Friday night. After supper, Joyce taxied Allen and Gordy to the high school dance in Lively on her way to the Legion bingo. Teresa was at her grandparents for the weekend. I was relieved that things turned out that way. Having the kids around just might change my mind.

I doubted if anyone or anything could reverse my decision now. I couldn't remember ever experiencing such a harmonious feeling of wellbeing. A wonderful sense of euphoria had elevated and freed me from the mire of gloom and depression. I believed suicide was the perfect solution. Why else would I feel so good about it?

So I spent the evening having my own farewell party, drinking beer and blaring out tearjerkers on my record player. Old standbys like *Blue Eyes Crying In The Rain*, and Kenny Roger's *Lucille* might sink a normal person into a bog of despair, but they carried me quite high.

I was smoking again. I had quit four years before because I was worried about cancer. Tonight I didn't care. What harm could tobacco do me now?

Around ten o'clock I fried up a huge moose steak smothered in onions and mushrooms. "Might as well go out in style," I said to myself. As I sat down to eat, I saw myself as a prisoner being granted his last request before facing the executioner. Well I was prisoner and executioner all in one. There was a certain wry humour in that.

I was just finishing up the last bit of steak and washing it down with a beer when Joyce walked in. She wrinkled her face when she saw the collection of beer bottles on the table and the air blue with smoke. I ducked her glare as she stomped past me on her way upstairs. "Don't look at me that way," I wanted to scream at her, "Don't you dare look at me like I'm some kind of shit."

What was the matter with me anyway? Until I got sick, until my body started coming apart, I was the axis of her world. Could it be true that she never did love me? She had said so herself. Could it be that she married me for all the wrong reasons hoping they would turn into the right ones? A father for her unborn child, perhaps? I had tried to be a good father, a good husband, a good person. But after all these years I never did get it right, at least in her eyes—where it mattered most of all.

After her look of disdain, followed by the slam of the bedroom door, I grew dispirited and sullen. I nursed another beer and smoked a few more cigarettes. When I thought she was sound asleep I staggered up the stairs and went quietly but purposefully into the bathroom. As I reached into the medicine cabinet for the pills, I caught myself staring into the mirror. I looked at my face for a moment. What I saw was the reflection of a beaten man— a man who had narrowly missed a life close to perfection. It seemed such a terrible waste of effort—to have been through so much—to have gone this far—and still to have failed.

I swallowed the full bottle of anti-depressant pills and a handful of valium, then stole quietly into the bedroom where Joyce lay curled into her side of the bed. Without bothering to undress I slipped in beside her, kissed her lightly on the cheek, and whispered: "Goodbye".

TWENTY-ONE

The weight of a hand on my head scattered my thoughts, bringing me back to the present."Mr. Horner, are you awake?" said a soft, female voice.

I felt as if I had stepped from a cold dark room into sunlight. I turned my head and opened my eyes to see a nurse standing over me. The hair under her white cap was auburn and her dark eyes concentrated on a clipboard she held in her hands.

"My name is Darlene," she said pleasantly, "we have a bed for you in room 512 on the fifth floor." With professional briskness, she scribbled something on a sheet of paper and hung the clipboard at the foot of my bed."I'll take you there now and introduce you to your roommate."

I was transported to the fifth floor into a brightly lit room that faced north and east into the morning sun. The man in the next bed was Gerry Thomas. His bed raised him to a half sitting position with pillows supporting his body. He was a good-looking man in his early thirties with a full head of afro-style brown hair.

"Light me up before you leave," he directed the orderly, who was in the process of draining the urine bag hanging at the side of his bed. The orderly went over to Gerry's bedside table and stuck a cigarette into a cigarette holder mounted on an ashtray. From the holder ran an arm's length of spaghetti-size flexible tubing. Gerry clenched the end of the tube firmly in his teeth. As he puffed, the cigarette glowed red in its holder. I thought the contrivance was fascinating. For a split second I wondered why he just didn't smoke his cigarettes the way other people did. Then it struck me that he didn't have the use of his arms.

Gerry had been a quadriplegic for more than eight years. I found out later that he severed his spinal column in six places in a car accident. His perspective on life made me feel even more ashamed of my cowardly act.

When the orderly left the room, Gerry turned to me. "I don't like that son-of-a-bitch," he said in a whisper that could be heard in the next room. "He's rough, got no consideration. You should see the bastard put in a catheter. You'd think he was shovin' a meat thermometer into a slab of roast beef, Jesus." He considered a moment.

"The other one though, Bernie, he's okay. Better than most, and believe me I know them all. Doctors, nurses, orderlies, aides. I should. I been here ten months, ever since July last year. I'm a regular. Seen three guys die in that bed," he said primly.

Darlene shot him a dirty look.

Gerry stopped talking a moment. He stared out at the sunlight and watched the wind shred the clouds.

"It's a great life if you don't weaken," he began again. "Hear you overdosed on pills. Probably did it over a woman or somethin' stupid like that, huh?"

Darlene stopped fussing at my bedside and turned sharply.

"That is none of your business, Gerry," she said. "I really don't think Mr. Horner wants to discuss it right now. Let it rest."

"Don't get your shit in a knot, Darlene. I just don't think there's anything in this world worth taking your life over. Nothing can ever be that bad."

Gerry continued to ramble on to Darlene. I was too weary to pay any attention. I turned my head away and closed my eyes abandoning myself to a deep sleep.

A rattling of dinner trays in the hallway awakened me. Darlene brought in a tray and set it down on my bedside table. She sang the words, "Chow time! I'll raise the head of your bed and we'll get some food in you. I suppose you're hungry?" She removed the stainless steel cover and the aroma of hot food made me realize just how hungry I was. "It's chicken and rice tonight," Darlene informed me, "they make it good here."

She had to feed me like a baby because I had lost all movement in my arms and legs. My entire body remained maddeningly feeble. I was terribly uncomfortable lying in one position too long. I realized most of my weakness was from the exacerbation, but a part of it had to be from the pills.

After supper, my doctor came in to see me. "That wasn't a very smart thing to do," he said stiffly, removing a pen-light from his shirt pocket. He drew the blind at the window and went to work. "Follow the light, please," he said, bending over me and breathing a gust of warm licorice into my face. I chased the light until my eye ached. "The other now. Very good." He snapped off the light. "When you were last in my office, you left me with the impression that you were coping. What happened? Was it the retirement?"

I shook my head.

The doctor extended his hand, "Can you squeeze it?" He saw that I couldn't so he lifted my hands from the bed, examined them, and gently laid them back down again. "Were there problems between you and Joyce?" he prodded.

I nodded, then looking him straight in the eye, I blurted out the whole story; Joyce's involvement with another man; our constant bickering; the exacerbation I felt coming on. My voice trembled in a sudden wave of self pity. I was on the verge of losing all self control, but the more I opened up, the easier it became. I told him that having multiple sclerosis didn't seem so bad as long as I had Joyce to lean on—she was my strength. I was handling the disease all right until she renounced her love for me. After that, I just couldn't cope any longer.

It was the first time I had revealed my troubles to anyone. Just talking about it made me feel as though a heavy burden had suddenly been lifted from my shoulders.

The doctor listened, visibly concerned.

"I'm sorry, Bill," he said. "I wasn't aware that you and Joyce weren't getting along. Why didn't you come to me? We could have talked about it."

"There was nothing anybody could do," I broke in. "No one could have made me stop feeling the depression and loneliness."

He patted my hand reassuringly. "Keep your chin up," he said with a ghost of a smile. "As far as we can tell no serious damage has been done. There are a few more tests to complete then we'll start you on ACTH. I'll be back tomorrow."

"Why?" Joyce said when she entered my room that evening. "Bill, I never expected you'd do something so stupid. If this is your way of getting me to feel sorry for you, it didn't work." She lit a cigarette and inhaled deeply. "I don't need that kind of surprise, coming home and finding you half dead. Did you even bother to think how me and the kids would be affected by all this?"

She paced in the short space between my bed and the wall, her voice growing angry, loud. "Do you know how awful this is for me. I don't know what to say to the kids. I'm embarrassed, everyone's talking."

She stopped pacing and turned to look down at me. Her cold eyes flashed anger. "I can't take any more of this. I want a separation." She crushed her cigarette in the ashtray and left the room.

As she walked away I wanted to cry out to her: "Please don't go. I'm sorry, Joyce. Can't we try again?" That was the part of me that still felt love and tenderness for her, but another part of me saw the hate and contempt on her face.

She didn't even bother to ask how I was, or want to know about the enduring pain and loneliness that led me to commit such a terrible act. "What about me?" were her exact words. She said I had destroyed her world. If only she knew how much I loved her, how much I needed her, to keep my own world from shattering.

From then on, I knew there would never be a reconciliation. We were two separate people.

I stayed six weeks in the Memorial Hospital. Friends and family came to visit—to scold.

"Why?" they all asked, over and over again. "Why did you do this? You who have such a good wife and three wonderful children, you who have so much to live for?"

My guitar-playing girlfriend, who had long since gone on another excursion, came to talk, to admonish, perhaps to reassure herself that this had nothing to do with her.

Joyce's parents came to remind me that what I had done to their daughter was unforgivable and if she were to leave me because of it, I only had myself to blame. I never saw either one of them again.

Joy Horner, my favourite sister-in-law, heavy with child, waddled in to visit me whenever she could get the car. The first time she came we talked for more than two hours after lunch. Her folded hands resting on an enormous pregnancy heavy in her lap.

That same afternoon Joy asked me to come to live at their house. "Joyce is talking separation," she said, "so Bryan and I discussed the idea of you staying with us."

I was touched by their offer but I didn't think it was right to intrude into their family life. Besides, the house was small, with only two bedrooms. Where would I sleep?

"We have it all figured out," Joy said excitedly. "We can partition off the living room then the dining area can be your bedroom. Please say you'll come. We'll be more than happy to have you."

I couldn't give her a definite answer, so I said I'd sleep on it for awhile. There were all sorts of thoughts running through my mind, decisions to make. It was going to be a slow and painful process getting my life back in order. I was faced with the loss of a love, the loss of a home, and on top of it all, I had a numb and broken body. It saddened me to realize there would never be magic moment when I could sit up and cry out, "It's okay. I'm all better now."

I looked at Gerry. He had a broken body too, much worse than me. Yet he had the guts to reach out and embrace the world, though his world had decreased significantly. I can't really say he inspired me, but in the few short weeks I spent with him, I realized I must start looking at life again through the right end of the telescope. I saw, through Gerry' eyes that to go on living one has to accept pain as a part of life.

After the first week of ACTH injections, my body began to improve. I could wiggle my finger tips. Then, I was grasping the rails of my bed, able to pull myself over whenever I lay in one position too long. Each day I gained a little more strength, until one day I raised myself to a sitting position on the edge of the bed. That launched me into a frenzy of determination.

On the eleventh day of my stay in the hospital I was back on my feet. True, with the aid of a walker and two therapists, but still I was on my feet. My legs prickled constantly, the right dragged numbly behind me. I couldn't manage more than a few steps without having to sit down again. As my strength and confidence grew so did the length of my strolls. In the evenings after visiting hours, the dull thump, thump, thump of my walker resounded along the hospital corridors. I lurched unsteadily onward in my relentless quest to get my body back to normal.

The last week of my hospital interlude, I had to spend some time with a psychiatrist. I did all the talking while he listened and smoked his pipe. I told him what I had told my own doctor about the causes of my suicide attempt; the ongoing conflict between Joyce and me; the impending exacerbations. After I stopped talking there was a thoughtful pause. He took a long puff from his pipe.

"I strongly suggest, Mr. Horner, that you and your wife live apart from one another."

It was this suggestion that made up my mind to sever my relationship with Joyce and leave the house for her and the kids. She was much more capable of taking care of them than me, at least for now. I asked her to break the news to them. I couldn't. Telling my children to their faces that I wasn't going to live with them any more was just too much for me to handle.

I was well enough to go home, and the doctors finally agreed. All morning, I sat on my hospital bed in street clothes anxiously waiting for Joy to come to get me. I had accepted Bryan and Joy's offer—but only until I regained my strength. Perhaps by then, I could get a place of my own.

On the afternoon Joy was due to arrive, Darlene wheeled me down to the lounge near the front door. She sat with me a moment and we chatted. She had talked to me from time to time when I needed someone—when I had been on the edge of depression, or lacking in self confidence. She had been firm, professional, and kind.

"Darlene, what is your opinion?" I asked. "Do you think Joyce and I could ever have a life together again?"

She looked surprised.

" Well, only you two can decide that," she answered.

"At the beginning we had so much love." I said earnestly. "We should be able to salvage something. I still have feelings for her."

"You never know, Bill," she said, "Maybe some day you and Joyce can become friends and perhaps get together again. But in the meantime the most important thing you can do right now is to get your health back in order. And don't be frightened. Everything will be alright."

TWENTY-TWO

"Good to be out, isn't it?" Joy said, as she watched me lurch out of the hospital on two canes. We walked through the double doors into a bright, sunlit afternoon. A slight rush of sweet-smelling air tickled my nostrils.

"Get a whiff of that air," I told Joy, who was putting my suitcase in the back seat. "It smells great!"

Through the window I watched the people dressed in summer clothes. Almost an entire season had passed while I was in the hospital. But, I didn't care. The excitement of being out of the hospital was much too thrilling to waste worrying about a lost spring.

When we rounded the corner by Meatbird Lake, I couldn't help thinking about my old life. We passed a group of high school kids frolicking around a diving float in the middle of the pond. Joyce and I spent many sunny days there, laughing and teasing just like these kids.

For a long time I couldn't look at anything without associating it with the memory of Joyce and the way things used to be. That's natural, I thought. You and Joyce were together since childhood. It's only natural.

Bryan and Joy did a wonderful job of fixing up a room for me. The dining area was partitioned from the living room with a wall of imitation pine panelling and a folding door was installed at the kitchen entrance, giving me complete privacy. A single bed, a pine night table, a chest of drawers, painted white, and a threadbare floral green armchair Bryan resurrected from the basement added the finishing touches to a cosy little room. I quickly disposed of the scatter rug in the middle of the hardwood floor. With my dragging foot, scatter rugs and loose mats were unwelcome obstacles.

That same day I made arrangements with Joyce to pick up my personal belongings. Our agreement was simple, she would get all the furniture, and I would keep the van. It was the most practical and logical way of dividing up the property. She had to have furniture, and I couldn't possibly manage without wheels.

The only other item of any consequence was the cottage, half of which belonged to her. It was a matter I did not want to discuss. Horner's Hideaway was very dear to me, and I couldn't bear the thought of ever having to part with it.

Next day while Joyce was at work, Bryan and I drove over to get my stuff. When we got there, the van was sitting in the driveway with the keys in the ignition. Inside the house, the rest of my stuff was lumped together on the kitchen floor. I was surprised to see how little I actually owned. There were some shirts and trousers, a black leather jacket and winter boots, my guitar and a few carpentry tools. Everything else in the house now belonged to Joyce.

"So this is it. It's all over," I thought, as I watched Bryan load the last of my belongings. It was terribly hard to look around the house for the last time and realize that this was no longer my home. There was no reason for me to come here any more.

On the trip back, I grew solemn and quiet. When we finished unpacking my things back at Bryan's, I excused myself and went to lie down. I tried to take a nap, but I couldn't sleep. If I closed my eyes I saw scenes of Joyce and me together. I saw past the quarrelling and disharmony to the years of happiness we shared. Now there was only emptiness.

I turned on my portable radio and listened to music for a while. I thought of making a phone call, but there was no one I really wanted to speak to. I just lay there for the rest of the day, excused myself from supper, and when darkness came, went early to bed.

If it had been just one day like that, it might not have been so bad. But day after day, I moped around the house wondering what to do with myself. What would I do with the days that stretched before me? How could I still give my life purpose?

It seemed to me I faced an empty, lonely existence and I saw no way to change it.

But thank goodness Bryan and Joy wouldn't let me languish. They knew how down I was, and decided to snap me out of it by planning a trip to Washagami for the weekend.

"It's darn time we got the old camp opened up, don't you think?" Bryan said. "Maybe we can stop at Ess Creek like we used to and catch some pike. What do you say?"

I didn't argue. There was no reason not to go.
And besides, I hadn't seen the place since we closed her up last fall. "Sure why not," I said.

We got there shortly before noon on Saturday morning. When we pulled up in the yard I thought about how this was the first time I had been there without Joyce. The sky was blue, the day was beautiful. I struggled to shake off my depressed feelings.

While Bryan and Joy opened up the cottage and put away the groceries, I relaxed on the porch in my easy chair. I watched a beaver in the bay make a widening V as he went about his business. I heard the call of the loon from the shadows where the huge pines hung over the water. It was refreshing to get away from the sounds of the mine compressors and the acrid taste of sulphur that enveloped our town for days at a time.

We had a lunch of bacon and tomato sandwiches. For the rest of the afternoon we sat around talking and drinking coffee laced with rum. The atmosphere was laid back. I enjoyed every minute of it. I even tried plucking out a few songs on my guitar but, with the numbness and lack of coordination in my hands, I soon gave up that idea.

During the evening, the three of us played cards while a brilliant sun set behind a ridge of pine trees at the far end of the lake. Up until then I was feeling pretty good except that every once in a while I winced from a stab of pain in my groin. When I went to bed that night I had to struggle more than usual to get undressed. I attributed it to the number of coffee royales I had earlier. The last thing I remember before the lights went out was the room spinning madly while I clung to the bed.

I woke up in the middle of the night with an uncontrollable urge to go to the bathroom. My bladder threatened to burst at any second but try as I might, I could not get up from the bed. The more I strained the more it increased the urgency. "Damn," I cursed under my breath. I didn't want to face the embarrassment of wetting my own bed.

I tried again. In one last desperate attempt, I managed to get off the bed onto a kneeling position on the floor. Then in a rush, my bladder let go. It streamed through my jockey shorts and drizzled down the inside of my leg onto the wooden floor. I couldn't move. All I could do was cling to the edge of the bed in a praying position as the warm fluid puddled around my kneecaps.

I put my head down into my arms on top of the bed until it stopped trickling down my legs. With the last bit of effort I could muster, I crawled weakly into bed, thoroughly disgusted with myself for making a shameful mess. What would Bryan and Joy think? The mess on the floor became only a minor concern compared to the weird sensations in my body. I felt hot and lightheaded, weak and feverish.

Was this another exacerbation? I was sure that it was. Yet it was different from my usual bouts. Now it seemed I was faced with the problem of incontinence, too. Right away Laurie flashed into my mind as I remembered her embarrassing moment down in physiotherapy. I had dreaded the possibility that it might eventually happen to me.

I didn't sleep after that, even though I was exhausted. I just lay there staring at the rafters until the morning grew light enough. Then I called Bryan over to my bedside. "I think you had better get me to a hospital," I said fighting back the tears, "I don't feel so good."

Early Sunday morning, as I lay wrapped in blankets on the floor of the van, Bryan guided us carefully but speedily back to civilization. Through the side windows, I could see tree tops passing by against a backdrop of pale blue sky. "I'll be okay," I said to myself over and over again. "This feeling of paralysis will wear off shortly. I'll be okay."

Soon I was looking at the city speeding by and then the van slowed and turned into the hospital parking lot. Two minutes later attendants were at my side easing me into a stretcher. By then the sun was directly overhead and my entire body was soaked with sweat.

Inside the emergency room, I was transferred to a hospital bed and wheeled into one of the many small cubicles. As the nurse pulled the privacy curtains around me, I again struggled desperately to move my arms and legs. They were numb and motionless. I felt so helpless, so frightened. Tears welled in my eyes.

I lay in the dim light of the cubicle feeling despondent and totally fed up with the whole mess. Grief, remorse and depression lay over me like a, suffocating blanket. At that moment, I wished more than ever I'd succeeded in my suicide attempt. By now I would be long gone from this miserable world.

After an hour or so, a familiar face poked her head through the curtains. It was Darlene.

"Hi, Bill," she said. "Just heard you were back in. It's only been a week since we discharged you on good behaviour. What is it this time?"

I managed a weak smile. "Looks like another attack."

And as I said it I felt tears hot and salty spill from my eyes and run down my cheeks. My nose became stuffy but I couldn't even raise my hand to wipe it.

Darlene wiped my nose with a tissue. She pulled another from her pocket. "Here. Blow. Feel better now?" "I'm sorry," I said. "Guess I'm feeling a bit sorry for myself. It's just getting too much for me to handle."

Darlene ran the back of her hand along the side of my face. Her gesture of concern felt good. It was reassuring and comforting to feel the touch of someone's hand. "Don't give up hope, Bill," she said softly. "Nothing is ever as bad as we first make it out to be. The fever and weakness could be caused by a number of things, not necessarily an exacerbation. Let's hear what the doctor says before we go thinking the worst."

"It isn't the disease flaring up," the doctor assured me.

A urine culture showed a serious bladder infection probably brought on from the body's rejection of the indwelling catheter on my last hospital visit.

"An infection of the urinary tract can cause high fever," he explained. "And because your resistance to infection was so low to begin with, it brought on a weakness so severe it was as if you were paralysed. Learn to recognize these symptoms, Mr. Horner, and see a doctor right away."

Following a week of urine and blood tests and high doses of antibiotics, I once again felt strong enough to be released from the hospital. I was ecstatic to find out it was not an exacerbation and as I gradually regained the use of my arms and legs, I felt sure I was ready to start living a meaningful life.

TWENTY-THREE

The world began to look fresh and alive again that summer. I groped through the warm days trying to think only positive thoughts. I was slowly putting my life back together.

Joyce and I remained aloof and unfriendly. Despite our mutual animosity, the rest of the family seemed to have survived the catastrophe with minimal damage. Living in the same small town had a lot to do with it. This way we could share the children who circulated easily between our separate quarters, seeming much more relaxed than they did in the past.

I didn't see much of Allen and Gordy but Teresa came by quite often—usually on a Friday night—sometimes with a bunch of giggling and buoyant teens like herself.

"Hey Dad," she might say after a short visit. "There's a dance at the club tonight. Can you spare two dollars?" Digging into my billfold, I was happy to give it to her even though I was reasonably sure she had already got money from her mother. Seeing her happy with her friends and "normal" meant a lot to me. I breathed a lot easier knowing that my kids were not seriously affected by our splitting up. It was up to me now to make a fresh start. As far as I was concerned my debts were paid. I owed Joyce nothing and I expected nothing in return.

Getting my life together meant getting control over my body. I tried to push it into healthiness, exercising regularly. My body remained maddeningly feeble, defiantly numb and uncoordinated. A simple manoeuvre like turning over in bed demanded patience and ingenuity. My gait was a sorry affair of shuffling and puffing. I lurched about on two canes, grasping banisters and furniture like the very old or nearly blind.

Besides coping with the disease, I had to cope with other people's reactions. When I first began walking with two canes I got into the habit of telling strangers who asked why I walked that way, that I'd been in a car accident. I shied away from admitting to multiple sclerosis after learning that a lot of people are scared of a disease but not of an injury. Later on, as I emerged from my cocoon of self-consciousness, I had my own answer for anyone who asked.

I hate to brag," I would tell them, "but I happen to have the disease of the handsome, brilliant, and famous—multiple sclerosis."

Both mentally and physically, I was more determined than ever not to give into the disease. Prior to my last attack, I had managed quite well with one cane which I only used for long distances and days when my walk became a stagger. Now that both legs were weakened and slowed even more with a dropped foot, I had to learn to walk all over again using two canes. It was no easy task at first. I endured bruised knees and cracked ribs from losing my balance by turning too quickly or my legs folding beneath me.

Eventually I got the hang of it. I learned to visualize each step before I made a move. If I took very short steps instead of my usual stride, I could manage without falling.

Not all falls were avoidable. I experienced a bad fall the morning I went down to Lively to cash my pension cheque. I had put it off again and again; mostly because I shied away from exhibiting my grotesque way of walking in public. Finally, when I was completely out of money, I went in to town.

I was feeling a little stronger that day, had even gone to the trouble of putting on a freshly-ironed shirt which Joy helped me to button up. Spiffy clothes and a clean shave always add a bit of vigour to my step.

"Maybe I should go with you," Joy said, handing over my canes, "you might need help."

I shook my head. "I'll be fine," I assured her. Joy would have gladly done my banking for me but I felt I could handle this job all by myself.

The mini shopping centre bustled with people in bright summer clothes moving in and out of stores as they went about their business. I eased my van into a parking spot directly in front of the bank, then I hesitated before going any further. Watching all these people shuffling back and forth suddenly made me awfully nervous. Maybe I should have brought Joy along.

"Oh well," I muttered aloud, "I'm here now. Might as well get it over with."

I grabbed my canes and climbed cautiously down from my seat, planting both feet firmly on the ground before making another move.

"Don't hurry, take short steps," I reminded myself as I focused my concentration of the glass doors of the bank. "You only have to lift your foot a few inches to clear the curb. The rest is easy."

Instead of lifting my foot high enough, I tripped over the lip of the curb and before I could recover my balance, I saw the sidewalk rushing up at me. I turned my head to protect my face and the last thing I remember was a muffled 'thud' and excruciating pain as my head struck concrete.

I don't know how long I was unconscious, but when I came to I was looking up at a blur of curious faces hovering over me. My head ached and black spots danced in front of my eyes. Realizing I was sprawled on my back in the flow of people, my face flushed with embarrassment. What must these people think of me, stumbling around like a drunken fool?

"Are you alright?" someone asked.

I didn't answer right away. I needed time to recover from the initial shock and try to determine if I had broke any bones. I felt dizzy and weak but there didn't seem to be any serious damage. "I think I'm okay," I managed.

I staggered to my knees attempting to get up on my own, but suddenly realized I couldn't. Without something to grab onto I was as helpless as a turtle on its back. I was used to having a sturdy chair, a sofa or even a doorknob handy to pull myself up again. I had to ask for help.

Two burly men who I recognized from the mines reached down and set me back on my feet. One of them handed me my canes.

"You want us to take you over to the medical centre?" he asked.

"No," I said, shaking off my fuzziness. "If you can get me to my van I'm sure I'll be fine in a few minutes."

After they eased me into the driver's seat I rested a while to collect myself. When I felt I had recovered enough to drive safely, I headed back to Creighton without cashing my cheque.

Home again, I staggered into the house and flopped down on a kitchen chair. At the sound of my footsteps Joy waddled in from Colleen's room where she had spent the morning putting a fresh coat of paint on the baby crib.

"Everything go okay?" she said, wiping her hands on a turpentine-soaked rag. Then she saw my skinned elbows and the tear in my freshly-ironed shirt. "Jeez, Bill, what happened? Did you get in a fight?"

I managed a sheepish grin. While Joy tended to my wounds, I told her how I bounced my head off the sidewalk right in front of the *Toronto Dominion* Bank. For added effect I got her to feel the lump on my head which still throbbed like the dickens.

Joy settled her pregnant body into a chair next to me and gently applied antiseptic cream to my raw elbows. Satisfied with her nursing job she looked at me with determination.

"Mr. Mulehead," she said severely, "I hope this teaches you not to go around trying to be so darn independent. I could have gone with you."

"It is not a case of being stubborn," I interrupted. "Trying things on my own is the only way I can find out my capabilities and admit my limitations. I don't want people doing things for me I can do myself."

Her eyes never left mine. "Yes, I suppose that's true," she said, "but don't feel ashamed about asking for help when you need it. And from now on, when you have business downtown, I'm going with you."

Joy was good that way, never hesitating to do things for me I couldn't do myself. Besides preparing my meals, she made my bed, washed laundry, and ironed my shirts without ever once complaining. I appreciated her kindness and it made me feel good knowing someone cared.

That summer Joy and I became close friends and her concern for me was real, never phoney. I valued the closeness we shared and that is why it bothered me so much when I began to see a distinct changes creep into our relationship.

In the early hours of an August morning I was awakened by rustling and hurried steps outside my bedroom door.

"I'm going to put on my shoes, and then I'll put the suitcase in the car," Bryan said, sounding a bit panicky. "You get ready."

"It feels like the baby's almost here," Joy said.

"That's why we have to hurry. C'mon."

I listened groggily to the whir of voices and rushing footsteps; a door slammed, then silence. I rolled over and drifted back to sleep thinking it was all a dream.

Bryan shook me awake later that morning to announce that Joy had given birth to a baby girl. Both mother and daughter were doing fine.

"We just got there and she had it," Bryan said, still trembling from the excitement. "Talk about close."

So now the little red house on Snider Street contained a family of four, Bryan and Joy, Colleen, the baby Stacey. And then there was me.

After the baby was born, Joy began to act differently toward me. Each day I noticed a gradual change in her behaviour. She became more withdrawn even sullen whenever we were in the same room. She could no longer face me squarely, speaking to me only when it was unavoidable. It wasn't too long ago that we used to sit down to lunch together, she and I, and perhaps afterwards play a few hands of crib or while away the afternoon in idle chatter. Now meals became an unavoidable clash. She would plunk down my sandwich plate in front of me then disappear into the living room to watch her soap operas. More often than not I found myself sitting alone at the table feeling like a stranger in a boarding house. Often I was too distraught to bother eating at all.

Why was she so annoyed with me? I had tried to be a star boarder; tried not to be a hindrance, paid my room and board on time, stayed clear of family arguments. The only explanation was that I was in the way now that she was tied down to nursing the baby. Perhaps, I could have taken care of more things, looked after myself more, made my own sandwich plates. I felt bad thinking Joy wanted me out and didn't have the heart to tell me what was bothering her. She didn't seem to have the courage to be completely honest with me. In the end I put it down to her wanting the house to herself and her husband and new baby. It was an intimacy I had no right to invade.

The uneasy atmosphere was wearing me thin. I felt uncomfortable and dismayed. I had to take some action.

One afternoon while reading through our local paper, I saw an ad for a two-bedroom apartment just a few blocks from our house. I decided to check it out.

The apartment was located at the back of an old rundown house that reminded me of the house Joyce and I first lived in when we moved to Creighton. In an attempt at rejuvenation, the outside of it had been covered in yellow siding that appeared to be the only thing holding the building upright. The porch leaned. Inside, the ceiling brushed the top of my head while the floorboards under the cheap linoleum creaked and sagged when I walked.

It disappointed me that the place was so old and shabby. But it had one great advantage—I could drive up close to the entrance with only six steps to the porch landing. Once inside, it was all one level. Getting around wouldn't be a problem. Still I worried about taking such a giant step on my own. "The rent's 150 dollars a month, including hydro," the owner said.

When I asked for time to think it over he gave me twenty-four hours. All through that night I fought with myself—a battle of indecision. One part of me said, "Don't be foolish, Bill. You're not strong enough to make it on your own. What if you fell down the stairs or in the bathtub? Who would be there to pick you up again? What about housekeeping? You can't shop for groceries or do laundry. Stay here where it's safe. Wasn't it just last week that you overheard Bryan telling Joy how your board money sure helped with their mortgage payment? They don't want to see you go, you're overreacting."

And another part of me would holler back. "Go on, give it a try. What have you got to lose? How many people worse off than you are making it on their own? And when you look back over your life are you going to be able to say you gave it your best shot? What if nobody knew the meaning of the word courage?"

By the time daylight came, I was still undecided. If only I could figure out what Joy was thinking. If only she would reassure me that I was more than welcome to go on living here. It would all be so simple.

After breakfast I caught her attention before she disappeared into another part of the house. I told her about the apartment and how I couldn't make up my mind whether or not to take it.

"Do you think it's a good idea?"

Her eyes widened in surprise.

"I had no idea you were apartment hunting," she said. Then she thought for a moment. "Be sensible, Bill. You know you can't live by yourself. You need someone to look after you."

"I think I can make it." I said trying to sound brave.

With a look of despair, she turned away to gaze at the kitchen window. When she spoke again her words were like weights on my heart. "When will you be moving?" she said.

So my intuition had been right all along. I had worn out my welcome.

"I'll move my things out this afternoon," I said. "As soon as Allen gets home from school I'll call him and ask him to help me with my things."

I needed Joy to push me in order to make this decision. I was hurt, but in the end I knew it was the right thing to do, for me as well as for Joy.

TWENTY-FOUR

My son Allen and his friend Mark loaded my belongings into the van. Before heading over to my apartment, we detoured around by the post office to get my mail. Then I remembered I needed groceries so I had the boys run into the *IGA* store and purchase a few necessary items. While I waited in the van, I leafed through the handful of mail Allen had deposited on the dash. My heart quickened when I recognized Joyce's handwriting on one of the envelopes.

Was she having a change of heart? Did she want to talk it over? I was all thumbs as I anxiously fumbled the letter out of its wrapping. It read:

> *Dear Bill,*
> *As you read this letter please try to understand the dilemma I'm faced with. I know what the cottage*

means to you and how you always said you would never part with it but something has to be done right away if the kids and I are to survive. I do not earn enough money working part-time at the IGA to support the household. I went as far as to approach social services for assistance but I was turned down because I own property, which they consider as income. I really don't want to hassle you about this matter, Bill. All I can hope for is that the welfare of the children will influence your decision.

Joyce

My first thought as I shoved the letter into my shirt pocket was that I wasn't about to give up the cottage for her or for anyone else. It was black outside and the wind velocity had picked up to almost gale force. The boys unloaded the van. They were anxious to be on their way. I was hoping they wouldn't rush off quickly, but I couldn't expect them to keep me company if they had other things to do.

"I'll check on you tomorrow okay, Dad?" Then Allan and his friend were gone, and except for the shrieking wind outside, a deadly quiet hung over the house.

It felt eerie being alone in that old house. Right away I dug out my portable radio and turned on some music to break the silence. Then I made myself busy unpacking some things from the pile of stuff lumped together on the living room floor. I had to get used to living alone. Whether I liked it or not, I had to accept the idea that this was the way it was going to be from now on.

A growling sound in my belly made me think about getting some grub together so I rummaged into the grocery bags and came up with a loaf of bread and a carton of eggs. I fried up some eggs in butter and devoured them between slices of bread.

"Mmm not bad," I thought to myself between bites and some hot coffee. I smiled proudly at my accomplishment. It was my first meal in my new apartment and the first time I had tried to cook anything since the night of my suicide attempt.

Having something to eat relaxed me a little, still I couldn't get used to the quiet. I got up and began putting things away, trying to keep my mind busy with tasks. But I really didn't know what to do with myself. I felt so alone, so abandoned. All my life I had lived with people. As a child I had grown up with a mum and a dad and a house full of brothers and sisters. Then after I married there was Joyce and the children to comfort me.

I looked around at the four walls. How do people manage alone? Who do they talk to? I thought of calling someone then remembered the phone wasn't hooked up yet. Not knowing what else to do, and feeling especially gloomy, I crawled into an unmade bed while a howling wind battered and shook the old house, causing the rafters to creak and moan and the windows drumming in their frames. Afraid and alone and faced with the uncertainty of tomorrow, I pulled the covers over my head and burst out crying so hard I felt as if my heart were one giant tear.

The next morning a blinding sun woke me as it streamed through a naked window. The storm had quieted, and in its wake the first dusting of snow lay on the ground, creating a world of white. It was a bright and cheery day and I felt a whole lot better as I got up from the bed. Even if my first night alone had been a dreadful, lonely experience, I had survived. I told myself that now I could make it on my own.

Fumbling with the buttons on my shirt I felt the crumpled letter in my shirt pocket and remembered its contents. I studied the letter intently after I put the kettle on for coffee. What was I going to do? Was I doing the right thing by trying to hang on to the cottage? After all, half of the property did belong to Joyce. Even if by some remote possibility I did manage to buy out her share, could I truly enjoy Horner's Hideaway as I once did? I remembered how difficult it had been just to walk over the uneven ground the last time I was there.

The whistling of the kettle interrupted my thoughts and almost automatically my mind drifted back to another time. I remembered how my head was in the clouds eight years ago when I first began building Horner's Hideaway. Ever since then it had been my dream to retire there someday—that is, until multiple sclerosis ravaged my body. Now, unless there was an overnight cure to restore my health, I could never hope to fulfil that dream. I stood up on shaky legs with barely the strength to raise the kettle high enough to pour a mug of coffee. When I sat back down again my mind was made up. I would make arrangements to sell the cottage.

Having to part with the cottage was one more example of how my life had gone downhill since I developed multiple sclerosis. First it was my job, then my wife, and now this. I started to laugh out loud. Who could I tell about the loss of these things that meant so much to me? There was no one, no one to share that with, no one to share anything with. Self pity began to well up in me. I hated that, and I knew that along with everything else I was going to have to fight self pity, too. It wasn't going to get the better of me any more.

A sharp knock at the door snapped me out of my melancholy. The door opened and in walked Carol and Ron, each carrying a cardboard box full of cooking utensils, dishes, and other odds and ends.

"We had these things hanging around the house and thought you could use them," Carol said, "at least to get started."

I was delighted by their thoughtfulness and more than delighted by their unexpected visit. Carol scolded me. "Boy, some brother you are," she said, facing me squarely with her hands on her hips. "I called you at Joy's last night, and she informed me that you had moved out. You could have told me."

"I didn't tell anyone," I said, "except Allen, who did the moving. It was a spur of the moment decision."

She looked around, her huge brown eyes dancing, they settled on the strewn clothes and stacked boxes.

"Well, he might have stayed to help straighten out the place a little." Carol removed her coat and began tidying things up a little. Ron rolled up his shirt sleeves and pitched in. While putting sheets on my bed, she stuck her head out the bedroom door. "Are you sure you can manage here by yourself," she said, her face showing concern. "The floor's not even level in here." Carol knew the difficulty I had with uneven ground. "You have to walk downhill to open the window. If I were you, I'd be awful careful."

I assured Carol that everything would be okay once I got used to the apartment.

"Well, Bill, if you ever feel you can't survive on your own, you're welcome to stay with us in Sudbury."

Ron nodded his approval. "We can always make room."

"No, but thanks anyway," I said firmly. I had tried living with family and found out that it only created an uncomfortable situation for everyone.

Yet I wondered to myself if Ron and Carol could adjust to living in the same house with someone who had a disease with no specific symptoms. I could be flat on my back one day and up walking the next. I had to live with it, but they would have to watch it happening.

Before they left to go home that afternoon I broke the news to them that I was selling the cottage. Carol's face grew sad but she didn't seem too surprised by this revelation.

"We kind of expected it to happen," she said, "even though we prayed it wouldn't. Ron and I couldn't see how you were going to hold onto the cottage now that you and Joyce are separated."

Ron had recently purchased Dad's cottage after Dad and his new bride moved to Nova Scotia. Ron and Carol would have been our neighbours on the lake.

"Oh well, you don't have to abandon Washagami altogether," Ron offered. "Anytime you want the key to your dad's old place, just say the word."

The dark side of living alone, I was soon to discover, was the loneliness. I kept thinking friends and family were the key because at first I was bombarded with their attention. Hardly a day went by when there wasn't someone popping in to check on me and end up staying for supper or a game of cards over beer and pizza. Sometimes I attended family parties but everyone came in pairs—Joe with Sue, Shelley and Sharron, Don and Marie, Bryan and Joy—and then there was me. I tried not to feel alone when I was surrounded by familiar faces, but I did.

Late at night, when I went home alone and climbed under the cold sheets, I longed for someone to hold in my arms the way I used to hold Joyce. Often during those moments, I thought of my father, spending five years alone after Mom died. I understood better now why he remarried. The loneliness had to have been unbearable for him too.

I yearned for female companionship, but I had no idea how to go about meeting someone after being out of the dating game as long as I have. More importantly, what woman in her right mind would want to get herself hooked up with a man who staggered around on two canes? These thoughts played havoc with my mind. Each new day saw me getting more and more desperate.

One morning a voice over the radio announced that a meeting for *Parents Without Partners* was slated for 8 o'clock that evening. Right away my ears perked up. I had never heard of the organization but from what I could gather, it sounded like some sort of singles club.

After a long inner debate, I decided it wouldn't hurt to give them a call. When I did, a soft female voice answered. Rebecca, was her name, and she was more than happy to answer my questions. "*Parents Without Partners*, is like a singles club," she said, "Only it's children oriented—which simply means that you must be a single parent in order to join. Do you have children, sir?"

"Three," I said, "but they're not with me."

"It doesn't matter," she informed me, "all that counts is that you are a parent. Why don't you come tonight and see for yourself what we're all about?"

Her voice sang so sweet and sensual over the phone that I was suddenly imagining her to be something out of a movie magazine. My curiosity got the better of me.

"I'll be there," I said.

"Now why did I go and do that?" I scolded myself after I hung up the receiver. It was hard enough staggering around in front of people that I knew without doing it in a room full of strangers.

"I don't have to go," I said out loud, but still, I couldn't stop the flutter in my stomach as I waited anxiously for evening to come.

The meeting was held at Marymount school in Sudbury. In the long corridor, the dull thump, thump of my canes resounded on the tiled flooring as I followed PWP signs with arrows pointing the way to the school auditorium. People dodging around me turned to stare quizzically. Some smiled graciously. I managed a weak smile in return, hoping no one noticed the beads of perspiration beginning to form on my forehead. I was getting awfully nervous and my legs were trembling more than usual. Still, I forced myself to trudge ahead, until I reached the doorway leading to the auditorium.

Inside I heard a cacophony of voices mixed with chairs being shuffled about. I hesitated and listened. It sounded like a full house. My palms grew damp and my knuckles whitened from grasping my canes too tightly.

"If I walk through that doorway," I thought, "everyone's eyes will be focused on me." I couldn't convince myself to take another step. Instead I did an about face and headed back the way I came as fast as two canes and two wobbly legs would carry me.

I had only retraced a few of my steps when I met with a silver-haired man in a wheelchair coming the other way.

"Not going in?" he asked.

I shook my head. "I must have the wrong place," I lied.

"Pardon me for being nosy," he said. "But I watched you walk as far as the doorway, then suddenly change your mind. I almost did it too, the first time I came here. I was scared out of my wits about wheeling into a room full of strangers."

He hesitated momentarily and glanced down at his own lifeless legs. "I know the feeling," he said. "But I can assure you there's really nothing to fear. Come on in and see what I mean."

The man in the wheelchair was John Bishop, president of the *Sudbury Chapter of Parents Without Partners*. John was had been in a car accident which left him paralysed from the waist down. He didn't show any signs of bitterness. His warm smile and soft-spoken manner relieved my anxieties. Listening to him gave me the nerve to turn around and walk back into that meeting place.

"If he can do it," I said to myself, "then so can I."

Still I was still nervous walking in. As I lurched through the doorway into the midst of at least fifty pairs of staring eyes, I imagined them saying, "What happened to him, who let him in here?"

Later, when I had a chance to survey the gathering from my seat at the back of the room, I didn't notice any throat clearings or elbow jabs, just smiling friendly faces. Best of all, as close as I could figure, the ratio of those faces looked to be about seven women to every man.

I was introduced to some of the members during a coffee break which followed the business part of the meeting. I met Rebecca, whose voice I recognized as the lady on the phone. She wasn't quite the movie star I imagined her to be, but she was very nice.

"Can I get you a coffee?" she asked me.

"I'd like that," I said.

"Cream and sugar?" I nodded.

She left and returned shortly balancing a styrofoam cup of coffee in each hand and two large donuts. I couldn't think of eating at a time like this but I yearned for a good cup of coffee.

"Been separated long?" she asked, as she settled herself down next to me, passing me the coffee.

"Six months." I said.

"One year for me," she said. "I couldn't put up with his drinking any longer."

She took a bite of her donut and a sip of coffee.

"Listen," she said, "after the meeting we all gather at the Frood Hotel for drinks and dancing. Would you like to come along?" She paused to take another bite and at the same time caught a glimpse of my canes. "On second thought, there are a lot of stairs, I don't know if you could manage. But we could get some of the guys to carry you down, the way they do with John Bishop. Would that be alright?"

I badly wanted to go but after thinking it over, I thought it best to go straight home afterwards. Just getting this far had zapped a lot of my energy and I wasn't about to push my luck tackling stairs.

"Perhaps some other time," I said.

Rebecca and I became close friends. In fact, she called the very next day and asked if I would like to go to a New Year's dance planned for the members. It was only three weeks away and I hadn't made any other plans. "Sure, why not?" I said.

TWENTY-FIVE

On the morning of Christmas Eve, Teresa, my fourteen-year-old daughter burst in with tears streaming down her face, her eyes red-rimmed and swollen.

"Mom is gone," she managed, verging on hysteria. "She got mad at the boys and me and said we don't deserve Christmas—all because the boys didn't shovel the driveway like she asked them to." Then she broke down completely and cried as if her little heart would break.

"Where did she go?" I said, after I calmed her down a bit. "We were both going to be there tonight when you guys opened your presents."

Teresa shrugged, wiping at her tears. "I don't know, Dad. She left a note on the kitchen table saying she would be back on Boxing Day and if we want turkey it's in the freezer."

"How could she?" I muttered under my breath. At that moment, I was steaming with fury at Joyce.

What had got into her? Okay, so the boys were prone to be a bit lazy sometimes. I had to give her that much. But how could she be that cruel? If she had thought for a moment, she might have realized that children do not forgive or forget easily when their mother abandons them, especially at Christmas.

Two weeks earlier, when the cottage was sold, Joyce and I had met in the lawyer's office to sign the papers required to finalize the deal. We had been civil enough to one another. She suggested I visit with the children on Christmas Eve and stay while they opened their gifts. I thought it was a great idea. Now, I wondered if she had already made plans to be somewhere else at Christmas?

As irresponsible as Joyce's behaviour was, I was determined she wasn't going to spoil Christmas altogether.

"Guess what?" I said to Teresa, who had her head bowed, sniffling into a hanky.

"What, Dad?" Teresa looked up at me with her round, sad eyes. She was fourteen, but she was still my little girl.

"We're going back to your house and we'll celebrate Christmas, together all four of us. How's that sound?"

Right away her hazel eyes brightened and a smile replaced the pout on her lips.

"In my bedroom, you'll find two boxes full of presents. See if you can carry them out to the van while I get my coat and boots on, okay?"

And so, that was how we spent Christmas. Gordy strummed the guitar while I blew on the harmonica. All together we played and sang Christmas songs like we used to. We hadn't had a get-together like that in a long time, and that night I realized just how much I missed those special times.

When we ran out of songs to sing, I got out my Instamatic and took pictures, while they opened their presents. Teresa was delighted with her black designer jeans and a red wool sweater. The outfit went well with her dark, auburn hair. Gordy couldn't wait to shove a heavy-metal tape into the tape player he received. And Allen's eyes sparkled like the tree lights when he got a screwdriver and socket set, similar to those used by TV repairmen. He was heading off to Radio College soon. The tools were exactly what he wanted.

As I focused in on each of their smiling faces, it suddenly struck me the greatest gift I could wish for would be that my children experience the wonder of a life brimming with good health—the way I used to know it. To me there was no better gift—a gift most of us take for granted.

I wondered about Joyce's heartless act. I later found out that she had gone away with her boy friend. How could she leave her children at the time when home and family meant so much?

Christmas passed and the next few days melted into one another, until New Year's Eve.

Tremors of excitement churned inside me most of the day as I waited for evening to arrive. Rebecca made the tremors worse when she called to say that three other ladies would be wanting a ride when I picked her up at eight. Afterwards, when I went down for my usual afternoon nap, I had all sorts of visions of what it would be like to be alone in the van with four women.

It was nearly dark when I awoke. I was disappointed to see the ground covered in new fallen snow, already piling up against my van. It fell in thick swirls, obliterating any sign of the driveway or the road a short distance away.

My spirits sank. Right away I thought about calling the whole thing off. No one in their right mind would be foolish enough to drive the ten miles to Sudbury in this kind of weather. Yet, the thought of being alone in my dismal room on New Years's Eve was even more depressing than taking my chances out there in the storm. Besides, four women were depending on me. I had to go.

Allen came over at seven and helped me into my royal-blue pinstriped suit. He did the buttons of my shirt and then fastened my shirt sleeves with a pair of gold cuff links. I looked at myself in the mirror afterwards and thought how good it felt to be dressed up again.

It's getting pretty bad out there," Allen said, adjusting my necktie. He was visibly concerned. "You'd better wear your overcoat."

"Oh, I'll be warm enough with just my suit jacket," I assured him. "I'll be in the van most of the time, anyway."

Truthfully, I didn't bother with an overcoat because I felt uncomfortable having to ask someone for help removing it later when I got to the dance.

"Well, just in case you get stuck or something," he said, "I'll put a warm blanket beside your seat when I go out to clean off the windows. Be prepared, that's what they taught us in Boy Scouts!"

My headlights barely penetrated the thickly falling snow as I drove into the storm with my face glued to the windshield. Snow streaked past, vanishing the roadside in a snowy fog. I was determined to keep going. As I neared the turn off to the highway, I felt myself stiffen. Through the blur of swirling flakes a pair of headlights suddenly loomed in front of me.

I yanked the steering wheel hard to avoid a head-on collision and the next thing I knew I was nose-diving over the edge of a three foot embankment. The van came to heel buried past the bumper in hard-packed snow.

"Son-of-a-bitch," I swore, pounding my fist on the steering wheel. "What in the hell do I do now?" I looked in my mirror and saw only blackness behind me. The other driver hadn't bothered to stop.

I shoved it into reverse but the heavy van wouldn't budge. The spinning wheels just made the traction more slippery. It wasn't far back to the apartment but it might as well have been a thousand miles. I couldn't even get out of the van without sinking past my knees in snow. My only hope was that someone would happen by and rescue me. I turned on my hazard lights and waited. The only sound that broke the silence was the soft drone of the engine and the whir of the heater fan.

A half hour went by. I tried to remain calm but at the same time my imagination was running wild with grim scenarios. The worst of these was the thought of running out of gas and being found frozen stiff behind the wheel. I had to grin when I looked down at my suit. I realized I was already dressed for my own funeral.

Then, out of nowhere came a set of headlights. My heartbeat quickened. I would be saved after all! I rolled down my window as fast as my wooden hand would permit and waved frantically at the approaching vehicle. The car stopped. A man in a fur-rimmed parka poked a full-bearded head through the open window.

"Can you help me?" I said. "I'm badly stuck. I can't walk. I've got multiple sclerosis..." My words ran into one another in my anxiety.

He scratched his beard thoughtfully. " Hmmm, I could try pulling you out," he said, "but I don't have a tow-rope."

"There's one in the back of the van," I quickly offered.

I could hear him wrestling with the chain as he tied our vehicles together. "Give her gas when I start to pull," he yelled above the roar of his engine. As the chain became taut, the rear of his car skidded and swayed. The air reeked of burning rubber from our squealing tires. After a few tries we both realized it was useless. His car was definitely no match for the heavier van.

"Sorry, friend," he said, unhooking the chain, "my car's way too light for this job." The sound of his words disheartened me, but my hopes brightened when he told me his brother owned a four-wheel drive jeep.

"You wait here," he said, "I'll go get it." His voice faded with the sound of his footsteps.

Wait! That was a laugh. What else could I do?

The minutes dragged on. Just when I began to wonder if he had abandoned me, he returned as promised. This time he was better equipped. The powerful little jeep gave one good jerk and in no time flat I was sitting back on level ground. What a glorious relief to know I wouldn't have to spend the rest of the night trapped in a cold van. I could be on my way again.

I took out my billfold to compensate this kind-hearted stranger for his troubles, but he waved it off. Instead, he yanked off his mitt and offered a friendly hand. I reached out and grasped it.

"All the best in the new year," the man said. He sauntered back towards his waiting jeep until he disappeared into the swirling snow. I had forgotten to ask his name. But to me he was a real live Santa Claus.

There were no more stops along the way save for a lone hitchhiker, whose car left him stranded on the side of the windswept highway. He couldn't thank me enough for the lift but I was more than grateful just to have his company. If I got into trouble again, at least this time there would be two of us.

Rebecca's house was a blaze of light when I got there. She and the other ladies had their heads poking through the curtains, probably wondering where I had got to. It was way past nine, but still not too late to have a good time. Rebecca introduced me to her three friends as they filed giggling and chattering into the van. In spite of the storm, everyone was in a holiday mood.

When we arrived at the dance, the small party room seemed to weave and dance with the movement of people; standing in groups, chatting, moving in and around the centre of the crowded room. The men wore dark suits, the women sparkled in their long evening dresses and fancy hairdos.

Somehow I got separated from the girls. I spied an empty chair next to the men's washroom and headed for it, trying to make myself as inconspicuous as possible while I stumbled shyly around the fringe of the crowd. I could never seem to shake this feeling of self-consciousness whenever I walked into a room full of strangers. Yet for some reason I was delighted to be immersed in this weaving mass of laughing, smoking, chattering people.

I hadn't been sitting long when I noticed a lady with a drink in each hand working her way in my direction. I blushed when she looked right at me with her shining eyes and warm smile.

Gee, she looked good. She had on a soft white dress, bare shouldered with fluff and sequins. She sat down beside me and passed me one of the drinks. I wasn't sure if it was rum or rye. Who cared?

We began our conversation talking about the party, agreeing it was wonderful considering how awful it was outside.

Her name was Shirley, and she had been separated for over a year. I couldn't believe it when she told me she had eight children, ranging from five to seventeen years—as young as she looked and with a little body like that—to me it was incredible.

The conversation got around to me. "Were you in a car accident?" she asked.

I shook my head. "Multiple sclerosis," I admitted.

She told me that her aunt suffered from MS. Strangely, whenever I mention multiple sclerosis to someone, it usually happened that they know someone, a neighbour or a relative who is a victim of the disease.

A waltz was playing on the record machine. "Care to dance?" said Shirley, setting her drink on the floor next to her dainty, pointed shoes.

Her suggestion caught me off guard. I didn't know if I could. It had been so long. The song they were playing was a real pretty one *When I Need Love*, it gave me goose bumps whenever I heard it and I loved dancing.

"I'd better not," I decided, although I wanted to badly. I was afraid that I might lose my balance and embarrass both of us. But she wouldn't take no for an answer.

"C'mon," she coaxed, "we'll dance real slow and if you get tired, we'll sit back down again."

The temptation was too much. I struggled unsteadily to my feet and, pulling her close, I teetered stiffly and awkwardly in small circles in front of our chairs. It wasn't a skilful blend of dips and glides like some of the couples were doing, but my feet were moving and I considered that to be dancing.

A sense of pleasure, like a sweet smell overpowered me as I held her warm body next to mine. She snuggled her head into my chest and I shook and quivered all over.

"You're doing just fine," she whispered softly, squeezing my hand. I believed her too. I was carried away by such unbelievable emotions, It was as if I was dancing a foot off the floor.

We sat down again, talking and laughing. I had such a wonderful time that the evening passed like the wink of an eye. Soon it was midnight and while the record machine blared out the words to *Auld Lang Syne*, I took Shirley in my arms and kissed her gently.

I was still holding on to her when Rebecca tapped me on the shoulder, bringing me back down to earth.

"Sorry to interrupt," she said, "but we have to go. The radio says the highways are closed, and they are advising motorists to stay off the roads."

Outside, it was worse than I had realized. How on earth was I supposed to get back to Creighton if the highways were closed?

Rebecca already had an answer. "The girls and I thought that if we can make it back to my place, we can crash there till the storm blows over. What do you think, Bill?"

I shrugged my shoulders. "Okay with me," I said, relieved to know I'd have somewhere to go. I bade Shirley goodnight with the promise that I'd call her soon. Then we had to part.

The city roads were barely passable. We finally made it back to Rebecca's. Now only one problem remained. How was I to get from the van to the house through all that snow? I had been so intent on getting this far I hadn't even thought of it till now.

It was Rebecca, always smart as a whip, who saved the day. She noticed the blanket beside my seat and that gave her an idea.

"Here is what we are going to do." she said, hardly able to contain her idea. "You lie down on the blanket here and we'll drag you into the house. There are enough of us here to do it."

I looked at Rebecca then at the girls and back to Rebecca again. "I don't know, Rebecca, I mean, do you think you can?" It seemed to me that these delicate ladies in their long slinky gowns and evening wraps were simply not strong enough to pull a full grown man like me across forty feet of knee deep snow.

Nobody was listening to me. Instead, they were already out of the van, spreading the blanket on the ground. Rebecca pointed her finger at it.

"Just get down on the blanket," she said firmly, "and we'll show you who's strong enough."

"Yeah, we'll show you," echoed one of the ladies.

As foolish as I felt, I resigned myself to my fate at the waiting hands of the four ladies.

If anyone had happened by, on that stormy night, I wonder what they would have thought as they watched a body, dressed in suit and tie, being dragged across the yard on a blanket by four charming, chattering, determined females. Had I been witness to such strange goings-on, I certainly would have suspected foul play.

TWENTY SIX

I plowed into the new year with hope and eagerness—as if made new again. I was happily involved with Shirley.

During the winter, I began a correspondence course in English literature. I wasn't thinking of going back to school, yet for some reason I had became very interested in reading and writing; something I hadn't bothered with much since I quit high school. Perhaps I would have enjoyed it all along but was too busy to notice before. It was good therapy, and jotting things down with a pen was something I could manage with a minimum of physical effort.

I was making progress in other areas too. Besides dating Shirley and studying, I took great pleasure in my work as a board member of the *MS Society*. I made quite a few good friends there, as we organized fund raising events together. Most satisfying for me, I spent time with newly-diagnosed patients using my own experiences to help them learn to live with the disorder.

Helping others must have had a good effect on me because even though I wasn't actually any better, I felt better.

When I was alone at home I began to think of myself as well, not sick. I watched my diet, guarded against fatigue, and exercised almost every day. For two months I tried in vain to touch my toes without bending my knees. I could never seem to get my fingertips past my ankles. Then, one day, I bent over and just barely touched my big toe. Some people might think it was a small thing, but it was a milestone for me. After that victory, I was sure I could do anything.

As winter mellowed into spring, I was learning and changing, adapting to my new life. There were no established patterns for me to follow in my daily schedule. How could I plan my days when I had no idea how my body might react tomorrow? I just figured it out as I went along.

On days that I lacked strength to button up a shirt I wore pullovers. When I didn't feel up to cooking a meal, frozen dinners were the answer. Any day that my legs felt steadier, and my hands had a firmer grasp, I just might do a bit of shopping or make a date with Shirley for lunch. I was slowly learning that the secret to living with multiple sclerosis was to think positively and never give up.

Sometime around the end of April, Teresa moved in with me for about a month. Apparently she and her mother weren't getting along that well. "She never lets me do anything," Teresa moaned.

"Well there are rules to follow here too," I warned her, "as long as you abide by them, you can stay."

Her stay ended abruptly when I arrived home unexpectedly one day and walked into the midst of a gang of adolescents drinking beer in my living room. This had been expressly forbidden.

If I could have lifted my foot high enough, each and every one of them would have received a swift kick, especially the one most responsible.

"You, young lady," I said angrily after I had cleaned the house, "are grounded for two weeks."

It didn't last two days. On the third day she came home after school and began stuffing her clothes into a green garbage bag. "And just what do you think you're doing?" I asked.

"If I'm going to be grounded then I'm moving back with Mom." she said flatly. She stomped into the bathroom and returned with her curling iron and hair dryer. She shoved them into the bag along with the rest of her belongings. "This place is worse than jail."

I was taken aback by this sudden turn of events. I had grown accustomed to having Teresa around, someone to talk to and care for. As desperately as I wanted her to stay I couldn't let her have things her way either. As far as I was concerned, she deserved the two weeks grounding.

I watched helplessly as she marched out the door dragging her green garbage bag behind her. I began to suspect that I had been used as a pawn in a game of playing one parent against the other.

A phone call to Joyce confirmed my suspicions.

"If you had called before you let Teresa move in with you," Joyce said. "You would have discovered that your scheming little daughter had already been grounded for drinking. A few of her friends had to carry her home from the skating rink one night. She was still serving out her grounding at home when she decided to move out."

I had been living alone for a year already and had done quite well on my own up until now. But lately, my condition was getting slowly but progressively worse. My gait was even more of a lurch, and I could barely lift my stiffened legs to climb the six steps into my apartment. Often, I was so exhausted after getting to the top of the landing, I was reduced to crawling the rest of the way on my hands and knees.

Driving, which had never been much of a problem in the past, was now very difficult as my arms and legs grew heavy and weak. My handwriting was little more than chicken scratchings because I could not grasp a pen firmly nor keep my hand steady. Every physical aspect of my life was affected. No matter how determined I was to stave off the deterioration, it continued relentlessly.

I had learned enough about multiple sclerosis by now to know that the end result could be paralysis—and that frightened me.

My fear and uncertainty steered me to my doctor for help. I knew there wasn't much anyone could do to halt the progression, but physiotherapy had helped me in the past. I asked the doctor about the prospect of a bed in the rehabilitation unit at Laurentian hospital—perhaps with a bit of physio and occupational therapy I could maintain what strength I had left. "It's worth a try," he said, "but all the beds at Laurentian are filled at the moment. I'll have to put you on the waiting list."

There would be a four month waiting period. In the meantime, I continued to function as best I could. Inside, I used a table, a chair, a wall, or anything else sturdy to steady me as I staggered around the house. Outside, I relied on my canes and had even tried crutches, because my wrists were getting too weak to support my weight. Eventually though whenever I was out of doors, I had to use a wheelchair.

I had fought it as long as I possibly could. Once I made the decision, my first reaction was relief. No more dragging reluctant legs, no more stumbling around with canes or crutches. Yet the wheelchair did not mean complete independence. I still needed someone to lift it in and out of the van and someone to push me around.

At first, I felt uncomfortable needing a pusher to take me wherever I wanted to go. It was Shirley who usually got harnessed with most of the pushing. Whenever we were shopping or going into a restaurant, I sensed that Shirley too, felt humiliated to have people stare or make comments.

In time, I settled comfortably into my chair on wheels and handled going out in public easily and with good humour.

As difficult as the chair was for me to accept, Shirley never could. Perhaps my deterioration threatened her femininity. I still don't know. But even at the start of our relationship I sensed that the poor women could never really deal with my disability.

This was confirmed on the eve of my thirty-ninth birthday. We were celebrating over beer and pizza at a local pizza place. It was freezing cold outside and Shirley was feeling it more than I. She was stuck with wrestling the cumbersome wheelchair from the back of the van, then wheeling me across the parking lot over uneven ruts of frozen snow. She was at the end of her endurance, edgy and tense when she finally got me inside. She screwed her face into a frown as she removed her coat and began helping me with mine.

"You know, Bill," she said at last, "you're lucky to have me. Very few women would go through all this trouble just to go out with you."

I suddenly felt hollow inside. All along I wanted to believe we were in the relationship on equal terms, that I was not the privileged one any more than she. I was seized with an angry impulse and before I knew what it was I wanted to say, I blurted out: "It's not my fault that I'm this way, Shirley. If you think I'm too much of a bother, then you needn't bother at all." My heart and my mind raged. "And don't bother to remove my coat either. I'm not staying. I don't need you. I don't need anybody."

It was not the first time Shirley had mentioned how draining my disability was for her, but I'd had enough. It wasn't her fault. I desperately needed to be wanted for myself, and this would require a very special kind of love. And so, with those bitter words of farewell, I wheeled myself out of Shirley's life.

* * *

Soon after I broke up with Shirley I moved out of my apartment and out of Creighton altogether. That spring, a flu epidemic spread through our area. As luck would have it, the bug hit me in the middle of the night. At least, that's what I thought it was. I awoke early in the morning feeling weak and feverish. My stomach churned, threatening to erupt at any moment. I tried to hurry to the bathroom but as soon as I stood up, my head began spinning crazily. Before I could sit back down again my legs caved beneath me, pitching me forward through the open door of the bedroom closet. My head landed in a pile of old shoes and I was stuck there coughing and gagging until I threw up.

I felt so helpless, so foolish, so degraded as I lay sprawled across the floor with my head jammed into the closet—unable to move my face and hair out of a stinking puddle of puke. The phone at my bedside started ringing and ringing. Carol had to be the one calling. Lately, she made it a daily duty to phone around this time to check on me. Help was only six feet away but all I could do was lie there and listen to the ring, ring, ring...

I began to sob from fear, frustration, and dismay. It was an unutterable moment of complete surrender, when the will drops from self like a robe from a naked body.

There in the darkness I lay in the stink of my own vomit for more than two hours. Finally, I summoned enough strength to get on all fours and then crawl, like a baby, back to my bed. I was too weak to do anything else. If I hadn't felt so miserable, I would have probably laughed out loud at my pathetic state.

The phone rang again soon after I got back into bed. It was Carol. "Boy you had me worried," she said, concern rising in her voice. "where have you been? I've been trying to get a hold of you."

I told Carol what had happened without being too dramatic. It would only upset her more. I didn't tell her how really sick I felt, nor how frightened I was.

"That settles it," she said with determination. "You are moving out of that barn and in with us. At least here there will be someone to take care of you."

I was in no mood to argue. "Yes," I said, fighting back more tears. "If you guys will have me, I'll get my boys to start packing my stuff."

I hung up the phone and sank my head into my pillow. This was the final blow—the loss of my independence. It came after many blows, each one heavier and more devastating than the one before. Whatever happened from now on, I didn't care. I just wanted to go to sleep.

TWENTY-SEVEN

That year, 1980, marked my seventeenth anniversary of living with multiple sclerosis. I thought of the many things that had happened to me during those incredible years. Taking inventory, I found it hard to believe that in that period of time I had transformed from a healthy, robust male into a pitiful weakling who barely had enough strength to roll over in bed. I could still remember, though it seemed ages ago, walking with my shoulders straight and determination in my stride. Now my movement was reduced to riding in a chair or, on the best of days, walking stiffly and grotesquely with the aid of a walker.

It was evident now that I would never regain the full use of my legs or my hands. I'd forever be dependent upon others for almost every physical function.

Once more I was living in someone else's home and once again there was someone to clean and cook for me. I felt comforted by the presence of these people who loved me. At the same time I felt awkward and out of place. I had grown accustomed to living alone. This time it wasn't as easy to adjust to living with another family—especially now that my body was weakened even more.

My room was a dining alcove off the kitchen with little privacy for dressing and undressing. When I needed a bath or when nature called, I hauled myself up to the bathroom on the second floor. This hazardous trek was especially frightening first thing in the morning when my legs were still stiff. For the days I wasn't up to climbing stairs, I kept a portable potty near my bedside.

I constantly wondered to myself if I had made a mistake in going there. Would I have been better off staying in my apartment? How much longer could I have survived on my own? These questions remained unanswered as each day I grew more uneasy living in Carol's dining room.

I had been determined to avoid going to live with relatives at all costs. But where else could I go? The only other alternative would be a nursing home, which I considered to be the end of the world. It was a place for the aged and infirm—not a place for a young, middle-aged man.

So I felt an enormous sense of relief two weeks later when the hospital called to say a bed was available. I looked forward to being in the hospital. Maybe there I would be able to think straight. Maybe, with rehabilitation, I might get some strength back into my feeble body.

On April 18, a nurse wheeled into the rehabilitation unit on the ninth floor. The corridors were brightly lit, the rooms spacious, almost elegant. The air smelled fresh, not the usual blend of antiseptic mixed with heavy odours of warm sweet decay.

My room was at the very end of the corridor. It had a magnificent view of Lake Ramsey, still frozen solid under blue ice. As the nurse unpacked my suitcase and hung my jacket in the closet, I settled in to my room. I had no idea this was to be my home for the next seven weeks, or just how eventful my stay here was going to be.

Later in the day I met the doctor in charge of the rehabilitation unit. He introduced himself then proceeded to examine me.

"Follow the light please, squeeze my hand, first the right. Fine. Now the left." He place a walker in front of my chair. "Please stand and walk for me."

I stood up on shaky legs and, leaning heavily on the walker managed to lurch my way stiffly across the room and back to my chair. I was out of breath and much relieved to sit down again.

The doctor stood there quietly, choosing his words carefully. Finally he said, "We will start you on physio' tomorrow, but there is no promise that you will improve all that much. We can only hope that exercise and therapy will help maintain what bodily functions you have left."

His words were not exactly what I wanted to hear but it was not terribly surprising news. I already knew that in most cases of multiple sclerosis, nothing short of a miracle reverses the disorder. Yet, in spite of this knowledge, I continually had hopes that I'd find some miracle cure at Laurentian Hospital.

I got right into the hospital routine; physio in the mornings, then occupational therapy, a needed rest in the afternoon, then supper.

My meals were taken with the rest of the patients in a spacious dining-room directly across the hall from my room. In all the other hospitals I ate from a tray brought to my bedside. So part of my therapy each day included getting up from my wheelchair and, under the watchful eye of a therapist or a nurse, walking with a walker from my room to the dining-room.

I was apprehensive at first about lurching into a room filled with patients who might be gawking at my grotesque way of walking. But the line of diseased and infirm who came to dine lurched in on canes or tottered along on the arms of nurses and when I looked around me and saw the state that some of these people were in, I thought of myself as not so badly off after all.

The guests at my table each day included a stroke victim named Nick who never spoke and constantly polished the table during meals with his napkin. Sometimes, between mouthfuls, he got up and polished the bookcase over by the window. Next to him sat a demented old man whose dentures slipped and clacked on shrunken gums, his mind damaged by the effects of alcohol. The only person at the table I could hold normal conversation with was Marilyn, a tall angular woman in her early thirties who always wore a *CCM* hockey helmet. Part of Marilyn's skull had been cut away to remove a brain tumour. The helmet was for protection.

Some of the patients snickered and made fun of her adornment, which did appear a bit ridiculous on such an attractive and delicate female. But Marilyn was not intimidated by anyone's rudeness. Instead, she carried herself straight and tall. I always felt honoured to have such a gallant lady at my table.

When I entered the hospital I took along my schoolbooks, planning to study. I needn't have bothered. For some reason I couldn't concentrate on school work. My mind kept running over what my doctor had said about not expecting miracles.

What if I didn't improve? What was I to do with my life if I couldn't get back to living independently? Where would I go when I left here? Carol and I had discussed the possibility of renting a house with a bathroom on the same floor, but was that really the answer? Was it fair to disrupt their family for my sake? She was content living where she was. I had no right.

I was at my lowest one Saturday night. The floor was quiet except for a few patients watching television in the dining-room. I was doing my wash in the utility room where they kept a washer and dryer. I was lost in serious thought, staring into space while the washer clicked and hummed and gurgled. Suddenly the sound of a voice from behind jolted me from my reverie.

"Mr. Horner," a soft female voice said. "There you are. I looked for you in your room but you weren't there. I have to take your blood pressure."

I swivelled my chair around and looked up at a pretty nurse with blue eyes and blond hair. Her nursing cap sat on a nest of soft curls. She smiled down at me and gently began to roll up my pyjamas sleeve; wrapping the black arm band smoothly above my elbow. While she inserted the earplugs of the stethoscope in her ears and studied the indicator gauge, I studied her. She looked to be in her late twenties. Her wide, sensual lips and the expressiveness of her smile attracted me immediately.

She expelled the air from the arm band then recorded some numbers on a chart. The nearness of her made my heart flutter. I had to say something.

"It's okay, isn't it? I mean the blood pressure."

"Your blood pressure is normal, Mr. Horner."

"At least something is normal," I muttered. Now why did I go and say that. I hate myself whenever I sound so damn futile. What must she think of me?

"Is something bothering you, Mr. Horner? You look so sad."

"Oh no," I answered sheepishly. "I was just thinking out loud."

She said goodnight and went about her rounds. As I watched her walk away, the room was suddenly much emptier. I knew that I had to see her again.

The next time I saw that particular nurse was around ten o'clock the following night. I was sitting alone in the dining room watching the late news on television when she walked in. Right away I felt that familiar flutter.

She commented on how busy the floor had been all evening. "I think I deserve a coffee," she said cheerily, "Would you like one?"

I said okay.

She plugged in the kettle on the nearby counter. When the water had boiled long enough, she brought over two steaming cups of coffee. She put a straw in mine.

"Careful when you take a sip," she said, "it's very hot."

I learned her name: Esther. At first we exchanged small talk in a casual manner, asking gentle but probing questions of each other. After I gave her a brief outline of my life, I wanted to know about her's.

She said she was married with two little boys aged two and three. They lived in Hanmer, a small town close to the airport where her husband worked as an air traffic controller. Esther was originally from Windsor.

"I met my husband down there and after he got a job at the Sudbury airport we got married. I worked at Memorial hospital for awhile, then I came here to Laurentian. So here I am," she finished.

That first night we chatted for fifteen minutes or so, sitting across from one another as the television groaned out the *National*. It was the first of many conversations we were to have as we gradually learned the details of each others lives.

Esther's life was not without its own sadness. She dearly loved her two boys and her husband was a good provider. But she was concerned about his habitual thirst for alcohol and the way he spent so much time "just drinking with the boys".

Esther's image of a happy marriage was to be a good wife and mother, and to share the good times and the bad together in a loving partnership. But most of her husband's interests lay outside the home and from these she was strictly excluded. As this reality eventually sank in she was left disillusioned, lonely and inwardly sad. Worst for Esther, he and his close-knit family had their own way of treating "the women", and it had little to do with sharing.

His concept of a marriage partnership was based on the wife as a chattel who was there to serve him, bare his children, cook, wash and iron. Yes, she could have a job to help pay the bills but heaven forbid that it interfere with his demands. Meals had to be on time and it was left to her to arrange for the babysitter each day. Every morning, before getting herself ready for the early shift, Esther would be expected to neatly lay out her husband's freshly ironed clothes for the day. At first she did this willingly but as it became obvious that he took it as his right, not a gesture of love, whatever small pleasure she had in doing it was taken away and it became just another unreciprocated duty.

Esther was reluctant to talk about these details but I don't think I posed any threat and slowly it all came out as we shared our woes and triumphs in life. It seemed to me that she felt almost guilty for finding out she had needs too. The subservient role she played in the marriage day after day left her feeling unfulfilled and inadequate. She had tried to express this to her husband by pleading with him to go to a counsellor with her. He dismissed her suggestion as out of the question. To him, their marriage was just fine and anyway you didn't talk about these things to outsiders.

Eventually Esther told me that her marriage had become so stifling and she so unhappy that she had tried to leave her husband. Not once, but twice. Never was another man involved. She just had to try to escape. They were short lived attempts. Her love for her children had driven her back each time.

For myself, I derived immense pleasure from just being in the same room with Esther; if only for the few moments she spent making my bed or helping me with my meals in the dining room. Sometimes, after her day-shift, she would wheel me downstairs to the coffee lounge where we could talk for a while before she went home to her family. The staff and the patients must have wondered if something was going on between us. After all, she was a married woman. But I wasn't interested in what people thought. Esther's friendship cut through all the emptiness and loneliness I had felt for months. The hours that stretched before me now had a purpose. I had a friend to talk with, someone who cared about the things I did. I spent two weeks in occupational therapy making a crib board for my sister Carol. When I showed it to Esther she was amazed that I could accomplish such exacting work with my numb and uncoordinated hands. I didn't think it was all that great, but her comments made me feel terrific.

In the warmth of our growing friendship, Esther and I found something else we could share. When she discovered I did volunteer work for the *MS Society*, Esther got involved too. She was enthusiastic about helping with a bake and craft sale our fund-raising committee was organizing at one of the downtown malls. "I'll get some of the other nurses to bake or knit something," she said. "They won't mind. After all, it's for a good cause."

As one day melted blissfully into the next, my whole world revolved solely around Esther. I thought of nothing and no one else. I existed for those few, magic moments when we could be together. In bed at night, when the lights were turned out, I thought of her gentle and quiet ways and I would fall asleep dizzy with delicious feelings. These feelings were not totally new to me. The only other time I could remember ever feeling like this was when Joyce and I first met. I was falling in love.

Questions of right and wrong ran through my mind, now that I was caught in the power of love. I thought, "For Christ's sake, Bill, she's got a husband and two little boys. What's the matter with you? Knock it off or you'll ruin a good friendship."

I tried. It was beyond me to stop my love from growing. In other circumstances I might have avoided further involvement, get away from the situation and fill my life with other things. As it was, I could do none of that. In my heart I didn't want to. Yet in allowing my love to grow, was I trying to climb a rainbow? Where would it lead?

TWENTY-EIGHT

While at Laurentian, I had been measured for a new wheelchair. The clunker I was in had been loaned to me by the *MS Society* until I could be properly assessed for a chair that fitted me comfortably. After skimming at length through the *Everest and Jennings* catalogue with Jill, my therapist, I settled on a sharp looking sports model with shiny black leather upholstery.

"That one is considered the Cadillac of wheelchairs," Jill commented.

"I guess six hundred and forty-five dollars is a lot of money, isn't it Jill?" "It's a bit more expensive than some of them. But if you're going to spend most of your time in a wheelchair, Bill, why not go for the best?"

That logic made sense to me. And it wasn't an impossible expense, because the *MS Society* had kindly offered to pay for it.

The chair came complete with caneholder and extra wide tires for easier handling in gravel and snow.

"We'll put a rush order on it," Jill said, "although it could take a while to receive this particular model. Let's hope it arrives before you have to leave the hospital."

Three weeks after entering the hospital, I talked to my doctor about a weekend pass. I needed a break from the hospital routine to get my thoughts in order. I needed to talk to someone.

I told Carol about Esther. Carol and I could always talk openly about such matters and I often sought her advice.

"Esther seems like a very nice person," Carol remarked, "when do I get to meet her?"

"You mean you think it's okay?"

"Why not? It sounds to me like you two would be good for each other."

"I didn't think you'd approve of my falling in love with a married woman," I said. I had also expected Carol to remind me of my illness, and the fact that I was twelve years older than Esther. But she didn't. She just seemed happy that I cared about someone.

"Does she love you?" Carol asked.

"Oh, I don't think so. She sees me as a friend, that's all. She has everything a woman could ask for. She's shown me pictures of a good-looking husband and two smiling fair haired boys. They live in a nice modern trailer home with a backyard full of flowers."

To myself I wondered, "Why would she jeopardize all that for someone in a wheelchair? Sure she has a few problems but nothing compared to having a partner who will always be dependent upon others?"

" Bill, a person can have all that and still be unhappy," Carol said, breaking through my thoughts. "Maybe they have marital problems. Has she ever said anything to you?"

"Yes, she's told me a bit about her problems, but as a friend you understand, not a potential partner."

When I thought about it some more, I remembered some of the hurts Esther had told me about. How, whenever there was time to spend together her husband left her at home as if she was part of the furniture. His nightly ritual was to run off like a kid and play ball with his airport buddies followed up with a bout of heavy drinking that lasted until the bars closed. It couldn't have been much fun playing babysitter to an amorous drunk night after night, especially one that could get violent if he didn't get his way. Maybe Carol had something there. Perhaps Esther wasn't so happy after all.

"Anyway, Carol, it's not my business to pry."

I told Carol that she would get to meet Esther this coming Saturday at the mall. She was going to be there to help with the craft and bake sale.

The outside world seemed totally empty without Esther. When the weekend ended on Sunday night, I could hardly wait to check back into the hospital. I had to see her again. I had to tell her once and for all exactly how I felt.

We met for coffee the next day down in the coffee lounge. When Esther had settled herself comfortably on one of the brown vinyl couches, I grabbed the moment to hand her an envelope with a card in it. My three day separation from her had inspired me to write a little bit of poetry—something about caring and sharing and how wonderful she made me feel. My hand trembled slightly as I presented it to her. I was frightened that I might lose her as a friend, yet I couldn't suppress my emotions any longer.

As she read the poem I tried to imagine what she might be thinking. I wasn't exactly sure, but as I watched her closely, I could have sworn I saw a tear glisten in the corner of her eye.

Then I did a very foolish thing. On an impulse I leaned over and kissed her softly.

"I love you," I whispered tenderly. She didn't turn away, she didn't respond, she just stared at me as if shocked by my behaviour.

I blushed with embarrassment. Public displays were not my style and I must have embarrassed her. For the first time in all the days and nights of talking with Esther, I found myself incapable of thinking of anything to say. I suppose the proper thing to do right then would have been to apologize for being such a romantic goof. But I couldn't find the words. I was filled with a shrinking sensation and felt like I wanted to crawl under the couch.

Esther glanced at her watch suddenly and stood up to leave.

"I'm sorry, Bill, I can't stay. I told my babysitter I'd be home by six. Thank you for the card. It's very nice." As she turned to walk away, Esther mentioned something about being off work until the following week. "I'll see you when I get back," she said. Then she was gone.

I wheeled slowly back to my room feeling humiliated and dejected, angry at myself for acting like a first class idiot.

"I told you you'd ruin a wonderful friendship," I thought inwardly. "Things will never be as they were between you and Esther, and it's all your fault."

The following Friday I got another weekend pass. This time it was primarily for business reasons. I had an appointment with a local garage to have hand controls installed in my van. With my stiffened legs and slowed reflexes, I was worried about being able to drive safely. I should have thought seriously about getting off the road altogether, but I didn't want to imagine how small my world would be if I couldn't drive my van any longer.

On the way over to keep my garage appointment, I detoured around by the mall to drop off my sisters, Carol, Joan and Marie, with a load of baked goods for the sale. Just as I pulled up at the main entrance, Esther came walking toward the van. Seeing her suddenly before me made my heartbeat quicken. After the hospital episode, I thought she would be staying clear of me and of anything to do with the *MS Society*.

After I introduced Esther to my sisters they excused themselves. They were in a rush to get set up at their booth inside the mall. Alone for a moment, Esther said to me almost in a whisper. "We've got to talk, Bill. When would be a good time?"

"I don't know. Is tonight alright, after the bake sale?" I answered nervously.

"That's fine with me," she said. "I'll drive your sisters home afterwards, then we can go somewhere." Then she smiled brightly and turned to go. That was all I needed, her warm, loving smile. A feeling of joy and relief filled me. I drove away with the feeling that more than ever, my whole existence was bound up in this girl.

That evening Esther dropped off my sisters as she had promised, then transferred me from the wheelchair into the front seat of her station wagon.

"Where to?" she said.

"We can drive over to Moonlight Beach," I suggested. "It's quiet there this time of year." Esther was understandably very cautious about us being seen together outside the hospital environment.

Esther parked her car under the canopy of a large spruce tree not far from the water's edge. At first, it seemed, neither one of us could find any words as we sat together, silently watching the waves lap against the shore.

"How was the bake sale?" I began nervously.

"Not bad at all," Esther replied, "Carol said we made around five hundred dollars."

We stared at each other then broke out smiling.

"Please forgive me," she said, "for walking out on you in the coffee lounge. I hope you weren't too upset."

"I'm the one who should apologize Esther. I had no right..."

"No, Bill," she interrupted. "It's alright. It's just that I was caught unaware—I have such mixed emotions. I suppose in a way

I loved you all along, but I couldn't tell you that right then. It's so complicated, I needed time to think everything out."

"Bill, I've decided to leave my husband. If I don't do something now, I'll end up having a nervous breakdown or worse. I didn't tell you before but I have already attempted suicide. I have to get out of this town altogether—go somewhere where I can make a fresh start as a real person. If it's okay with you, I'd like us to leave together. Will you come with me?"

I was stunned. I actually couldn't believe my own ears. "Do you mean you want me to go with you—forever?"

She nodded. "For as long as you'll have me."

Wow, this was almost too much to handle all at once. It had to be a dream. Things like this don't happen in real life, only in movies. I touched myself to make sure I was awake. It was real, not a dream, not a fantasy. After months of loneliness, of nothingness, here was someone willing to fill the vacuum of my life. I wouldn't have to go back to live at Carol's, after all. I had nothing to lose and everything to gain.

But was my illness too great a burden to place on Esther's shoulders? Was it fair to her?

"Do you realize what you're saying, Esther? I mean look at me. Think of the commitment, the consequences..."

She smiled warmly, taking my hand gently in hers. "I don't see the disability or the wheelchair. I see a warm and wonderful man—someone I can see myself growing old with. I promise to take good care of you, Bill, I am a good nurse, you know. And as long as I'm around you'll never have to worry about going into a nursing home. Ever!"

"But what can I offer you?" I said, gazing into her sea-blue eyes. "I can't even dance."

"As if it matters to me whether you can or can't dance," she broke in. "That's not important. I just want someone to be there for me. I need someone who cares about me the way you do."

My heart jumped when Esther leaned over and kissed me lightly on the lips. Then we were touching, feeling, holding each other, our bodies side by side. When we paused to look up, the sun was disappearing over the black ridges at the far end of the lake.

"Oh my," Esther exclaimed. "I've got to go. My husband will be wondering."

"About your husband," I said. "Does he suspect anything?"

"As far as I know he doesn't. In fact, I hardly ever see him now that ball season is here."

"When will you tell him?"

"Only when I'm safely out of the house. He is so unpredictable I'm afraid of how he might react or what he might do."

"What about the children?"

"I love my boys very much and it's been tearing me up inside that I'll be leaving them behind for now. But what kind of stability can I offer my babies within this marriage. And when I'm not even sure of where I'm going or what I'll be doing I can hardly take them with me. It would put them through the kind of insecurity I am trying to avoid for them? At least I know they will be safe at home with their dad. After we get established somewhere I will get in touch."

For the next two weeks Esther and I planned our departure. Every detail, including sneaking the sewing machine out of her house, had to be done secretly. We thought first of making our home in Ottawa, in the end we settled for Thunder Bay. It is six hundred miles northwest of Sudbury, at the very top of Lake Superior. Neither one of us had ever been that far west, but just the name 'Thunder Bay' had a ring of excitement and adventure. Besides, the cold dry climate was better suited to my condition.

However, we couldn't leave the Sudbury area right away. The wheelchair I'd ordered would delay our journey for five whole weeks. In the meantime, Ron offered us the use of his cottage at Washagami as a temporary hideaway.

We figured the best time to make our getaway was on June 9th, the night of the *MS Society's* annual wine and cheese party. By volunteering to help with the party, Esther had a good excuse to be out of the house that night. On the previous Friday, I was to be released from the hospital while Esther would continue working her regular shifts throughout the weekend. That way, we wouldn't create any suspicion by leaving the hospital at the same time.

Esther and I had spent hours talking about where we would go, what we would do, hours of fantasizing about being together. Now at last, the day arrived when we could finally make that fantasy come true.

TWENTY-NINE

After six weeks in rehabilitation there was no noticeable improvement in my physical ability. It was certain now that I could never again live independently—that I would always have to rely on someone. In the past, this in itself would have been enough to trigger another bout of self pity and depression. Instead, I left the hospital feeling as though I could cope with anything now that I held the promise of a future with Esther. Outside the hospital doors a meaningful life waited for me and all I had to do was reach out and grasp it with willing arms.

When I arrived at the wine and cheese party, Esther was already there, helping Carol set out the cheese trays and the wine glasses. She looked entrancing, dressed in a red blazer over a white, satin blouse. She wore a bit of makeup to accent her sparkling blue eyes, but she could have got away with wearing none at all. Esther is a natural beauty.

"You look wonderful," I said, wheeling alongside her. She reached for my hand, squeezing it gently. Right away her eyes communicated warmth and openness.

"Let's leave right now," I teased. "I can't wait any longer."

She smiled, nodding her head. "Yes, I'm getting anxious too," she said, "but I promised I'd help serve the refreshments. We're short on able-bodied volunteers. Besides, it's a good opportunity for you to visit with these people. You never know when you might see them again."

During the course of the party I tried to relax and enjoy the warmth of my friends and family. My cousin-in-law, Bob, brought in his guitar and started a sing-along. Everyone was encouraged to join in, but I couldn't get into the mood. All evening my stomach had been acting nervously, like it did on my first day in the mines. It still seemed almost too good to be true that in a matter of hours, Esther and I would be sharing a new life together.

Doubts kept popping into my mind to disturb me. What if Esther suddenly lost her nerve? What if we got down the road, and she suddenly realized she had made a mistake? What if she was just leading me on? Although I didn't honestly believe she would.

It's not that I didn't have confidence in Esther, it's just that I couldn't help wondering. After all, how many women would walk away from a secure marriage and everything else they had striven for, to face an uncertain future with a man in a wheelchair? If Esther had backed out at the last minute, I wouldn't have blamed her one bit.

So when I talked to my kids on the weekend, I said, 'might be' not 'would be' when I mentioned moving away to Thunder Bay. I felt they had a right to know if I was leaving but when I brought it up, it didn't seem to affect them one way or the other. Lately, all three of them seemed to be caught up in their own worlds.

After the party Esther drove her station wagon to the bus depot while I followed in my van. She parked her car in the depot parking lot, leaving the car keys and her wedding rings on the front seat. Back at Carol's, we changed into camping clothes. Finally, Esther couldn't put it off any longer. She excused herself and went into the next room to call her husband.

When she came back into the room, her face was solemn and tense. "How did he take it?" I asked.

"I'm not sure." she said. "He was more concerned about who he would get to baby sit. And he wanted to know if his clothes were ready for tomorrow. Can you believe it? He never said he loved me or wanted me to come home. Perhaps all I ever was to him is a babysitter!"

She burst into tears. I took her in my arms and held her close. At that minute we felt like co-conspirators and I suppose we had stolen, lied, and manipulated to make this union come into being. But, that night there was no longer any doubt in my mind that Esther was truly mine. I finally had someone who sincerely believed we could share the rest of our lives together.

We lingered at Carol's just long enough to pack a suitcase of clothing and other essentials, then we headed off in the direction of Washagami.

From now on Esther would do the driving. She was a good driver, but that night was the first of many that I had to watch her closely whenever she drove after dark. We had only gone a few miles past the lights of the city when her head began to nod onto her chest.

"Esther, wake up!" I yelled sharply. She sat bolt upright just in time to gain control before the van veered off the pavement. She suggested I drive after that. It had been a long day for me, too. I had a better idea.

"There's a motel just a bit further on Es. If you can make it that far we'll stay there tonight and head out first thing in the morning."

A few more minutes brought us to the *Paradise Motel.* Esther went into the office and booked a room.

Esther and I knew almost everything about each other, but we knew nothing of each other's bodies. We were nervous and shy when we undressed and crawled into bed together. We kissed and held each other. We looked, explored, touched, and whispered words of love. I forgot about my sickness, my months of loneliness, of nothingness. I was a man again, holding a woman in my arms. I had Esther and nothing could hurt us, at least not on this night.

Off and on through the night I fell asleep and woke thinking it had been all a dream. But there was Esther beside me, real, tangible. I watched her sleeping, and drifted back to sleep again, wondering if I had ever been more at peace, if I had ever been so happy.

THIRTY

"How much further is this Washagami?" Esther asked, casting me a sidelong glance. She was especially pretty when she was disturbed. "It seems to me like we've been driving on these bush roads forever."

I had to chuckle to myself because that's exactly how I had felt the first time I drove in here. "Just around the next bend we'll cross the bridge over Ess creek," I informed her. "Then it's only two more miles to the lake."

"I'm glad you know where you're going," she worried, "because I was lost when we left the highway."

I smiled to reassure her. I knew exactly where we were going and the closer we got, the more excited I became. Ever since the day Ron offered us the key to his cottage, I could hardly wait to show off Washagami to Esther.

The distant blue hills and the soft green shoreline seemed more beautiful than I remembered from the last time I had been here, over a year before. The sun sparkled on the water.

"Oh Bill, it's gorgeous," Esther exclaimed, as she pulled the van off the road close to the beach.

She jumped out and glanced around her. "I have never been anywhere so quiet and remote. It's as if we're the only two people in existence." Then she noticed a white cottage perched on a hill overlooking the lake. "Is that Ron's cottage up there?" she asked, shading her eyes with one hand and pointing with the other.

I nodded.

"Which part of the lake did you build your cottage?"

"About a mile up the lake," I said, nodding in the direction of the tree-studded shoreline.

"Can you take me there right now?" Esther said, the excitement rising in her voice. "I've heard you talk so much about this place. I can hardly wait to see it."

I shrugged my shoulders. "If you want to," I answered. "It's only a ten-minute drive from here."

Although I didn't let on to Esther I wasn't all that anxious to see my old cottage again. I worried about old memories lingering there to haunt me. But it wouldn't be fair if I didn't take Esther there. After all, I was the one who had roused her curiosity about it in the first place.

Except for a new coat of yellow paint on the porch, the cottage looked the same as when I sold it the fall of '78. There wasn't a hint of human life anywhere so we thought it wouldn't hurt to have a quick look around.

Esther wheeled me over a carpet of pine needles to a smaller building nestled under a canopy of white pines.

"That's the steambath," I said, "and over there, I nodded in the direction of the lake, is a sun deck. It was my favourite place to sit in the evenings and the last thing I built before everything started to go wrong."

Esther detected the sudden sadness in my voice. She wrapped her arms around me. "Everything is as lovely as I pictured it to be, Bill. There has to be a great feeling of satisfaction to have accomplished all this by yourself?"

"Not by myself Es," I corrected her. "Joyce and the kids did their part."

"Still, it is quite a feat when you think about it; to carve a road through all that bush with an axe and shovel takes strength and determination. What a shame to have to give it up after all that work. You must be bitter at times toward Joyce, about the cottage, about her leaving you?"

"Not any more," I said, "the way my health was going downhill, selling the cottage seemed to be the logical thing to do. Oh, I suppose there's some bitterness. I really did love this place. It brings back a lot of old memories. And deep down I'll always be angry at her for letting me down when I needed her most. I can't completely erase that feeling."

"I can understand that it would be terribly hard to forgive her for what she did," Esther said. "And I suppose my husband is feeling the same way about me, right now. But in your case, Bill, there will always be that question. Would your marriage have ended up in separation even without multiple sclerosis? After all, in her own words, she claimed she never was happy.

"Yes," I agreed. "I've often thought about that. And you're probably right. Perhaps it would eventually have ended up that way anyhow. But I don't dwell on it much any more. Actually, when I think about it now, she did me a big favour by leaving me. How else would I have met you?"

Esther squeezed me tightly. "I'm sorry for stirring up old ghosts," she said, "I don't even know why I brought it up in the first place."

"No need to apologize, Es. In fact, I like the way you're not afraid to say what's on your mind."

And what I said was true. To this day I admire Esther for her wisdom and her candour. To be near her makes me feel good and quiet inside, for you always know where you stand. Now her eyes held mine.

"Let's go back to Ron's cottage and have lunch, she said, "I'm starved."

As Esther helped me back into the van, a warm breeze rustled through the trees and brushed my cheek like a human hand. For a second, I imagined I could hear the sounds of children playing in the water, squeals of laughter fading on the wind.

We set up housekeeping at Ron's camp and settled in for five glorious weeks. Now that we were living together I was even more impressed with Esther. I had never met a woman who could match her enthusiasm, her zest for life, and her innate talent for doing so many things so well.

In the remote world at Washagami, we began to lose all sense of time. Es and I went on picnics and long drives exploring seemingly endless logging roads. Sometimes we'd park beside a river's edge or a lake shore, Es would spread out a blanket, and we'd have a picnic lunch and enjoy the view.

On a hot, sunny day in July, Esther held up my bathing suit. "We're going swimming," she said.

"I'm not up to swimming much any more," I told her.

"Well, put on your suit anyway, we'll go down to the beach and take some sun. You can watch me swim."

Down at the beach the sun burned hot on our exposed bodies. Esther stood beside my chair in her black bathing suit as we inhaled the breeze off the lake, fresh with the tang of cedar and pine. At our intrusion, a mother duck prodded her ducklings toward the safety of the weed beds uttering deep, guttural sounds.

Memories returned of long ago summers spent here with my family—the feel of sand between my toes when I walked on this very beach, the exhilarating feeling of splashing into the cool, clear lake. I sighed and sat in my chair prepared to get vicarious enjoyment from watching Esther swim.

But suddenly, Esther grabbed the front of my chair and began tugging it towards the lake. The chair bogged down, but she was amazingly strong and virtually plowed furrows through the sand to the water's edge. Here the sand was packed and the traction easier.

Esther didn't stop! She plunged onward with controlled recklessness until I was all the way out in the water, up to my knees.

"Es-Esther! What are you doing?" She looked up at me laughing, her eyes gleaming. She kept on going till the wheels of the chair were completely submerged in the lake. I was both shocked and thrilled at the impromptu excitement.

"Guess what," she said with a sly grin.

"Wh-what?" I asked, my voice trembling with laughter and excitement.

"You're going swimming." With that she grasped me firmly under the armpits and pulled me off the chair. Being submerged up to my neck in cold water without the support of the wheelchair, took my breath away momentarily and made my heart pump madly. I had no reason to be scared. Esther's strong grip held me safely as I floated on top of the water. Who ever would have thought I'd be swimming again in Lake Washagami?

After that experience I was floating on air. The wheelchair was no object to get in Esther's way. There was not a hint of pity or awkward uncertainty to inhibit her actions. She joked, played, challenged and provoked me as she would if I were not disabled.

Towards the end of July, Ron sent word to us that my new wheelchair was waiting for me at the hospital. This bit of news meant that our stay at Washagami had regrettably come to an end. It was time to move on to other places.

On the morning of July 25th, while I basked in the shade on Carol's front lawn, Esther began the tedious job of loading our possessions into the back of the van. We agreed to take along only the practical items that would pay their way in usefulness—like my sofa that made into a double bed and an old coloured TV that blew up in smoke the first time we tried to use it again. Carol said she could make use of the furniture I was leaving behind. As it was, Esther had to remove the back seat and lash it to the roof to enable her to cram everything else into the van.

Finally, around noon, Esther got down to loading the last and most important item—my new set of wheels, complete with shiny chrome and black leather upholstery.

At last we could be on our way. As I made myself comfortable in the passenger seat, Carol came around to my side of the van.

"I'm really happy for you, Bill," she said. "You have found someone who is neither afraid or put off by your disability. If anyone can handle the physical problems of your handicap, Esther can. You take darn good care of her. She's priceless."

Carol then climbed up on the running board and hugged me like she never expected to see me again. I returned her hug, promising to write often and inviting her to visit once we got settled. Before we left Sudbury I had Esther drive over to the bank where I drew out all my savings, a total of about fifteen hundred dollars. Along with our possessions in the van, that's all we had between us in the whole world.

Driving past the outskirts of Sudbury, heading west, I peered up at the Coppercliff Super Stack belching clouds of grey and yellow sulphur smoke high into the clear blue sky. The rolling hills along the highway were black and bleak, as I had always known them to be. Long ago the fumes from the smelter had killed the grass and trees; then with no roots to hold the earth it was washed away, leaving miles of bare, windswept rock around the city. It was like no earthly sight. Only man could interfere with the green earth with such devastating effect. We may as well have been on the moon, and the black and barren landscape symbolized the bleakness I had experienced in and around Sudbury these past few years.

There had been a lot of happy times, I grant you, but then so much wretchedness. As I reflected on some of those grim memories, I glanced over at Esther, who at this moment represented freedom and my chance to start over. Would I ever regret leaving this place? I didn't think so. Not by a long shot.

THIRTY ONE

After we passed Sault Ste Marie and turned north, civilization thinned out. In its place was mile after mile of some of the most spectacular country Esther and I had ever seen.

It was a land of mountains in miniature, of crags and forest, dominated to our left by the world's largest body of fresh water, Lake Superior. The highway rose and fell and curved beside the magnificent lake. There were vistas of jutting shoreline and coves and expanses of white beach. It was a natural paradise.

Esther and I said little to one another. We were absorbed in our private thoughts, silently surveying the panorama around us. Esther was the first to break that silence.

"I've been thinking, Bill," she said. When I find a job and have to work all day, how will you keep busy? I mean it could get awful boring sitting home with nothing to do."

I shrugged my shoulders. "I hadn't really thought about it," I said, wondering what she was driving at. "But I'm sure I'll find ways to amuse myself. I can help with the cooking and cleaning."

"What about writing? Have you ever thought about making it a hobby?"

"Writing? What made you think of that?"

"Well, when I was clearing out your desk drawer I came across a story written in your handwriting. It's not bad, you know."

"You think it's okay, do you?" she was referring to a story I had written about a fishing trip with my two boys.

She nodded. "Yes I do. I think you have something there that's just waiting to get out. You should keep at it."

"But that story was written when I could hold a pen in my hands," I protested.

Esther shook her head. "Doesn't matter. Hands are tools. That's all. The skill, the talent is in the mind. We'll get you a typewriter and if you can't use your hands, use a mouth-stick. If you can write, it would be a shame to waste that talent."

I enjoyed writing. I had begun to dabble in it when I was living alone. It was a simple pleasure I pursued for fun and to occupy myself during those long, idle hours. Then, when I couldn't grasp a pen any longer I gave it up in frustration. But now, Esther's idea about using a mouthstick renewed my interest. I could hardly wait to try my hand, or mouth at the art of writing again.

We spent the night in Wawa and reached Thunder Bay the following day in mid-afternoon. The date was July 26, 1980.

Approaching from the east, we first saw the city from one of the viewpoints along Highway 17. The sky was cloudless, the air cool, refreshing. We looked across a bay of wind-streaked water at the huge rock formation in the distance. It's called the Sleeping Giant. About six miles long and one thousand feet high, it rises from the lake cloaked in rich hues of brown and green.

This was not the bleak and barren landscape of Sudbury.

Thunder Bay was a city surrounded by green forest and mountain ranges called the 'Nor Westers'. The beauty hit you right between the eyes. The air reeked with vitality.

We marvelled at the skyscraper grain elevators towering high above the harbour, and at the lake freighters loading their holds with golden cargo—each freighter longer than a football field.

We felt like royalty surveying a new empire. For weeks we had planned for this moment, and now we were here. "Well, what do you think, Es?" I said, tingling with excitement. "Do you think we can make a home here?'

Esther's blue eyes sparkled like the sun on the water. "I can hardly wait to get started," she said.

We stayed in a motel for three days until we found a cottage on Lakeshore Drive to rent. It wasn't much of a house but it was a start. There were two tiny bedrooms, a tiny kitchen and a surprisingly large living room. We looked it over and right away said yes, we'd take it.

But we weren't accepted as tenants right away. In fact, the landlady's face wrinkled as she surveyed Es and me. We must have looked an incongruous couple when I think back. Here we were, newly arrived in town, hauling with us everything we owned in the world, and both of us unemployed. Risky tenants, I would say. Still, we kept our fingers crossed.

In the interrogation that ensued, she asked me if I had an accident. I told her it was multiple sclerosis. "Isn't that a shame," she said, shaking her head sadly. "I have a brother-in-law with MS." After that she seemed to warm to us, and the following day we were notified that the house was ours.

Not long after we moved in, Esther landed a job as an industrial nurse at the Ontario Hydro Plant—starting wage, $8.00 per hour—more than she had made working in the hospital and more than I ever made down underground.

We were living in heaven, I thought. With her income and my pension cheque we could afford to buy furniture and whatever else we needed to make our little white doll house cosy and comfortable.

There was money left over for luxuries, too. One day she came home from work and plunked an electric typewriter on the kitchen table. It was a *Smith Corona* portable. "What's this?" I asked.

She smiled down at me, hardly able to contain her excitement. "It's time you got to work too." she said. "I saw it in the second hand store window. Everything's automatic. All you have to do is feed it paper and punch the keys."

So as the first cold winds began to blow in off Lake Superior, I was pecking out stories with a stick in my mouth. It was Esther's confidence in my ability that gave me the courage to try to get my work published. My first story was accepted for publication a year later.

Es and I had no regrets about choosing Thunder Bay as our home. With its picturesque beauty came the friendliness of its inhabitants. Maybe it was just me, but somehow they seemed more comfortable around handicapped people than in other places I'd been. People would almost trip over themselves to open doors when Es and I approached an entrance to a mall or a restaurant. Sometimes if Esther happened to be having a hard time transferring me into the van, a kindly gentleman might happen by and say, "Can I help you, ma'am?"

Yet, no matter where you go there are those who think that if you are physically handicapped, you are mentally deficient too. For instance, when ordering from a restaurant menu, there was always that certain waitress who would ignore me altogether and say to Es, "And what will he have?"

Esther's usual reply was, "Why don't you ask him? He's right here."

I'd look up and smile sweetly but always felt like telling the waitress my real feelings—which weren't exactly sweet.

However, if some people had a problem with the chair, it was their problem, not ours. Esther's attitude about pushing me was so casual that it was fun for both of us, a game. She'd push me one-handed or give the chair a hard shove then jump on the back, resting her foot on the cane holder.

We lived together in blissful harmony. Even when I'd been on my feet, I had never been this happy. But it was becoming more and more evident that something was bothering Esther. It was her children. Her spirits seemed to ebb and flow like the ocean tides. Some days she was brimming with chatter and bounce, on others there were long periods when she sat quietly, her eyes sad. Often during the night, she would toss and turn, talking in her sleep about her boys, Craig and Dean.

One evening I caught her sitting at the kitchen table staring into space. It disturbed me to see that lost child look on her lovely face. Her eyes were mournful, on the verge of tears.

"It's the children, isn't it?" I said.

My words startled her. She buried her face in her hands and cried uncontrollably. She was entirely broken up, desolate. I wanted her in my arms.

"Oh, Bill, I miss them so much." she managed, wiping at her tears. "I thought I was doing the right thing by losing all contact with them, but I realize now, I just can't abandon them altogether. I have to at least be able to visit them."

The pain was real. We talked it all out and in the end, it was a great relief. We decided that before her divorce became final in the fall, she would talk to her lawyer about getting visiting rights.

* * *

It was all working out. Just before Christmas in 1981, I received a very special gift from people I hardly knew. Actually the gift was for both of us. It came from the guys at the hydro construction site—Esther's co-workers and new found friends. The men took a shine to Esther right off, and when they discovered that her boyfriend was in a wheelchair they became curious. Their questioning led to how I managed to get in and out of the van.

"It's not that easy," Esther explained, "on good days, he manages okay, but on others, I virtually have to lift his full weight."

Nothing more was said on the subject. Then one day, one of the men asked to borrow our van. He said he needed it to move some furniture. When he drove it back into the yard later, a brand new wheelchair lift had been installed.

"The boys thought it might make things a little easier for you guys," he said.

Tears filled my eyes at this unexpected surprise. I couldn't believe it! We had dreamed of buying a lift someday but we simply couldn't afford the four thousand dollar price tag. Now, thanks to a crew of construction guys, Esther can get me in and out of the van with a mere push of a button.

When Esther's divorce became final, I began to think of marriage. I never loved anyone as much as I loved her, and I knew she felt the same about me. But there were days when I ardently wished for more than just living together—I wanted Esther for my wife.

Still, I hesitated to propose. I wondered if I was being unreasonable to ask for such a commitment; to place the burden of my disability on her shoulders. What if I had another attack, and ended up bedridden? In my heart, I didn't believe that would ever happen, but if it did, what then? It wouldn't be fair to her. The way it was now, she was free to leave anytime she had a mind to.

As I weighed the problem in my mind, I came to the conclusion that if anyone could handle such a marriage, Esther could. All I had to do was ask her.

Finally, one night after supper, I broached the subject. I seized the opportunity when she made a comment about an application form she was filling out.

"I'm never quite sure whether to sign my name Esther Robertson or Esther Horner on these darn forms," she said. "Sometimes, it can be so confusing."

"Well, there's an easy way to fix that," I said, "marry me."

She chuckled. "That seems a simple solution."

"I'm serious, Es. Why don't we? You're a free woman now. Usually when two people fall in love they marry and spend the rest of their lives together."

"No, Bill. I'm sorry. I can't think of marriage right now. I need more time."

"How much time do you need? We've been living together over a year and a half."

"We're talking about a terribly important commitment, Bill. Not the commitment of your disability. I don't have a problem with that. I just want to be absolutely sure this time."

So we let the subject drop then and there. Although I was a little disheartened by her decision, I respected her honesty Perhaps I was being a bit hasty. If she needed more time then I wouldn't press her. I was willing to wait.

THIRTY-TWO

"What is it Bill? What's wrong?" Esther said, switching on the bedside lamp.

"I don't know," I muttered faintly. "I tried to roll over but my arms or legs won't budge." It felt as if someone had bound me while I slept.

Before going to bed that night, I had been feeling overly tired and weak. So weak in fact that I was incapable of holding a toothbrush to clean my teeth. "God," I thought, "It's happening again." I hadn't even wanted to think of the word exacerbation. Not now, not when everything was going so well in my life.

* * *

Esther and I had returned to Sudbury in January. Arrangements had been made for Esther to see her children—the main purpose for the trip. Her former husband had a live-in girl-friend, almost from the day Esther left, but he was reasonable enough about the visit. While we were there, I had plans to visit old friends and family members, especially my three children.

We declined Carol's kind offer of accommodation. Instead, we set up headquarters in a motel room. I felt more comfortable having my own space and that way people could visit me while Esther was gone all day with her children. Every day that week, and often late into the night, friends dropped in—to chat, to share a glass of wine, to dine in the motel restaurant.

When I saw my kids again I couldn't believe how much they had grown up. Where did the time go? There was so much to talk about, so many questions to ask. Allen was going on twenty-one, finished Radio College and had his own apartment in Sudbury. Gordy too, was out on his own. He brought his girlfriend over to meet me. She was a lot like Gordy in her reserved and bashful way. Teresa, my baby, had turned sixteen in the fall. She was at home with her mother and still in school.

All in all they were doing fine, as well as could be expected, I supposed, coming from a broken home. Seeing for my own eyes that they were alright was a great relief to me. I considered it a blessing that my children were older when I contracted multiple sclerosis. Otherwise, I don't know if they could have survived as well as they did.

During the days Esther was with her boys. It was so good for her to see them. Esther told me word for word about the reunion:

"As soon as Craig saw me he ran into my arms. 'That's my mum! That's my mum!' he yelled to anyone that cared to listen. But Dean, the younger one held back, uncertain. 'That's not my mum' he said slowly. Then a look of recognition and a big smile filled his little face and he ran forward and hugged me and I showered him with kisses."

Every day for four days they visited together. They exchanged belated Christmas presents. The boys proudly showed Esther their new room and bunk beds. They went shopping and skating together. On the way back to Thunder Bay Esther told me:

"We crammed so much into those few days. But I feel much better having reestablished contact with Craig and Dean. Now I have more good memories to last till the next time."

In all it was a wonderful week but it left me totally exhausted. I was used to a routine with scheduled afternoon naps. By week's end I was anxious to get back to Thunder Bay to regain my strength.

As if the trip itself hadn't been tiring enough, late at night on the way back, we ran into a heavy snow squall blowing in off Lake Superior. The gale force winds shook the van and whipped blinding snow across the highway, cutting our visibility to zero. Esther was doing the driving, but I was so nervous I could feel numbness and tingling all over.

After sixteen long hours on the road we managed to arrive home safely. However, the numbness and tingling hadn't ended then. A week had gone by and it persisted throughout my entire body. Now, as I lay in bed full of fear and uncertainty, I was too weak to lift my hand to scratch my nose.

* * *

"I'm calling the ambulance right away," Esther said, her face full of concern. "We're not taking any chances."

That night is one I would rather erase from my memory. I was sweating one moment, my teeth chattering the next. Despite my fever and weakness, I was stunned to realize I was sick again. I hadn't been this sick in a long time. My thoughts were on Esther too, her worried face hovering over me, waiting for the ambulance to arrive. She had never seen me like this before. She had to have been frightened out of her wits.

I was lying in a stretcher in the hospital emergency ward when a grey-haired doctor came and leaned over me. He checked my eyes, heartbeat, and pricked my legs and arms with a pin. "Can you feel that, Mr. Horner?"

I told him I couldn't.

After completing a few more tests, he told me what I already knew. "It appears that you are having an exacerbation," he said. "We'll start you on ACTH right away."

When the doctor left, I felt a hand touch my shoulder. Esther was standing over me, her face tear-streaked and pale. "Feeling better, darling?" Her hand ran over my forehead.

"Not bad, really." I was lying. My worst fears had been confirmed. I was in a state of despair and self-pity. What would happen to me? All these big, strong wise doctors who where supposed to be in charge, why couldn't they stop this disease from tearing my body apart?

After two days in the hospital, my condition remained unchanged. I was paralysed from the neck down and completely dependent upon the nurses who spoon fed me and bathed me. Esther came after work each day. That reassured me, despite her shaking hands and reddened eyes. When she left, only blessed sleep saved me from my misery.

On the third day, I noticed movement in my fingers, and if I tried hard enough I could make a fist. I was excited and relieved. Maybe I wasn't going to be bedridden after all! By late afternoon I could lift my arms over my head.

Esther arrived at supper time with that same worried look on her face. I gave no hint that I had any movement in my limbs. "How about a hug," I said.

She leaned over the bed and cautiously held me as if I were porcelain. At that moment I wrapped my arms around her and squeezed her tight. She was dumbfounded. Her eyes above mine opened wide in surprise. "My God, Bill! You can move your arms. You're getting better."

I nodded, grinning from ear to ear. "You bet I am. And I'll be up and around soon, I can promise you that."

"Well, I've got news for you too," she said. "You had better get your butt out of here so we can get married!" I stared up at her, wide-eyed and dumbfounded. When I could finally speak again I said, "Esther, my little Austen heater, (Esther's maiden name was Austen) are you asking me to marry you?"

"Yes," she replied, "I want to be your wife and grow old with you."

I was transferred over to the rehabilitation unit at St. Joseph's Hospital to begin my physiotherapy. At first, it was difficult to get out of bed or even sit up in my chair for any length of time. I felt like a zombie.

But I was determined to beat this thing. Esther was out there waiting for me and I wasn't wasting any more time. I worked myself to the edge of fatigue, exercising on the floor mats, strengthening my arms on pulley weights. I also tried walking with a walker, but failed miserably in that attempt. I could stand all right, but my stiffened legs would not allow me to lift my feet off the floor. It was like having cement blocks for slippers.

I realized there would probably be no escape from the wheelchair this time, but that didn't mean I was licked altogether. I could still transfer from wheelchair to chair or bed on my own and I had regained enough use of my hands to shave and feed myself. My vision remained intact and I could still type with a mouth stick. Even though I had lost my ability to do some things, it was not what I had lost that mattered, but what I had left. I was content with that.

Esther was jubilant at my recovery. For the six weeks I stayed in the hospital she came every day after work and on weekends. How I hungered for those visits, gazing out my window at the rush hour traffic, watching for the green van to pull into the parking lot. She was there to accompany me to the dining room for dinner, to wheel me to the sun room, and to reassure me that our future was still bright. We made plans for a fall wedding. That would give us time to save some money and allow Esther time to make her wedding dress.

We were married on November 13, 1982 in a small church in Lively, the town in which I grew up. It was my idea to have the wedding there. I wanted to share my happiness with my friends and relations, and to show off my new bride.

I remember the day as vividly as if it were yesterday. I recall how I waited nervously at the altar. My head clouded with doubt and fear. I wasn't afraid for me, but for whether I could give Esther the life she deserved, the happiness and security I wanted for her.

Next to me sat Allen, my best man. Only the minister stood. An empty chair, decorated with pink and white carnations, waited for the bride, who began her wedding march on the arm of her father. "My God, she's beautiful," I said to myself, as I swivelled my chair to see her walking toward me. It was the first time I had seen her in the flowing gown she had made. Suddenly, I became so overwhelmed with emotion, tears spilled from my eyes.

I tried to stifle them but I couldn't. The happiness I felt at that particular moment was more than I could handle all at once. I had hardly dared to dream that anyone would want to marry me when I was in a chair. Now it was happening. I was about to be blessed with the sort of love and joy denied to many—even to those who are without physical handicaps. Surely anyone else in my place would have cried, too.

Before the reception ended that evening, Esther requested that the band play Anne Murray's *Can I Have This Dance* as the home waltz. When the music started to play, I asked Esther to wheel me to the centre of the dance floor. Much to her surprise and to the surprise of the people around us, I stood up from my chair and took her in my arms. Suddenly, everyone stopped dancing, and instead, began clapping and cheering. With both feet planted firmly on the floor, I held onto Esther and we swayed to the rhythm of the music. In the blur around me, I caught glimpses of people wiping tears from their eyes.

When I couldn't stand any longer, I sat back down again with Esther on my lap. We finished the dance holding each other close while her mother wheeled us around the dance floor. "Who says you can't dance?" Esther whispered, as we looked into each other's eyes and laughed till the tears ran down our cheeks.

EPILOGUE

My condition has progressed to the point where I must depend on other people for my day to day living. To explain further, Esther and I live in an apartment which offers attendant care for physically challenged people. When I am by myself, the staff help with my meals, give me physiotherapy, transfer me into bed when I get tired from sitting too long. Attendant care has worked out well for both Esther and me. She can go to work feeling secure that someone is there to watch over me, while at the same time I have the privacy I want yet someone is nearby if I need attention.

When Esther heads off to work, I wheel down to our spare room where I have a word processor and a printer. How thankful I am that technology has arrived. I spend most of my day there putting together words in one form or another.

Writing a book began as a form of therapy, something to do when I was left alone. I had no intention of making my life open to the public. It was too private, too painful, and in some cases too embarrassing. I still carry guilt feelings about my suicide attempt.

As I started to record the many things I wanted to say about my life, I began to wonder: Am I alone? Certainly I was not the only one who, stricken with a disease, almost took his own life. Whether it was multiple sclerosis or something else that struck them down, I couldn't be that unique. There had to be others.

All of a sudden it became very important to write about what happened. Perhaps by telling my experiences I could help others find the strength and courage to keep on striving.

* * *

Today Esther's boys are just into their teens. She is in frequent contact with them. Both are happy, healthy and well adjusted. My children too are healthy and, I believe, happy.

We often drive down to the waterfront, Esther and I, where we like to sit and watch the sun slip down inland, behind the mountains and the forest. From my seat in the van I can look out at the ever changing colours of the mightiest of all lakes, Superior. In summer I see the ocean freighters anchored here in mid-continent. They seem to be drinking in the fresh beauty of Northern Ontario before they start on their long journey to the industrial cities of the east, then on through the Gulf of St. Lawrence to the Atlantic Ocean and foreign ports. In fall, the colours of the surrounding forests make us gasp. And in winter the foreboding black and white landscape fills my senses with a deep respect for this country's harsh extremes.

But always, at the lake, I can look out beyond my little world to the distant horizon.

APPENDIX I

UNDERSTANDING MULTIPLE SCLEROSIS:
with George Rice MD., FRCP

What is MS?

Multiple sclerosis, known widely as MS, is the most common serious neurological disease that affects the central nervous system of young adults in Canada. The known prevalence across Canada and the northern United States is about one in every one thousand in the general population. If unsuspected or undiagnosed cases are considered, the prevalence might well be considerably higher, as high as one in five hundred. More than twice as many women are affected than men, a ratio of two and a half to one, a finding typical of most autoimmune diseases. We believe that the incidence has been unchanged in the last one hundred years. MS is most common in individuals of northern European ancestry. Some sub-populations rarely develop MS. For example, cases among the Inuit and other aboriginal Canadian peoples are all but unheard of. The worldwide distribution of MS reflects in part the migration patterns of peoples with genetic susceptibility for the decease.

The part of the central nervous system affected by MS is the insulating covering around the nerve fibres in the brain and spinal cord. This substance is known as myelin and is made up of lipids (fats) and three major proteins. Myelin is vital in the transmission of nerve impulses through the nerve fibres. Even slight damage to the myelin may cause nerve impulses to be completely disrupted. The name of the disease is derived from this process: "multiple" (many) since it occurs in a number of places within the nervous system, and "sclerosis" (scars) because of the hard tissues which replace the damaged myelin. Thus multiple sclerosis means "many scars".

What causes MS?
Despite tremendous research efforts, little is known about the cause of this baffling disease. Two major factors do however appear to be at work: an abnormal immune response pointed at some undefined target within the central nervous system and a genetic predisposition.

There has been intense study of the immunological abnormalities in people with MS, however, most appear to be isolated and only a few observations are reproducible and thus confirmed by other researchers. What has been confirmed is that there appears to be an over-production of certain kinds of antibodies (the substance produced by the body to fight bacteria, viruses and other antigens) and those which are produced have a characteristic banding pattern. The target of these antibodies remains unknown. The second reproducible observation is that activation of the immune system, as can happen following viral infection, surgery, or administration of gamma interferon, can cause the disease process to flare. The third observation is that some forms of "immunosuppressive" treatment such as cyclophosphamide, and azathioprine appear to have a very modest benefit, at least for a short period, in controlling the progression of the disease.

Some researchers have suggested that lymphocytes (white blood cells) of people with MS are unusually reactive to two important brain proteins, myelin basic protein (MBP) and proteolipid. (MBP and proteolipid protein are both components of myelin.) A variety of other observations, some of which are theoretically attractive, have incriminated "immune activation" in the central nervous system however, they have not yet been established as bench marks.

For example, researchers have found that people with MS have an over representation of certain histocompatibility antigen (HLA) types, these are protein molecules found on the surfaces of white blood cells, however, the contribution of HLA to MS is very likely to be small because bearing a certain HLA type is neither sufficient nor essential for the development of MS.

People with MS and their doctors have learned to temper their excitement about scientific advances in clinical immunology since all too often the research eludes reproducibility.

Is the disease hereditary?

Yes, several observations lead us to believe that the decease is genetically influenced. If one twin has MS, the identical twin will have a 40% chance of developing MS. If the twin is not identical, the chance is two per cent, which approximates that found in siblings of patients with MS. Twenty per cent of the close relatives of MS patients are also affected by MS.

The rarity or absence of MS in certain populations also suggests a genetic role in the determination of susceptibility. The higher incidence of MS in temperate climates more likely represents the geographic distribution of individuals at risk for development of MS, than any peculiarity in the environment.

Is it caused by a virus?

It does not appear so, all attempts to implicate viruses in the cause of MS have failed. At least ten viruses have been claimed to be associated with MS; but all claims have failed the test of reproducibility.

In summary, the etiology of MS appears to be a self-directed immune response directed to an unidentified brain determinant, occurring in individuals with a genetic predisposition to this kind of self-reactivity.

What are the symptoms of MS?

The commonest symptom of multiple sclerosis is numbness in the arms and legs. Other common symptoms that can herald the diagnosis are: weakness, fatigue, visual loss (optic neuritis), clumsiness (ataxia), difficulties with bowel and bladder control, vertigo, double vision and facial weakness. These symptoms, when present in people with MS, almost always last for more than 24 hours.

A frequently described symptom is the complaint of numbness in the trunk or extremities occasioned by bending the head forward. This is known as the l'Hermitte symptom and occurs in about fifteen per cent of people with MS. Extreme heat sensitivity is also common.

Occasional symptoms are: seizures, episodic facial pain (trigeminal neuralgia). Sudden, paroxysmal motor and sensory disturbances are rare but can also be symptomatic of multiple sclerosis.

How is the diagnosis confirmed?

The diagnosis is most confidently made on clinical grounds.

A solid history of at least two separate episodes of "white matter" dysfunction (visual loss, sensory loss, weakness, ataxia, brain stem dysfunction), with supporting evidence, from the neurological examination, of trouble in at least two anatomically discrete white matter regions, afford the greatest diagnostic confidence. This presupposes that no better explanation can be found for the findings.

In people whose histories and neurological examinations are less complete, (e.g. history of two attacks, with only one neurological sign, or a history of one attack, with two or more neurological signs), diagnostic confidence can be bolstered by spinal fluid analysis, magnetic resonance scanning, and certain electrophysiological tests.

The commonest abnormality in spinal fluid is the presence of a banding pattern in immunoglobulin. This condition is present in ninety per cent of MS confirmations. The magnetic resonance imaging scan is a useful adjunct for the demonstration of inflammation in patients with MS, but is not necessary for most diagnoses. Electrophysiological tests of white matter function can be used to assess nerve conduction time in the visual (VER), auditory (AER), motor and sensory pathways, but extreme caution should be observed in interpreting these tests which are of moderate sensitivity and low specificity.

In the best of hands, diagnostic accuracy will reach about 95%.

What should the person with MS expect for the future?
Life span is rarely shortened by MS, but disability, to the point of requiring some kind of walking assistance, develops in approximately half of people with MS around 15 years after onset. The disease can be extremely variable. The clinical course will pursue a pattern of relapses and remissions in the majority of cases. In another thirty per cent the clinical course is progressive from the outset. A further fifteen to twenty per cent have an extremely benign course, with no further attacks after the disease begins.

The factors which identify a more or less progressive pattern are only partly understood. One study states that if there is an early onset of disability, the occurrence of frequent attacks in the first two years, and a shorter interval between attacks, then more aggressive course is likely.

What is the present treatment for MS? Do drugs help?
MS researcher, Noseworthy concluded in his 1984 study that unfortunately most early, encouraging reports from almost all pilot studies have not been corroborated by well designed, prospective, randomized, placebo-controlled trials. This should engender a healthy scepticism for any observations about new drugs for the disease. His advise is worthy of note and while tremendous research efforts continue no cure is yet known.

For people with acute attacks, corticosteroids (oral prednisone, intravenous methylprednisolone) remain the mainstay of treatment. The acceptance of this treatment is not universal however, and these drugs do not appear to alter the natural course of MS. The long term complications of steroid therapy are important for persons with MS and their doctors to take into consideration.
For the prevention of acute attacks, azathioprine has been known to have a modest effect. Several other drugs that modulate the immune system "immunomodulatory" are under study. Two promising ones, Beta interferon and bromocriptine are currently being tested. In patients with progressive disease, studies show that azathioprine appears to have less effect. Considerable interest has been focused on cylophosphamide and its effect on the immune system following a Harvard based study in 1983. However due to an inability to corroborate the Harvard findings the treatment has been abandoned in Canada. The search continues for drugs that unequivocally alter the progress of MS, can be better tolerated and lend themselves to administration under chronic circumstances. For example clinical trails are in progress with beta interferon, methotrexate and mitoxantrone.

How are complications treated?
Because of the devastating impact that MS can have on the lives of patients, we highly recommend referral to one of the thirteen MS clinics in Canada where comprehensive care and support is offered. Marital strife, depression, unemployment can be anticipated, indeed they might be termed as the most common side effects of MS. They can however be helped by knowledgable counselling and psychiatric intervention. These services are available through MS Clinics.

Rehabilitation, and activity programs can be coordinated by the physiotherapy team at the MS clinic. Therapeutic devises, and support equipment can be made available. The occupational therapy staff can design a program that can help coordinate the integration of the disability into workplace and the home.

The urological problems that frequently accompany the condition can be identified and treated with medical or surgical approaches.

The Multiple Sclerosis Society of Canada, its seven divisions and more than 120 chapters are also an important source of assistance for people who have MS and their families. *The Society* provides up-to-date information, support counselling, seminars and workshops, recreation programs, and self-help groups and loans mobility equipment in parts of the country where government funding is unavailable or insufficient. Information on the clinic or support group nearest you can be found in Appendix II of this book.

Dr Rice is a neurologist. He has dedicated eleven years to MS research. He is associated with the MS Research Clinic, University Hospital, London, Ontario, Canada.

APPENDIX II

FINDING THE HELP YOU NEED

THE MULTIPLE SCLEROSIS SOCIETY IN CANADA

The *Multiple Sclerosis Society of Canada* was founded in 1948. It presently has chapters in more than one hundred cities across Canada and is affiliated with similar Societies in 30 countries around the world. The *Society* offers a number of services for people who have multiple sclerosis and for their family members. These vary across the country depending on the provincial government and community programs available since the *Society* does not wish to duplicate services already in existence. Examples of services are:

- up-to-date information about MS
- support counselling
- lending of equipment
- educational seminars
- workshops
- self-help groups
- recreation programs

The *Society* also supports a medical research program aimed at finding the cause, effective treatment and cure for multiple sclerosis. Researchers are concentrating their efforts in four basic areas: immunology, immunogenetics, virology and the biochemistry of myelin. At this time much MS research is targeted at trying to understand how the complex nervous system works and why it malfunctions. Once these questions are answered, finding the cause and cure of MS will be much easier.

A network of MS clinics across Canada is funded by the *Society*. The clinics are affiliated with hospitals frequently university hospitals and offer diagnostic and assessment services, information and treatment. Potential treatments for MS are tested through the clinics, and clinic patients may have the opportunity to participate in these studies.

Addresses and telephone numbers of MS Society offices and clinics in Canada can be found in this appendix as can information on MS support Groups in other countries.

Canadian Offices of the Multiple Sclerosis Society

National Office:

250 Bloor Street West Suite 820
Toronto, Ontario, M4W 3P9
Phone (416) 922-6065

Divisional Offices:

Atlantic
45 Alderney Drive
Suite 612
Dartmouth, NS. B2Y 2N6
(902) 465-7251

Quebec
279, rue Sherbrooke ouest
Bureau 401
Montreal QU. H2X 1Y2
(514) 849-7591

Ontario
250 Bloor Street East
Suite 820
Toronto, ON. M4W 3P9
(416) 922-6065

British Columbia
6125 Sussex Avenue
Suite 205
Burnaby, BC. V5H 4G1
(604) 437-3244

Manitoba
825 Sherbrook Street
2nd Floor
Winnipeg, MB.R3A 1M5
(204) 783-8585

Saskatchewan
2329 - 11th Avenue
Regina, SK.
S4P 0K2
(306) 522-5607

Alberta
11203 - 70th Street
2nd Floor
Edmonton, AB.
(403) 471-3313

Multiple Sclerosis Society Clinics in Canada:

Atlantic:
MS Clinic of Dalhousie U.
Camp Hill Hospital
1763 Robie Street
Halifax, NS. B3H 3G2
(902) 422-7817

Quebec:
MS Clinic
Montreal Neurological Hspl.
3801 University Avenue
Montreal QC. H3A 2B4
(514) 398-1931

Montreal East: MS Clinic,
Notre Dame Hspl., CP 1560
1560 Sherbrooke Street East
Montreal, QC. H2L 4K8
(514) 876-6848

Ontario:
Hamilton MS Clinic
Room 3N11-F, McMaster Div.
Chedoke-McMaster Hospital
Box 2000, Station "A"
Hamilton, ON. L8N 3Z5
(416) 521-2100 Ext.6073

Kingston MS Clinic
c/o Dr. D.G. Brunet
EEG Department
Kingston General Hospital
Kingston, ON. K7L 2V7
(613) 548-2308

London MS Clinic - 70P33
University Hospital
39 Windermere Road
London, ON. N6A 5A5
(519) 663-3697

Ontario Cont...
Ottawa MS Clinic
Ottawa General Hospital
501 Smyth Road
Ottawa ON. K1H 8L6
(613) 737-8532

Toronto MS Clinic
St. Michael's Hospital
30 Bond Street
Toronto ON. M5B 1W8
(416) 864-5377

Manitoba:
Neuroscience Clinic G.E.- 2
Health Sciences Centre
700 Williams Street
Winnipeg, MA. R3E 0Z3
(204) 787-5111

Saskatchewan:
MS Clinic,
University Hospital
University of Saskatchewan
Saskatoon, SK. S7N 0X8
(306) 966-2447

Alberta:
MS Clinic
9-101 Clinical Sciences
University of Alberta
Edmonton, AB. T6G 2G3
(403) 492-6430

British Columbia:
MS Clinic
UBC Site, University Hospital
2211 Westbrook Mall
Vancouver, BC. V6T 2B5
(604) 822-7131

Affiliated International Societies (IFMSS)

ARGENTINA
Argentina Anti-Esclerosis Multiple,
Avenida Belgrano 485, Piso 10,
Buenos Aires
Tel: (54) 331 2512

AUSTRALIA
National MS Society of Australia
34 Jackson Street, Toorak,
Victoria 3142
Tel: (61) 3 828 7222

AUSTRIA
Osterreichische Multiple Sklerose
Gesellschaft Neurolog.
U. Klinik, Waehringer Guertel 18-20
A-1090, Wien, Tel: (43)1 40400 /
3121

BELGIUM
Bergische Multiple Sclerose Liga
173 Avenue Plasky,, B- 1040,
Bruxelles
Tel: (32) 2 736 1638

BRAZIL
Brasileira de Esclerose Multipla
Rue Demostenes 168,
Sao Paulo, CEP 04614
Tel: (55) 11 531 19 28

CANADA
MS Society of Canada
Suite 820, 250 Bloor Street,
Toronto, Ontario, M4W 3P9
Tel: 1 (416) 922-6065

CYPRUS
Cyprus MS Association
1 Theseos Street, Flat 43,
C.B.C. Area, Nicosia
Tel:(357) 2 426943

DENMARK
Landsforeningen til bekaempelse af
dissemineret Sclerose
Mosedalvej 15, DK-2500 Valby
Tel: (45) 31 170466

FINLAND
Suomen MS-yhfdistysten Liitto,
Finlands MS forenin-gars Forbund
r.y., Seppalantie, PL 15 21251 Masku
Tel: (358) 21 820311

FRANCE
Ligue Française Contre
la Sclérose en Plaques
15 Blvd. Auguste Blanqui, 75013
Paris
Tel: (33) 1 40 78 69 00

GERMANY
Deutsche Multiple Sklerose
Gesellschaft, Rosental 5, 11 Aufgang,
4. Stock, D-8000, MÜnchen 2
Tel: (49) 89 2608058

GREAT BRITAIN
MS Society of Great Britain and
Northern Ireland,
25 Effie Road, Fulham, London SW6
Tel: (44) 71 736-6267

ICELAND
MS Felag Islands
Aland 13,
108 Reykjavik

INDIA
MS Society of India,
c/o Voltas Ltd. NKM Intl. House,
178
Backbay Reclamation, Bombay 400
021 Tel:(91) 22 202 8360

REPUBLIC OF IRELAND
MS Society of Ireland
2 Sandymount Green, Dublin 4

ISRAEL
Lsrael MS Society
8 Schatz Street, Tel Aviv
Tel: (972) 3544 9739

ITALY
Associazione Italiana Sclerosi Multipla
Centro Servizi Nazionale,
Via Riboli 20, 16145, Geneva.
Tel: (39) 10 310291

JAPAN
Japan MS Society
c/o Sanyai Corporation, PO Box
Tokyo Asakusa 28, 4-1-2 Kotobuki,
Taiko-ku, Tokyo lll Tel: (81) 3 3847 3504

LUXEMBOURG
Ligue Luxembourgeoise de la Sciérose en Plaques, Boite Postale 1444,
Luxembourg 1014 Tel: (352) 400844

MEXICO
Association Mexicana Contra la Esclerosis Multiple,
Apdo Postal M-7255, Delegacion
Cuauhtemoc, 06000, Mexico DF

NETHERLANDS
Nederlandse MS Stichting
Postbus 30470, 2500 GL's
Gravenhage Tel (31) 703 648804

NEW ZEALAND
National MS Society of New Zealand
PO Box 2627, Wellington,
Tel (64) 4 499 4677

NORWAY
Multiple Sklerose Forbundet
1 Norge, Jac. Aallsgt. 26, Oslo 3
Tel: (47) 2 604960

POLAND
MS Society of Poland
c/o Marriott Hotel, Al. Jerozolimskie,
Warsaw. Tel (48) 2 630 7220

PORTUGAL
Sociedade Portuguesa de Esclerose Multipla, Rue da Horta Seca,
11-1, 1200 Lisboa
Tel: (351) 1 346 6904

REPUBLIC OF SOUTH AFRICA
South African MS Society
295 Villiers Road, Walmer, Port
Elizabeth 6070 Tel: (27) 41 51 2900

SPAIN
Asociacion Espanola de Esclerosis
Multiple L/Calaf 19 pral.2A
08021, Barcalona Tel: 34-32017519

SWEDEN
Nerolgikst Handikappades Riksförbund,
MS-forbundet Box 3284, S-103,
65 Stockholm, Tel: (46) 8 140 320

SWITZERLAND
Schwiezerische MS Gesellschaft
Brinerstrasse 1, CH-8003 Zürich
Tel: (41) 1 4614600

UNITED STATES OF AMERICA
National MS Society
733 Third Avenue, New NY 10017
Tel: 1 (212) 986-3240

YUGOSLAVIA
Savez Drustava MS SFR Jugoslavije
Buleva AVNOJ-a 104, SIV-2
soba 44-b, Beograd Tel:(38) 195 244

ZIMBABWE
MS Society of Zimbabwe
PO BOX 8214, Causway, Harare
Tel; (263) 796957

APPENDIX III

Books and other useful reading on Multiple Sclerosis

Brack, Joyce., 1981: *One Thing for Tomorrow*. Western Producer Press, 2310 Miller Avenue, P.O. Box 2500, Saskatchewan S7K 2C4.
ISBN 0-88833-080-4 $8.95 CAN. Paper. Autobiography

Burnfield, A., MD. (1985): *Multiple Sclerosis: A Personal Exploration*. Demos Publications, 386 Park Avenue South, Suite 201, New York, NY. 10016
ISBN 0-28565-018-1 $12.95 US. Paper. Autobiography

Frankel, D., Bunbaum, R., editors (1982): *Maximizing Your Health*. National Multiple Sclerosis Society, 733 3rd Avenue, New York NY. 10017 .
$2.51 US. Paper Exercise and Meditation

Ginther, J.R. (1978): *But You Look So Well*. Nelson Hall, 111 N. Canel Street, Chicago, IL., 60606
ISBN 0-88229-399-0 $19.95 US. Paper. Autobiography

Horner, William (1992): *The Last Dance is Mine*. Optimum Publishing Inc. PO Box 237, Victoria Station, Westmount, QC. H3Z 2V5 Phone:(514) 937-8038
ISBN 0-88890-228-X $21.95 CAN. Paper Source Book and Autobiography

Kalb, Rosalind, Ph.D. and Scheinberg, Labe, M.D.(1992) *Multiple Sclerosis and the Family*. Demos Publications, 386 Park Ave South, Suite 201, New York, NY 10016
$21.95 US Help for the Family

Le Maistre, JoAnn., (1985): *Beyond Rage, The Emotional Impact of Chronic Physical Illness*. Alpine Guild, P.O. Box 183, Oak Park, IL. 60303, USA. .
ISBN 0-93171-203-3 $28.90 US. Paper with audio tape, Six case histories

Mathews, B., (1980) (1985): *Multiple Sclerosis——The Facts*. Oxford University Press, 70 Wynford Drive, Don Mills ON., M3C 1J9
ISBN 0-19286-011-9 paper (1980) $8.50 CAN. Paper (1980)
ISBN 0-19286-523-8 cloth (1985) $30.50 CAN. cloth (1985) Information

Risidore, L. (1987): *Multiple Sclerosis: The Kinder Side*. Chadwich Macdonald Publications, 3529 Walmer Road, Burlington, ON. L7N 1C9
ISBN 0-96929-850-1 $14.95 CAN Paper Autobiography

Rosner, Louis, J.M.D. and Ross, Sally, (1987): Multiple Sclerosis: *New Hope and Practical Advice for People with MS and their Families*. Prentice Hall Canada,1870 Birchmount Road, Scarborough, Ontario, M1P 2J7
$26.95 CAN Information

Schapiro, R.T.,(1987): *Symptom Management in Multiple Sclerosis.* Demos Publications, 386 Park Avenue South, Suite 201, New York, NY 10016, ISBN O-93995-703-5 $12.95 US Paper
ISBN 0-93995-702-7 $19.95 US Hardcover Information

Schapiro, R.T., (1992): *Multiple Sclerosis: A Rehabilitation Approach.* Demos Publications, 386 Park Avenue South, Suite 201, New York, NY 10016
$21.95 US Rehabilitation

Shaw, Carole, BSR (PT), MCPA, MCSP, Low. Barbara, BSR, MCPA (1989): *Multiple Sclerosis: An Exercise Guide,* University Hospital UBC Site 2211 Westbrook Mall, Vancouver, B.C. V6T 2B5 Phone: (604) 228-7269.
$25.00 CAN Exercise and Relaxation

Silby, W.A., MD.and Board of Editors from International Federation of MS Societies (1992): *Therapeutic Claims in Multiple Sclerosis, 3rd Edition.* Demos Publications 386 Park Avenue South, Suite 201, New York, NY. 10016
$21.95 US Hardcover $13.95 US Paper Therapy and Treatment

Strong, Maggie (1988): *Mainstay: For the Well Spouse of the Chronically Ill.* Little Brown and Company (Canada) Ltd. 148 Yorkville Ave. Toronto, Ontario. M5R 1C2
ISBN 0-316-81923-9 $23.95 CAN Autobiography of Spouse

Waksman, M.D., Reingold, Ph.D., Reynold, M.D. (1987): *Research on Multiple Sclerosis, 3rd Edition.* Demos Publications, 386 Park Ave South, Room 201, New York, NY. 10016
ISBN 0-939957-07-8 $9.95 US Information,Diagnosis,Research Treatment

Wolf, John K. (1987): *Mastering Multiple Sclerosis: A Guide to Management 2nd Edition*, Academy Books, P.O. Box 757, Rutland VT. 15701
$22.95 US. Equipment and housing

A list of booklets available on all aspects of the disease Multiple Sclerosis is available by writing to:

Multiple Sclerosis Society of Canada
250 Bloor Street West Suite 820
Toronto, Ontario, M4W 3P9
Phone (416) 922-6065